Praise for April Henry's
Square in the Face

"Engaging. . . . The vanity license plates sprinkled
through the book are great."
Seattle Times

"Highly readable. . . . Ms. Henry is an accomplished
writer who orchestrates her plot with skill. The story
moves briskly to a satisfying—and surprising—
conclusion."
Dallas Morning News

"Oregon sleuth Claire Montrose comes of age in this
second outing. Definitely a new series with staying
power."
Margaret Maron, author of *Home Fires*

"An absorbing, and at times, moving mystery with a
lively heroine."
Publishers Weekly

"Agreeable prose, a steadily engaging plot, and a few
vanity plate puzzles thrown in for good measure."
Library Journal

"A tour de force of skill and perception."
Shirley Rousseau Murphy, author of *Cat to the Dogs*

"The suspense is superb and makes for a real nail-biter
of a tale."
Romantic Times

And Her Debut Novel
Nominated for the Agatha and Anthony awards
A Booksense 76 Selection
Circles of Confusion

"*Circles of Confusion* is a thoroughly entertaining debut mystery. Claire Montrose is a heroine you can root for."
Phillip M. Margolin, author of *Wild Justice*

"An amateur sleuth with an unusual day job debuts in this lively, romantic mystery. . . . An off-beat, vital first outing."
Publishers Weekly

"A delightful book."
Mystery News

"Wonderful!"
Poisoned Pen

"In her first novel, April Henry has created a cracker-jack plot that is intelligent, internally consistent and interesting. She has created an attractive protagonist and the tale is told in a strong voice that never drifts toward cute."
Drood Review of Mystery

"*Circles of Confusion* supplies ample entertainment and tremendous potential for the continuing Claire Montrose mysteries."
Mystery Reader

"April Henry is attracting attention as a new writer to watch with this fast-paced debut mystery."
Eugene (OR) *Register-Guard*

Also by
April Henry

CIRCLES OF CONFUSION

And in Hardcover

HEART-SHAPED BOX

SQUARE
IN THE FACE

A Claire Montrose Mystery

APRIL HENRY

AVON BOOKS
An Imprint of HarperCollins*Publishers*

AVON BOOKS
An Imprint of HarperCollins*Publishers*
10 East 53rd Street
New York, New York 10022-5299

Copyright © 2000 by April Henry
ISBN: 0-06-109716-0
www.avonbooks.com

First Avon Books paperback printing: March 2001
First HarperCollins hardcover printing: February 2000

Avon Trademark Reg. U.S. Pat. Off. and in Other Countries,
Marca Registrada, Hecho en U.S.A.
HarperCollins ® is a registered trademark of HarperCollins Publishers Inc.

Printed in the U.S.A.

10 9 8 7 6 5 4 3 2 1

STUMPD?

Each chapter of *Square in the Face* contains vanity license plate puzzlers. At the end of the book is a glossary so that you can check your sleuthing skills.

1 ● Standing in front of the kitchen sink in Dante's co-op, Claire slid another plate into the wooden dish rack. The view from his window, eight stories above Fourth Avenue, was still something she had a hard time believing. If she pressed her cheek against the cold pane, she could even see a slice of the Empire State Building.

"I have a feeling we're not in Portland anymore, Toto," she murmured to herself. Even without the Empire State Building, a glance across the street would be enough to let her know she wasn't in Oregon. Buildings here were squeezed up against one another, without even an alley-way for breathing room. Directly across the street, two brick buildings bracketed an older one of stone, complete with carved gargoyles on the corners. Behind each window was another life she could scarcely imagine. Actors, editors, students, and dancers. Old women who could talk for hours about seventy years before, when the streets bustled with fat Checker cabs and people had streamed into the Horn and Hardart Automat on the corner. Palm readers, chanteuses and cellists, writers of advertising catchphrases. People from every country in the world, be-cause this was New York City, after all. And Claire was just one more person among seven million.

In a way she was glad that she was just visiting. New York demanded the persona she had perfected during years of riding the bus in Portland (and happily discarded as soon as she got a car). No smiling, no chance eye con-tact, no talking to yourself, no making yourself stand out from the herd. It was the only way to stay safe from the wolves. You walked fast and didn't let your eyes catch on anything.

Behind her, the CD player switched to another of the discs Dante had loaded before he went to a meeting at the Met, a meeting that was unavoidable even if he was officially on vacation. When he came back, they were going to a photography exhibit at a gallery downtown. To Claire, everything in New York felt like what Portlanders called downtown, i.e., tall office buildings and crowded sidewalks, but to Dante the city lay neatly divided into downtown, midtown, and uptown. Afterward they were going out to dinner with some of his old friends. The idea filled Claire with a barely suppressed nervousness that went far beyond wondering which fork she should use. Every time she met an old friend of Dante's she would wonder again what Dante saw in her. Their conversations were filled with references she barely caught. Like Alice in Wonderland, in New York Claire sometimes felt as if she had to run in place just to keep up. She told herself that dinner would go fine, but the part of her that still thought in the language of license plates added a sarcastic SHRSHR.

As her mind moved from thought to thought, her hips began to move, too, echoing the beat of the music, a hard-to-pin-down mix of folk, Celtic, and Middle Eastern sounds. Claire walked over to the empty CD cases and flipped through them until she figured out which one it was. Loreena McKennitt. The singer's long red curls looked something the way Claire's hair used to, until she had been forced to cut it all off last fall and dye it black to keep herself from being so easily recognizable.

Susie, Claire's hairdresser sister, had done what she could to restore her. She had dyed Claire's hair back to its original color, and the match was so close that the roots of the new growth couldn't even be seen. But Susie couldn't do anything about the length, which now brushed Claire's shoulders instead of the middle of her back. Claire missed the familiar weight of it. Sometimes, after she put on her coat, her hands would automatically reach back to pull her hair free from the collar and meet only air.

The next song was a ululating melody, a Middle Eastern sound complete with bells and drums. She turned the music up a tick and began to walk back to the sink. Without conscious thought, Claire's body found the pattern of the camelwalk. The memories of the dance were steeped in her bones, laid down in eighth grade when she had taken a five-dollar beginning belly-dance class from Minor's Department of Parks and Rec.

The teacher had not only taught them how to dance, but how to dress the part. After stops at FabricLand and Newberry's, Claire had made her own belly-dancing outfit. The skirt was sheer nylon, layers and layers of black with a final hidden underskirt of scarlet. She sewed silver bells on a heavily padded black bra and then in class she was taught the secret of making them jingle. Surrounded by housewives and secretaries, Claire learned how to snake her arms and shake her hips and even how to hold her curved arms overhead, back of one hand pressed to the back of another, while she slid her head from side to side. For the first time in her life, Claire began to feel that she might be graceful and coordinated.

Although she was by far the youngest person in the class, for once she didn't mind feeling different. The other women fussed over her as if she were exotic and special. No one teased her for being too skinny or too tall. Instead, they touched her curls, marveled at her pale skin, exclaimed over her flexibility. When the talk turned to men and babies and blood, as it always seemed to do, they hadn't shooed her away, but let her listen.

The dishes forgotten, Claire thought about all this as she camelwalked across the faded scarlet of Dante's Oriental rug. The camelwalk was a dance that required coordination. As you walked forward heel-toe, your breasts and hips moved in opposition, going toward each other and then away, in a movement that reminded Claire of a clamshell opening and closing. It was the belly-dancing version of a strut.

Claire's mind was in the past, and her body was lost in the music. She didn't know Dante had come in until she felt his hands on her hips.

"Slow down there, Slim."

A hot flush ran up her neck, but Dante had already turned Claire around and pulled her to him, his lips seeking hers. In her mind's eye, she saw how ridiculous she must have looked, gyrating spastically in yellow dish-washing gloves. But maybe Dante hadn't seen her in the same way, because he leaned down, swung her into his arms, and carried her into the bedroom.

10SNE1

• • •

Shrunken and somehow pathetic, the yellow dishwash-ing gloves now lay inside out on the white-oak floor. The floors had been built with Siberian oak before the turn of the century, Dante had told Claire, nailed into place by men who were little more than Siberian serfs.

Dante lay stretched out on the white-cotton sheets, his body turned toward Claire, his head propped up on one elbow. With his olive skin, black goatee, and a gold hoop in his left ear, he looked like a gypsy or a pirate, certainly not like a Met curator who specialized in old masters. There was an amused gleam in his black eyes.

"How many other tricks do you have up your sleeve? Can you do jujitsu? Three-dimensional calculus? A triple axel? How come you never told me you knew how to belly dance?"

"When was that ever supposed to come up? It's not

like I get a lot of opportunity to practice. But you never forget how to camelwalk. It's like riding a bicycle." Still lying on the bed, Claire raised her hands above her and began clicking imaginary finger cymbals in time to the music. "And you also never forget how to do belly rolls." She took Dante's free hand and put it on her stomach. Cheating, because you really weren't supposed to use breathing to accentuate the movements, she sucked in her abdomen, then rolled it up and over with a kick that made Dante's hand jump. He jerked it back.

"Wow! That felt just like when my sister was pregnant. How'd you do that?" He rolled on his own back, eyeing his perfectly flat abdomen, and tried to duplicate her maneuver. He succeeded only in sucking his stomach in and out, without any hint of a rolling motion. Defeated, he turned back toward her. "I was going to tell you I saw a good plate today."

"What was it?" Sometimes Claire still couldn't believe how much her life had changed. Only six months before, she would have been in her gray-burlap cubicle at Oregon's Specialty License Plate Department, REJECTED stamp poised over yet another application for 6ULDV8, submitted by someone who thought a government bureaucrat would be too stupid to understand his clever substitution of the number 6 for the word *sex*.

Dante spelled it out. "K-I-D space K-R-8. On the back of a minivan."

She smiled. "That's pretty good."

"Do you ever hear that clock they talk about?"

Claire was staring thirty-six in the face, so she knew what clock Dante meant. "That biological one? I don't know. Sometimes. Maybe when I look at Eric." Eric was her sister's son. "He was resting his head on my stomach the other day and he asked me what the sound he heard was. It turned out he was hearing my heart."

"That's a good idea." Dante scooted over so that his head lay on her stomach. He closed his eyes. When he spoke next, his voice was so soft Claire could barely hear him. "Do you ever think about us getting married?" He must have felt her tense, because he waved one hand. "Rewind. Forget I said anything."

"It's not—I don't think—no." So many thoughts crowded into her mind that Claire couldn't complete any of them. Dante rolled away and put his feet on the floor. By the hunch of his shoulders, she could tell that he was upset. "It's not like I don't want to be with you. It's just that I don't know if I believe in marriage. The only marriage I know that works is J.B. and Susie's, and they aren't even married. I come from a long line of people who either don't get married—like my mom—or get married five times—like my grandmother. Neither one's the greatest role model. Don't you like what we have now?"

"Of course I do. But it's hard for me to enjoy it, knowing that you're going back to Portland in two days."

"You know I don't like to leave Charlie alone for too long. She's nearly eighty." Claire noticed that neither one of them had brought up the real sticking point in their relationship—that they both had families and settled lives in cities three thousand miles apart.

Dante scrubbed his face with his hands, then got up and walked to the bathroom in silence.

Claire watched him go. Her gaze fell on the painting that faced the bed, a large oil created with swift, sure brushstrokes. It showed a nude woman, or rather just her torso, beginning just below her bent knees and ending just above her breasts. She straddled a wooden chair turned backward. One arm rested on the top of the chair, the fingers thick strokes of color that suggested rather than articulated. Her body was half-turned, one shoulder twisted back, as she leaned back on her right palm, which rested on the seat behind her. A nipple peeked between the wooden slats, and the other breast was seen in profile. Her figure was nearly perfect—that of a young woman as yet unmarked by time, pregnancy, breast-feeding, or years spent slumped in an office chair.

It was titled *Passing Through*, and Claire had never asked Dante if the title he had chosen referred to the model herself, or the brief window of perfection that she inhabited.

The bathroom door opened. "Claire, I—"

The ringing of the phone interrupted them. Dante looked at the Caller ID box next to the phone. "It's a Portland number—do you want to get it?"

Fear swamped Claire's heart. Something must be wrong with Charlie. In two strides, she was at the phone. "This is Claire."

"Claire—it's Lori. Charlie gave me Dante's number." Lori and Claire had spent eight years working in adjoining cubicles at Specialty Plates. "I'm sorry for intruding."

"No, you're not intruding, Lori." Claire used her friend's name to let Dante know the call wasn't about Charlie. Still, she could already tell by the tremble in her friend's voice that it was bad, whatever it was. "What's wrong?"

"It's Zach. He's really sick. I'm calling from the hospital. They say he's got leukemia."

"Oh, no, Lori. No. I'm so sorry." It was hard to imagine Zach, a dark-haired three-year-old who sang and hopped through life, sick. "Tell me what I can do for you. I'll be home in a couple of days."

"I've been thinking and thinking." Her next words were so soft they were nearly drowned out by a crackly background voice paging a doctor. "If Zach doesn't go into remission soon, or if he does go into remission and it fails, then he's going to need a bone-marrow transplant. And they've already told us there's no match in our family, no match on the donor registry. But remember how I told you about," Lori hesitated, her voice so soft it was nearly inaudible, "about his sister?"

Claire remembered. They had gone out to eat Mexican

food at Acapulco Gold's one Saturday, a "girls' night out" while Havi watched the couple's two boys. Lori had ended up crying into her empty margarita glass. "I remember."

"I need you to help me find her. In case she's a match."

"But Lori, I—" This was ridiculous. Claire wasn't a private investigator. What did she know about tracking down a child from a ten-year-old private adoption?

"Don't say no to me, Claire. Not now." Lori's voice was near tears. "Just promise you'll talk to me about it when you get home."

What choice did she have? "I promise."

"Good. Call me as soon as you get home." Lori sighed as if a boulder had been rolled off her chest. "And thanks, Claire."

Claire hung up the phone, wondering what she had gotten herself into.

"What's wrong with Lori?" Dante asked. The winter daylight was already fading, turning Dante into a dark shape against the white sheets.

"Her three-year-old son has leukemia. He might need a bone-marrow transplant, but there isn't a match available." Claire put her hands over her eyes and sighed. "She wants to talk to me about finding his sister to see if the girl is a match."

Dante looked confused. "I thought she just had two boys."

"When Lori was in college, she got pregnant and gave the baby up for adoption. The guy she's married to now was the father, but they had broken up before she knew she was pregnant. Later they got back together and got married, but Lori never told him what happened."

"And she hadn't wanted to have an abortion?"

"No. She and Havi had always been like this"—Claire held up two fingers wrapped around each other—"so she felt really connected with the child. Connected and angry at the same time, because she had broken up with Havi and didn't want to be reminded of him. That's why she decided to give it up for adoption rather then keep it."

"What kind of a name is Havi?"

"He's Mexican-American, so his real name is Xavier. But no one here knows how to say it right, with an H sound at the beginning and an A sound at the end. They always say Ex-ave-ee-air. So he tells people to call him Havi, and he spells it with an H."

"So how come this Havi guy didn't ever know Lori was pregnant? Even if they weren't going out anymore, wouldn't he have seen her during that nine months?"

Claire shook her head. "After they broke up, Havi joined the army. He only looked her up when he got out four years later. They got back together, ended up getting married. They had Max right away. He's six now, and Zach is three. She was always afraid to tell him about their other child, so she kept it a secret." Claire thought that Lori must be frightened indeed, to think she must trade her secret for her son's life. Claire leaned over and kissed Dante, then they both got up and began to get ready to go out.

● ● ●

"And you'll have . . ." The waiter paused expectantly. He was all capped teeth, artfully streaked blond hair, and too-good-to-be-true turquoise eyes. He was probably one of those waiters-slash-models. Everyone in New York seemed to be a hyphenated blend of what they were doing temporarily and what they were meant to be.

What Claire wanted was the fresh-caught tuna served with aioli, but even though she knew that aioli was fresh-made garlic mayonnaise, she didn't know how to pronounce it. Did you say all the vowels? Unfortunately, none of the other people sitting at her table had ordered it. Claire compromised. "The tuna."

The waiter nodded and scribbled without saying anything, so Claire remained unenlightened. His gaze moved on to Tabitha, who was seated next to Claire. He added a few dozen more teeth to his smile, taken in by Tabitha's jet-black hair and tip-tilted eyes. "The tia pila. Rare," Tabitha said. Handing her menu back with a snap, she continued the monologue the waiter had interrupted. "So they won't fund the segment on the death camps unless I can get footage. But how can I get footage without any funding? The whole thing's circular, but they just won't see it."

Tabitha was a documentary filmmaker who specialized in war—specifically its effects, not on the main combatants, but on women and children. (Of course, as a war ground on, it wasn't unusual to find that the person holding the gun was a twelve-year-old, or that a camp follower had scavenged a weapon and turned it on the enemy.) Lately her beat had been extremist Muslim conflicts, and unfortunately, she had a number from which to choose. Disguised behind a floor-length black chadoor, her blue eyes covered by a screen of mesh, Tabitha ventured into the field with a tiny camera hidden in the voluminous folds of her head scarf. Because she was an American infidel who risked stoning or a headsman's sword, she also kept a revolver strapped to her ankle and a stiletto tucked in her bra.

Unfortunately for Claire's self-esteem, Tabitha was typical of Dante's old friends. They were all vivid, fascinating, and more than slightly exotic. Claire sat silent, listening to the play of conversation around her as it touched on war, politics, dance, theater, art. At one point, Dante gave her shoulder a squeeze, but it didn't make her feel any more sure of herself. What was Claire Montrose—who one year ago had never been farther east than Boise, Idaho—doing in New York City, eating food she couldn't pronounce?

The answer was that she had sneaked in when no one

was looking. Six months earlier, she had inherited a mysterious oil painting from her great-aunt. After gathering up all her courage she had gone to New York City, taken her painting on the rounds of auction houses and museums. At the Metropolitan Museum of Art, Dante had offered to look at it.

Later Dante had admitted to Claire that he had instantly fallen in love with both her and her painting of a woman in an ermine-trimmed yellow jacket. The little painting turned out to have been looted, first from its original owners by the Nazis, and then by Claire's great-aunt's US Army boyfriend. Haunted by the thought of the thousands of Jews whose deaths had allowed both Hitler and Göring to amass enough art for a dozen museums, Claire had turned over the money from the painting's sale to the World Jewish Restitution Organization. It was only at the insistence of her elderly roommate—herself a concentration-camp survivor—that Claire had kept just enough to free herself from the drudgery of Specialty Plates.

The waiter took Aryeh's order and departed. Aryeh, who was sitting next to Tabitha, was an Israeli artist who referred to his works as "installations." They seemed more designed to shock than to beguile. His latest was a pig, freeze-dried whole, which had then been sliced by a laser beam into one-sixteenth-inch segments. Reassembled in the order they had held in the original pig, the slices were displayed in formaldehyde, each one dangling from a piece of fishing line. Visitors were invited to agitate the Lucite box in which they floated and watch the weird and somehow lifelike way the whole thing rippled.

Next to Aryeh was sara (she insisted on lowercase), a publishing executive who had just returned from a solo trek in Nepal. She wore a black dress the size of a postage stamp and heels high enough to make her a good three inches taller than Claire's five-foot-ten. Claire wondered if the air was better up there.

Ant was seated next to sara. A silver ring pierced his right eyebrow, and the white tablecloth hid his kilt. His shaven head showed not a trace of stubble. How much work did it take to maintain, Claire wondered. Had he shaved off his five o'clock head shadow before joining them for dinner? Ant played lead guitar in the band Muck. Claire had never heard of Muck—but the way Dante's friends talked about it, she felt as if she should have.

The four of them were now engaged in an animated discussion of Aryeh and Tabitha's newly remodeled condominium. Only in New York could an apartment encompass more than two floors, and it seemed as if this one had at least four. Claire gathered that the basement housed a triple-width Italian-marble lap pool lined with Spanish tile, and on the third floor was a screening room that seated sixty. At one point, Dante rolled his eyes in Claire's direction, but still, she felt intimidated just hearing about it.

To Claire, the four were representative of Dante's old friends from Harvard, the kind of people who climbed Everest and spontaneously flew off for weekends in Paris. They had grown up using Mommy's charge card at Bloomingdale's, and Daddy was either on Wall Street or a senior partner at a white-shoe law firm. The one time Claire had ventured this theory, Dante had gently chided her, reminding her that his family had made its money in the bakery business, and that their success had come only after years of hard work. Dante was the anomaly, though. Most of his friends had been born with the benefits that only old money, the best education, and family connections could bring. Now they knew people—or sometimes even *were* people—Claire had only read about *in People*. When she was around them, she felt herself receding behind her face, while always maintaining an interested expression.

"How are you enjoying our fair city, Claire? Do you

miss Oregon?" sara was all sweetness, but Claire noticed how she continued to pronounce the state's name as *Ory-gone* instead of *Ory-gun*, even after hearing Claire say it the right way. sara specialized in editing ghost-written celebrity books, and, Claire had quickly figured out, had once dated Dante. Even though her left hand occasionally grazed Ant's pate, Claire sensed an undercurrent of jealousy from sara's direction whenever Dante leaned over to whisper in Claire's ear. Claire could see herself through the other woman's eyes. Some creature from the piney woods who hardly wore makeup.

"I like it here; I like it there." She realized her words unconsciously echoed the rhythm of *Green Eggs and Ham*, one of Rainy's favorite Dr. Seuss books. Once a week, Claire spent an hour struggling to teach seven-year-old Rainy to read at one of Portland's inner-city elementary schools. Rainy was one of four siblings who had one mother and four different and absent fathers. "Oregon has things that New York doesn't. Then again, I went to MoMA today, and that's not an experience you can duplicate in Portland."

There was a pause while Tabitha and sara exchanged a sideways glance. sara speared a pumpkin ravioli and leaned forward. "Claire, you should know that the acronym is pronounced 'Mohma.' Not 'Mama.'" Her smile didn't reach her pale eyes. Dante shifted. Out of the corner of her eye, Claire saw him shake his head slightly, but sara's too-intent expression didn't change. "So what does Oregon have that New York City doesn't?"

Dante squeezed her shoulder. Claire could have launched into a list for the rest of them, one that would have started off with the word *friends*. She could have talked about living in a green lushness cradled by forested hills and snowcapped mountains, of being less than a two-hour drive from the ocean, the mountains, the desert. She could have talked about the different pace and attitude. Instead she put on her own false smile and added a country twang to her voice. "Oh, you know, sara, maybe Oregon's not much different than here. We just got more pine trees, pickup trucks, and poverty. That's all."

Even Ant laughed.

URBSTD

2 • Claire stepped over the foot-wide dog dish that lay on the porch. Emblazoned in gold script along the edge was the word *Duke*. Charlie had gladly paid the extra dollar to have it personalized when she bought the dish at Portland's Saturday market. She said it was cheaper than a burglar alarm—or a real dog. Claire put her key in the lock, picked up her suitcase, and pushed the door open with her hip.

In just a few seconds, a tiny white-haired woman bustled into the living room. "Clairele! It's so good to have you at home again!"

Charlotte Heidenbruch—Charlie to her friends, which was pretty much anyone—opened her arms wide. Claire put her bags down just inside the door and gave her roommate a hug. It was impossible—given that Charlie was a foot shorter and more than forty years older—but for a moment Claire swore her feet left the ground. Then again, Charlie *was* the star of her Self-Defense for Seniors class.

"Careful there, Charlie." She straightened up. "You don't want to break anything." Claire wasn't sure which of them she was referring to.

"Come back into the kitchen and tell me how is your flight? New York City? Your lover?" Charlie pronounced it *luffer*. Even at seventy-eight, her Marlene Dietrich accent and casual European acceptance still drew men to her.

"The flight was okay." Claire had tried to lose herself in a paperback mystery, hoping to forget a recent *60 Min-*

utes episode that basically demonstrated most airport control towers were run by ancient computers far less sophisticated than Claire's digital watch. "And Dante's—well, Dante." After the awful dinner with his old college friends, he had spent her remaining time in New York trying to make it up to her. They had stayed up well past midnight the night before, eating Chinese takeout in bed and watching kung fu movies on TV. When a piece of mu shu pork had escaped her chopsticks and landed with a plop on her chest, one thing had led to another. They hadn't gone to sleep until after three. She and Dante had barely made it out of bed in time to make it to the airport. Claire smiled to herself as she followed the older woman.

Charlie's house was about the same age as she was, and both were well maintained. There was fresh white paint on the high-ceilinged walls and a touch of coral on Charlie's lips. The kitchen was modernized with stainless-steel appliances, just as Charlie wore, not an old lady's polyester pantsuit and twenty years out-of-date shoes, but a rose-colored cotton knit tunic and pants accessorized by her trademark pink tennis shoes.

"And will you tell me anything about New York, Clairele?" Charlie picked up an already open bottle of red wine. She refilled her own glass, then poured one for Claire. The affectionate "le" ending was one of the few things Charlie had kept fifty years after leaving her hometown near Stuttgart, with a two-year stopover in Dachau. The country and the language had been left behind, but the green embroidery of the concentration-camp tattoo on her arm would never fade. Strangers who heard the way she talked sometimes insisted on knowing what she was, but Charlie's answer was always the same: She was an American.

"Times Square looks even more like Disneyland than the last time I was there. Artificially shiny and colorful. But I guess it's better than porno theaters." Claire took a sip from her glass, enjoying the bite of tannin that spread over her tongue. "Something smells good."

Charlie took a cast-iron pan from the cupboard and set it on the gas stove. "I've roasted a chicken, so I thought to sauté onions, red bell peppers, and mushrooms for the side of the plate. And of course rösti. Does that sound good?"

Claire's mouth watered. "Let me help. How about if I cut up the vegetables? You're the only one who can make rösti right." Rösti, a dish taught to Charlie by her Swiss grandmother, was like the most perfect version of hash browns, brown and crisp on the outside, tender in the center of every strand.

By the time they sat down to eat, Claire was starving. "Did you eat any good meals in New York?" Charlie asked as she set a plate in front of Claire. Although she kept a trim figure, Charlie liked to talk about good food as well as prepare and eat it. Claire had read that the concentration-camp inmates had been so hungry that they boiled weeds for soup, and she could imagine how such a hunger could not be sated, even after fifty years.

As she savored a mouthful of roast chicken, Claire thought about the food she had eaten, both alone with Dante and with his friends. "We went out to Chinatown for dim sum. You know, I've read about dim sum, but I've never actually eaten it. It was great." Dante had ordered a half dozen little plates of Chinese dumplings—pork, chicken, shrimp—from the passing carts. Tiny Chinese women dressed in black pants and white shirts piloted the carts through the close-set tables filled with people all talking at once in what Claire supposed was Cantonese. The noise had been nearly deafening, but the tastes had made up for it. Plump sweet shrimp, sharp ginger, greasy and flavorful pork—every treasure wrapped in a bland dough wrapper. When they finished eating the waitress counted up the empty plates and charged accordingly.

"You know what I liked about it? It made me feel like, yes, I may be thirty-five, but there are still great things out there that I haven't tried yet."

Charlie shook her head, her tone gently chiding. "Clairele, if you think you are old, then what does that make me?"

Claire set her fork down on her empty plate and let out a deep breath that bordered on a sigh. The quiet of the old house enfolded her, allowing her to relax as she never really could in New York, with its constant background hum of horns, sirens, and tires having intimate congress with potholes.

"You still haven't told me how things are with Dante."

"He talked a little bit about us getting married."

Charlie divided the last of the wine between their two glasses. "And that is not what you want?" Charlie never judged, which was why people revealed themselves to her.

"I don't know. I don't know what I want. Maybe we're too different. I think that's what his friends think. Especially the women."

"Women can be territorial. And it is what is underneath a person that counts." Charlie closed her eyes for a moment. Her skin was so translucent that Claire could see the delicate blue threads of veins in her eyelids. She wondered if her friend was thinking of Richard, the young husband lost to the camps. Charlie had only spoken of him a handful of times in Claire's hearing. Was it that Charlie no longer remembered him or that she remembered him too well? And then there was their son, the child whose name Charlie never uttered, as if she were afraid to draw him into the world again.

The thought of Charlie's long-lost son made Claire remember her promise to Lori. She stood up from the table. "I need to call Lori."

Charlie's faded blue eyes opened, and she regarded Claire from the distance that nearly eighty years on earth had given her. "She told me about her son, how something was wrong in the marrow of his bones. He is—how old?"

"Three."

Charlie closed her eyes again. Her mouth jerked down to the left, once. Claire thought again of the boy who had been just a year older than Zach when he was pulled from his mother's arms forever. But Charlie had somehow found a way to go on. If Zach died, could Lori do the same?

3 • Even from the outside, it was clear that something was wrong at Lori and Havi's house. The curtains were drawn, their porch was dotted with a week's worth of rolled-up newspapers, and an empty yellow recycling bin lay overturned in the middle of their dandelion-speckled lawn. If she hadn't seen Lori's maroon Honda Accord parked in the driveway, Claire would have driven right on past, still looking for the neatly kept-up ranch house she remembered from previous visits.

Taped on the front door was a sign written on notebook paper in Lori's distinctive, backward-slanting cursive. "If you've just been sick, are sick, or feel as if you might be getting sick, please visit another time." Claire raised her hand and knocked softly.

It was a different Lori who answered the door, too. Instead of a designer suit, she wore Levi's and a plain black turtleneck. Without saying a word, she pulled Claire inside the shadowed hall and hugged her fiercely. "God, I've missed you!" Claire had the weird feeling that Lori was comforting *her*, and she wondered just how bad things were.

Lori pulled back without meeting Claire's eyes. Her voice was fast and breathless. "Oh, Claire, the gal they hired to replace you, she's driving me up the wall. She has some new weird symptom every day. She itches or the air conditioner is giving her a stiff neck or she needs her karma readjusted. I could live with that, except she wants to tell me about everything in detail. I can't escape. She follows me into the break room or even the bathroom, yak, yak, yakking. And now that he's been promoted, Roland's worse than he ever was. He's taped warning signs all over the coffee machines to make sure we don't make any good coffee in them. He found out that it's written in the coffee supplier's contract that we have to use the state-supplied coffee. You know, the stuff that tastes like it was brewed in an ashtray? He's been checking out the freezer, even sniffing people's mugs, looking for illegal Starbucks." Lori still had not paused for breath. She was like a speeded-up, bad imitation of herself.

Fearing that her friend might drown in the torrent of her own words, Claire gave her another hug. "Ssh, ssh," she whispered in her ear. A black cat with one white foot walked in the half-open door and wound around their legs before jumping on the couch in the darkened living room.

Lori pulled away and turned to close the door. The daylight caught her face, revealing a paper construction of hollows and shadows.

"And Zach, Lori? How's Zach doing?"

Lori's voice arced higher. "Okay. He's okay. Right now he's sleeping." Her eyes got wider, and she blinked them rapidly. She turned and started down the hall to the kitchen. "Speaking of coffee, would you like some? I'm practically living on the stuff. I'm thinking of seeing if I can just buy a case of Vivarin."

They both came to a stop in the kitchen doorway. The sink was filled with dirty dishes, the counter littered with wrappers from McDonald's and Burger King. The red-tile floor was dotted with dried spills, as well as a green-rubber duck, a Speedy Gonzalez Pez dispenser, a child's blue-suede tennis shoe, and a squirt gun. The refrigerator, decorated with children's crayoned drawings, had been wrapped lengthwise with silver duct tape, so that it looked like an odd outsize present. Claire only had eyes for her friend.

"And how about you? How are you doing?"

"Bad," Lori whispered without looking at Claire. "Real bad." She walked into the kitchen, leaned her back against the refrigerator, then slid down until she was sitting with her mouth pressed against her knees. Tears leaked from her closed eyes.

"I just keep thinking, I'm his mother, you know? I'm his *mother*. How could I not know that something was wrong? Instead I just had an excuse for everything. Zach was crabby, well, that was because he was finally getting his two-year molars. And sometimes he complained his bones hurt, but I figured that was just growing pains. He picked at his dinner, but I thought he must be eating a lot at day care, 'cause he still had this little potbelly. Now the doctor tells me that Zach's liver and spleen are *enlarged*, and that's why he didn't eat. He *couldn't* eat because there wasn't room." Lori took a deep, shuddering breath. "I told myself all these lies, and the whole time there's a cancer, a goddamn *cancer*, in there, chewing on his bones. I'm his mother, I should know when something is wrong." Her words dwindled to a sharp whisper. "Why didn't I take him in to the doctor six months ago?" Her lower lip turned white as she pressed her teeth against it, so hard that Claire was afraid it might begin to bleed.

Claire knelt down next to a little heap of spilled coffee grounds and patted Lori's knee. "But you didn't know, Lori, you didn't know. I've watched you with your kids. You're a *good* mother." Lori responded with a polite grimace. Claire saw that she wasn't getting through. Getting to her feet, she took a blue sponge from the sink, wrung it out, and began to wipe off the kitchen counter. She wanted to do something to help her friend, and it was the only thing she could think to do. "And what's past is past. You have to concentrate now on Zach, on helping him get better. How is he doing?"

Lori answered with a question of her own. "Do you remember when he was born?"

Claire nodded, thinking of the photo Lori had kept on her cubicle wall, Lori's three guys together. In the picture, a three-year-old Max stood holding Havi's hand while they stood in line to see Santa at Washington Square Mall. Zach nestled in a front-pack against Havi's broad chest. He was just a week old, his tiny bowed legs like a plucked chicken's.

"At first, I wondered how I could ever love Zach as much as I loved Max. But your heart, you know"—Lori thumped her closed fist on her chest—"your heart always makes room." She shook her head, her bangs hiding her eyes. "Zach's—changed. Do you remember when he first started to talk? It was always 'Me do!' even when he couldn't. Now he just wants to be carried every place. And he throws up a couple of times a day. It's a side effect from one of his drugs. And he's also on prednisone, which makes him crazy hungry all the time. That's why the fridge is taped shut. Havi put the duct tape on there after Zach got up in the middle of the night and spilled an entire gallon of milk."

Using the refrigerator door handle, Lori pulled herself to her feet and began to pick at the duct tape with her fingernails. "He's gained five pounds in the last month. But he has to stick to bland stuff because his mouth is all full of sores." She peeled the tape back, opened the refrigerator door, and began to rummage around inside, her words muffled. "He's living off noodles, plain tortillas, and family-sized cans of chicken noodle soup poured straight from the can. But he's still so hungry he's been waking me in the middle of the night asking me to feed him."

"You do look a little tired," Claire said, as Lori emerged with a liter bottle of Diet Coke in one hand and a carton of orange juice in the other. Which was an understatement. Lori would no more go without makeup than she would go without clothes, but now against her pale, nearly translucent skin her foundation and blush stood out like a mask—or war paint.

"I don't sleep much anymore." Lori pushed aside a stack of dirty dishes and set the pop and juice down on the little table in the breakfast nook. Claire picked up the dishes and began to load them into the dishwasher. "Zach mostly sleeps in our bed now. We do a little shuffle. First we put him in his bed, which lasts about twenty minutes, tops. Then I hear him climbing up the stairs, and he comes crawling into our bed. Then Havi feels crowded and goes downstairs to sleep in Zach's bunk. That wakes up Max, and he comes up to the big bed."

Lori dragged a chair from the dining room into the kitchen, then stood on it to reach into a cabinet high above the refrigerator. It was half-full of dusty serving pieces, but in front of them was a selection of junk food. Claire realized she was looking at Lori's secret stash. "And Zach likes to sleep with his arm draped over my neck, but since his arms are about six inches long, that means I have him breathing in my face all night long. Half the time I end up climbing into Max's bunk bed— anything so I can get a couple of hours. In the morning we all wake up in the wrong beds, feeling confused." Holding a box of Wheat Thins and one of Ritz Crackers, as well as a half-empty bag of Lay's barbecue potato chips, Lori climbed down off the chair. "Want any of this?"

Claire shook her head. "What does the doctor say? I'm afraid I don't know a lot about leukemia."

"Leukemia screws up the bone marrow, which I guess is like a factory for blood." Lori stuffed a handful of chips in her mouth and continued talking around them. "When you have leukemia, the bone marrow starts churning out bad white cells called blasts. They crowd out all the good parts of blood. The reason people with leukemia die"— she crammed more chips into her mouth—"is from organ failure or an infection that can't be stopped. Sometimes they just bleed to death."

Her hands began to chatter over the tabletop, her index fingers creating a little pile of potato-chip crumbs. "The kind of leukemia Zach has is called ALL. That stands for acute lymphoblastic leukemia. When the doctor told us that, my mind went blank. He was going on and on about treatment modalities, and all I was thinking of was that old commercial where they used to sing out A . . . L . . . L. He was talking about how my baby might die, and I was sitting there thinking about detergent."

Claire opened her mouth to interrupt, but closed it when she saw the look on Lori's face.

"I only snapped back when the doctor told me he was going to admit Zach into the hospital that night to start chemo."

"That soon?" Claire asked. Her hands were filled with balled-up fast-food wrappers, but the garbage can under the sink was full. She found a paper bag and began to toss all the trash into it.

"The whole idea is that you jump on this thing fast and with both feet. They kept him in the hospital for a week, filled him up with four different chemo drugs plus transfusions. I slept with Zach every night in his hospital bed. And every time I woke up I would just—just look at him." Lori's voice broke. "Last month I was drying him off from his bath and teasing him, calling things the wrong names, you know, saying his feet were his knees and his hands were his cheeks. And he got mad, and said, 'You say the left words, Mama, and I say the right ones.'" She stuffed a final handful of chips into her mouth, then balled up the empty bag and threw it in the direction of the sack Claire was filling with garbage. It fell short. "He made me laugh so hard that I forgot to ask him about where he had gotten this huge purple bruise on his knee. That's the kind of thing that can make you crazy, thinking maybe he would be in remission now if I had brought him in earlier."

"Do they think he'll go into remission?" Claire was beginning to feel desperate for good news. She picked up the crumpled potato-chip bag and put it in the garbage.

Lori shrugged. "Dr. Preston said ninety-five percent of kids will go into remission. But then when I asked the doctor what Zach's chances were, and he said he wanted to wait until after he was in remission to talk about 'long-term survival.'"

Lori's face contorted as she repeated the words *long-term survival*. Claire thought it sounded so awful framed that way, the germ of failure already contained within it. Weren't those the stories you always heard about kids with leukemia, of failed remissions, of borrowed time bought at great cost? "Isn't leukemia curable?" Claire took a pink-plastic pig from the dishwasher's utensil basket and added it to another paper bag half-filled with the other toys she had collected. "Or, you know, more curable than some things?"

"Those brochures the doctor gave me are filled with all these cutesy little drawings and these scary little facts. Like only sixty percent of kids are alive after five years." Lori poured herself a glass of orange juice, then opened up a roll of Ritz Crackers and stuffed four into her mouth. "I used to play the lottery for a lot worse odds than that. But that was only for money."

"How can they tell if he's in remission?" Claire turned on the dishwasher, then leaned against it as it began to fill with water.

"Every couple of days they take some of his marrow and start counting blasts. He's officially in remission once they can't find any more." Lori rubbed her hand across her mouth. "I have dreams about those numbers, about those people tucked away back in the lab, bending over a microscope. They know what's happening even before you do."

She shut her eyes, but Claire could see them still darting beneath lids as fragile as tissue paper. "It's like if you went to a fortune-teller who could *really* see the future. And she looks at your palm and knows that in the next month your house will burn to the ground, your dog will run away, and you'll find out that your best friend is sleeping with your husband. She holds your palm in her hands, and she sees all this in an instant. And meanwhile you sit there, you've paid your ten bucks, and you're smiling, oblivious. Because you don't know shit. And that's what it's like waiting to hear the counts." Lori opened her eyes and looked up at the ceiling. A tear spilled down her cheek. "And I don't know if it will feel any different even if he does go into remission. Because even then I'll worry. Because one day we could go in for a routine checkup and have the rug pulled right out from under us again. How do you ever let go? Because you know now that the way things *seem* can be a lie."

Claire couldn't imagine trying to pass the days without knowing what lay ahead. How could you sleep, how could you eat, knowing your child might be taken from you? Lori's hollowed-out face answered her question.

"And what if everything we're putting him through doesn't work—or it only works for a little while, and then the remission fails? If that happens, then they stop talking about a cure. Then the only hope is a bone-marrow donation. Only we don't have any options. Like I told you on the phone, Max isn't a match, and there isn't one on the national bone-marrow registry."

"Couldn't you or Havi donate?"

"It doesn't work that way. Kids get half their genes from each parent, remember? Havi and I would have to be cousins before that had a chance."

"Could you sponsor a bone-marrow registration drive?" Claire had seen signs for one once on the bulletin board at the Mittleman Jewish Community Center, Jewish parents from back East seeking a match for their daughter. A few months later, she'd heard that the girl had died.

"Dr. Preston says your ethnic heritage is reflected in your bone marrow. Where am I going to find a bunch of half Irish-German, half Mexican-Americans—with maybe a little Mayan Indian thrown in?"

"What about having another child?" Claire asked. "Didn't I hear about a couple whose daughter had leukemia and then they had another baby who turned out to be a match?"

"I asked Dr. Preston about that, but he said that girl had a different kind of leukemia than Zach does, one that was a lot slower." Lori's words were calm, but she was eating crackers so fast it seemed as if she wasn't even chewing. "There probably isn't enough time to have Havi's vasectomy reversed, get pregnant, and have a baby. That's assuming they could reverse it. And the doctor asked me—what if I got pregnant and we did an amnio and found out the baby wasn't a match? Would I be willing to have an abortion just so we could try again?" Lori shook her head, her lips thinned down so much they nearly disappeared. "I told him yes, which I think shocked him a little. But I guess that's not even really an option."

The cat came into the room, tail held high, and uttered a questioning purr. Claire leaned over and ran her hand down over the arch of the spine, then began scratching behind its ears. It eyes slitted with pleasure. "What about getting a lawyer or a private investigator to find your daughter?"

"By the time this finished dragging through the courts, it wouldn't matter anymore. Besides, we don't have the money. We were in debt even before Zach got sick. Now our eighty percent insurance coverage no longer looks like such a good deal. One day in the hospital is fifteen hundred dollars, and Zach was there for a week. We're one step away from those people who appear in the Consumer Credit Counseling ads," Lori said, mimicking the man with protuberant teeth and a *Hee Haw* accent who was a staple of late-night commercials. "'Thanks to Consumer Credit Counseling I got me a *caahr* again.'"

"And there's no chance the place where you had the baby will tell you where she is?"

"The Bradford Clinic? I called them while Zach was in surgery getting his Port-A-Cath." Lori's fingers rubbed a spot on the left side of her chest, just below the collarbone. "I talked to Vi Trumbo, the head nurse. I still remember her. She's one of those small women with a lot of personality."

Lori bounced the flat of her hand rapidly on the tabletop. Her wedding ring made a clicking sound. "She had this husky voice, and she always wore these ridiculously high white high heels. Sometimes when I was leaving she used to slip a Reese's peanut butter cup into my hand and give me a little wink. See, Dr. Bradford was always wanting you to eat this impossibly healthy diet." Her lips twisted. "And I know Vi remembered me. She told me the records are completely sealed, and that she 'could neither confirm nor deny the birth of any child at the clinic.' I started to argue with her. Then she told me that she was sorry she couldn't be of any help. And then she hung up. When I called back, she threatened to sue me for harassment, and hung up again."

"How'd you find out about these people, anyway?" Claire asked. The cat had jumped on her lap and was now kneading her belly with unsheathed claws. "Ouch, stop that!" Claire said, and tried to hold the cat's paws still.

"Sorry, One Sock got weaned too early or something. Kick her off your lap if you want." Lori's nails clicked as she picked at the seam in the tabletop. "The Bradford Clinic ran an ad in the campus newspaper, along with everyone else who wanted a baby. Guess they all figure it's a better bet that a college girl's kid might be smarter, or at least not born addicted to crack. Even back then, most of the ads promise open adoptions. You know, be part of your kid's life, celebrate his birthdays with his new family, get a monthly packet of photos." Between fine, hard, bracketing lines, Lori's mouth trembled. Her fingers touched her lips, the table, smoothed the edges of a discarded napkin, picked up the box of crackers, and put it down. Claire wanted to take Lori's hands in hers and hold them until they quieted. "I didn't want any of that. I knew that the only way I could do it would be to do it clean. And then I saw this one ad promising to pay all your living expenses, plus what they called a "life scholarship," in exchange for a completely closed adoption. There I was, working twenty-four hours a week and trying to go to school full-time when I turned up pregnant. I thought I had found the solution to everything."

"Wasn't it hard to do it?" The cat was kneading harder. Claire pulled the edges of her jacket until the fabric overlapped, hoping to protect herself from the cat's claws with a double layer of fabric over her belly. One Sock saw right through her strategy and began to knead ever higher, aiming its claws straight at her heart.

"Not when I made the decision. The baby didn't seem real to me. I told myself I was helping out some couple that couldn't have a kid, and if they were rich enough to pay the clinic's fees, they would be rich enough to give it the good life. Besides, Dr. Bradford made you work for the money. I got tested more with that baby than I ever did with Max or Zach. You got your diet sheet about what to eat, and you came in every week to be weighed, measured, and to have drug and alcohol tests. Once a month, you got an ultrasound, only they never let you keep the picture. I have nothing to show that I even had a daughter. You should see the boys' baby books. Ultrasounds, footprints, hospital wristbands, little locks of hair."

"What about Havi? Have you told him yet?"

"No. And I don't want to tell him now unless I need to. What if I tell him and then we can never find her? What would I gain then?"

Claire thought, but didn't say, that it must be a terrible burden to carry alone.

"What are the chances that your daughter would be a match for Zach?"

"Twenty-five percent." Lori saw the starkness of the number register on Claire's face. "But if Zach needs a transplant, then *his* chances right now are zero. That's why I need you to find her for me. I mean, you've done this kind of thing before. There must be some way of—" Lori stopped, her head cocked. She was up and on her feet before Claire even heard a sound. "He's calling me."

The cat jumped off Claire's lap and followed Lori. Only then did Claire hear the faint wordless cry from the back of the house. Uncertain, she stood in the kitchen for a moment, then walked back into the hall.

The door at the end of the hall stood open, and inside Claire could see the boys' room. The bunk beds were painted a glossy red. Two child-sized chairs stood on either side of a low wooden table covered with a half-dismantled wooden train set. One Sock was at the foot of the bed. The first sight of Zach's face pulled the breath from Claire's chest. Most of his hair was gone. His face was pale and bloated, his eyes half-open. The neck of shiny blue-and-gold pajamas was pulled down. Just above the face of a cartoon Hercules, looking desperately out of place, a plastic plug was embedded in the wall of his chest.

Lori knelt by the bed and put her arm under her son's shoulders. She helped him half sit up to take a drink from a white-plastic sipper bottle. His head seemed too big for the rest of his body. "Hey, Zach," Claire said softly from the doorway, but she couldn't tell if he had noticed her or not. When he was done drinking, he let his head fall back. Lori gently lowered him back down to his pillow. She leaned over him and lightly ran her hand over his head, barely brushing the few strands of black hair that remained.

When they walked into the hall, Claire put her arm around her and gave her tight shoulders a squeeze. "I don't know how you handle it."

The face Lori turned toward her was full of fury. She was a lioness ready to defend her cub, but with no place to sink her claws. "Nobody *asks* if you can handle it. You just handle it." Then she sagged against the wall. "Find her for me, Claire. You've got to find her. She may be the only chance he has."

4 ● How would she ever find Lori's daughter, Claire wondered as she set out for her daily five-mile run. Since quitting Specialty Plates, she had tried to be careful to maintain a productive rhythm to her life. She did volunteer work, spent time with Charlie, and was thinking about taking a class at Portland Community College. Still, she was afraid that she might end up sitting on the couch eating Chee-tos and watching two women wrassle on the *Jerry Springer Show*. To help ensure that that didn't happen—or at least that if it did, she wouldn't get terribly fat—she tried to run each day.

Still missing the swinging-metronome weight of a ponytail, Claire trotted down the street. The sky was overcast, the clouds threatening rain. Just judging by the weather, it was hard to tell if it was February or November or some month in between. It was the kind of day that made even native Oregonians like Claire long to live in a place with real seasons.

As she ran, Claire remembered the day she and Lori had become friends seven years before. Even though Lori had been the new employee in Specialty Plates, she had been the one to ask Claire to lunch, suggesting a new Thai restaurant in Northwest Portland. Claire had envied the direct way Lori had extended the invitation, as if she never worried about whether anyone liked her or who she was. She also didn't seem to worry overmuch about the department's rules, not even glancing at her watch as they ate up more and more of their allotted time making ever-widening circles, seek-

ing a parking space somewhere in the same zip code as
the restaurant.

In the years Claire had lived in Portland, the northwest
corner of the city had gone from being slightly seedy—
filled with ramshackle old houses, thrift stores, and sad-
eyed alcoholics pushing stolen shopping carts—to
relentlessly gentrified, with reborn candy-colored Victo-
rian houses, chi-chi shops, and beautiful girls on
Rollerblades being towed behind Irish wolfhounds.
Sometimes Claire missed the old Northwest Portland,
back in the days when it had not yet started looking like
an outpost of San Francisco.

As Lori's Honda threaded the narrow, crowded streets,
she had said, "I think this situation calls for a sacrifice to
the Parking Goddess."

"The Parking Goddess?" Claire echoed. At the time,
she still hadn't quite decided how she felt about Lori.
Lori dressed as if she were ready to prowl down a run-
way, not the orange-carpeted corridors of Oregon's Specialty License Plate Department. Next to Lori, Claire felt
practical and plain. Lori wore a lime green wool suit with
matching four-inch Via Spiga heels. Claire was wearing
black-cotton pants and a white Gap T-shirt. Her hair was
twisted into an impromptu bun, secured with a pencil.

"If you can't find a space, then you must make a sacrifice to the Parking Goddess, and she will reward you."
Without any further warning, Lori leaned on the horn.
And then again. People on the sidewalk turned to stare.
The man in the car ahead of them held up his middle finger. Claire sank low in her seat and covered her eyes with
one hand so that she could no longer see the world outside her window.

"It only works if you do it at a time when you'll draw a
lot of negative attention." Lori smiled unself-consciously
at the people gawking at them. "Now the Goddess will
reward our sacrifice."

Under the shelter of her hand, Claire could feel her

face burning. This, she decided, would be her last lunch with Lori. Then, two seconds later, a spot opened up directly in front of Beau Thai. It was even on the corner, so Lori could pull right in without parallel parking and tying up the already slow traffic.

At lunch, the rest of Claire's reservations evaporated as Lori launched into a wickedly funny imitation of their boss, Roland. Roland was known for his collection of elephant figurines, and his conviction that with enough catchphrases (*Quality Is Our Watchword!*) and computer-generated graphs, he could whip Specialty Plates into ultraefficiency. Lori steepled her hands in front of her and spoke through her nose in a high, prissy voice. "Claire, your effort as a self-directed work unit has maximized output and avoided redundancy. If only the other associates would model your paradigm." Still in character, Lori favored Claire with a sideways leer. Claire had to laugh. Lori had Roland's number, from the way he spoke incomprehensibly in a vain effort to seem smart, to his fumbling attempts at flirtation that might have qualified as sexual harassment if they weren't so pathetic.

The fact was that with or without Roland's slavish devotion to the latest management guru, their department grossed a lot of money for the state of Oregon. For a fee, Oregon motorists could order license plates containing their chosen word or phrase, up to seven digits. People were vain, but that vanity brought in a lot of money for the state. There were 78,988 vanity plates on Oregon vehicles, each of which had cost fifty dollars initially and then thirty-five dollars a year.

Most requests for personalized plates were for a person's hobby, occupation, or first name. Others were more creative. That was where the problems began. People were always trying to slip something past you. The whole task of rejecting or accepting these messages involved detecting perceptual crime, a difficult area for the government to regulate.

Until she had quit last fall, Claire had spent eight hours a day approving or denying applications for vanity plates, deciding if the abbreviated or encoded messages were obscene or otherwise objectionable. Her tools were a set of dictionaries (including specialized ones for slang and obscenities), the bathroom mirror (to make sure that something didn't take on a whole new meaning once it was seen in a rearview mirror), and a good eye for vulgar and otherwise offensive words.

In the ten years she worked for the state, Claire learned how to say *fuck* in thirty-eight different languages. Unfortunately, most people didn't go to the bother of using a foreign language when they decided they wanted to communicate something titillating. They simply requested plates like HOTMAMA (or, more rarely, the mirrorized AMAMTOH), and then were surprised when their applications were rejected.

After Lori started working at Specialty Plates, Claire realized she had found a kindred spirit. Like prairie dogs, they began to pop their heads over the shared cubicle wall to snicker at the general strangeness or stupidity of the public, with their all too frequent requests for BITEME. While their friendship had loosened in the months since Claire quit Specialty Plates, no longer fueled by daily coffee breaks, it still remained strong.

Now Lori wanted Claire to help her find her daughter. As a hedge, she explained. Just in case. That was what she said, anyway, but Claire had heard the edge of desperation in Lori's voice. But what could Claire do? Maybe Lori should run an appeal in the newspaper. Maybe the adoptive parents would come forward if they knew Lori wasn't going to ask for her child back.

But would a newspaper appeal work? Any parents who craved secrecy enough to go through the Bradford Clinic would be unlikely to come forward ten years later. Clearly, the answers to Lori's questions could be found in the clinic—but how could Claire get her hands on them?

Claire decided to check at the neighborhood I Spy Shoppe. Jimmy had helped her out in the past. Maybe he could give her some "off the record" tips about procuring something that wasn't technically yours.

A twinge of guilt pricked Claire as she neared her mother's apartment building. They hadn't talked since Claire had returned from New York. In many ways, Charlie was the mother Jean had never been. Deciding to say hello, Claire hit the STOP button on her watch.

Claire didn't need to worry about finding Jean at home—Jean was always home. Her days were structured around the listings in *TV Guide*. Judicious use of her two VCRs and five TVs meant she never had to miss a program. On birthdays and Christmases Jean gave Claire copies of shows she had taped off PBS (while watching something else entirely) that she thought might appeal to Claire. They were usually shoestring documentaries about elderly beekeepers or the closing of a cardboard box factory.

A square brown UPS truck waited for her to cross the driveway before pulling into the apartment's parking lot. She was surprised when she and the driver arrived at Jean's door at the same time. His hand truck was loaded with a stack of a half dozen cardboard boxes, the largest about a foot square, the smallest only about three inches across.

"Are those all for my mom?"

"You're Jean's daughter?" The smile he gave her, white even teeth in a tanned face, made Claire realize why so many women fantasized about UPS drivers.

Claire nodded and pressed the buzzer. "You know my mom?" Alarm bells were beginning to ring in the back of her head.

"Yeah, lately I'm here nearly every day. Say, does she own stock in them?"

"In who?"

He held up one of the boxes so she could see the return address. "QualProd."

"What's that?" Claire pressed on the buzzer again, wondering why her mother wasn't answering the door. She could hear the muffled sound of the TV, but that didn't necessarily mean anything. Jean left her TVs on even on the rare occasions she did leave the house.

"Oh, you know. One of those home-shopping channels."

"Oh, crap," Claire said. She tried the knob and found it unlocked. She pushed the door open.

The living room was dim, the shades drawn so that nothing competed with the forty-inch Goldstar with separate twin speakers that held pride of place. Her mother sat on the ratty green-velvet couch wearing a white bathrobe with gold appliquéd butterflies. In her left hand she had a cup of coffee, and in her right hand she held a pencil poised over a notepad open on her ample lap. On the arm of the couch next to her lay the cordless phone.

"Mom—," Claire started, but Jean shook her head without answering, her eyes riveted on the screen. On a little revolving black-velvet pedestal lay a tennis bracelet, lit up so that every stone sparkled. In a slightly panicked tone, a man rattled off, "Only a handful of these bracelets remain in stock, and our phone lines are sizzling." In the corner a digital display counted off seconds, going from thirteen to twelve to eleven as Claire watched. Her mother picked up the phone and punched in a number.

The UPS man put the clipboard into Claire's hands and pointed at a line. "Could you sign for your mom, please? She looks busy." Claire scribbled her name, anxious to have him leave. Maybe he had seen weirder sights in his deliveries, but Claire was embarrassed by her mother, the moth-eaten couch, the garish appliquéd butterflies, and, most of all, by the TV, where a knock-off Hermès silk scarf had now appeared on screen. "This scarf is not available in stores," the announcer said. *Probably because any one who could examine it under a bright light would realize it isn't worth fifty-nine dollars,* Claire thought. On the fine white print running along the bottom of the screen, she noticed the scarf wasn't even made of silk, but of something called Zilk, which had a little trademark symbol after it.

"Got it in the nick of time!" said her mother triumphantly, setting down the phone. "The operator said it was one of the last five left."

"See you soon, Jean," said the UPS guy as he finished stacking the boxes against the wall.

Claire waited until he had closed the door behind him. "Mom, what in the heck is going on?"

"What do you mean?" Her mother opened her eyes wide, but then was unable to stop herself from transferring her gaze from Claire to the TV set, where a set of nesting dolls was now on display. Instead of Russian grandmothers in babushkas, a fat-looking Clinton doll swallowed up Hillary, Monica, Linda Tripp, and even a tiny Socks.

"All this stuff, Mom." Claire waved her hand at the boxes the UPS man had left, as well as the knickknacks that now covered every horizontal surface. "The guy said he was making deliveries nearly every day. Why are you buying all this stuff?"

Her mother pressed her lips together. "I haven't seen you in six weeks, and the first thing you do is start yelling at me."

The twinge of guilt was back, only now it was more of a spasm. Her mother was right. What gave Claire the right to come into Jean's home and immediately start lecturing her? She sat down beside Jean on the couch and picked up her mother's hand. Jean kept it limp, but she didn't pull away.

"I'm sorry. You're right. I shouldn't just waltz in here and start interrogating you. I was just worried that maybe you were spending a little too much."

"Oh, no. Not at all. The prices are very reasonable. Better than you would find at any store. Although most of the merchandise they sell is so special it's only available through QualProd. I'll give you a catalog to take home." Jean brightened. "Come look at what I've done with the bathroom!" She got up and pulled Claire to her feet.

The bathroom counter was crowded with a dozen white-beeswax candles and an open white-ceramic jar of potpourri. Next to the sink, an ornate white soap dish held balls of white soap sculpted to look like many-petaled roses. On the wall, an ornate white-and-gold clock looked like something that should have belonged to a Louis The Something Or Other, if French kings had had access to batteries. The old blue towels were gone, re-placed by white towels with gold appliquéd butterflies that matched the ones on Jean's bathrobe. Claire thought it must be uncomfortable to rub the butterflies over wet skin, but Jean's face reflected nothing but delight as she surveyed what she had accomplished.

Claire scrambled for something neutral to say. "Wow—it's so, so, so different!"

"Isn't it beautiful?" Jean looked up at her, her face open.

What could Claire do but nod? And maybe the fact that Jean spent her days watching QualProd was better than watching the soaps. And besides, when Jean had been re-decorating the bathroom, she must have been out of view, if not earshot, of the TV. After promising to visit more of-ten, Claire turned down the offer of the QualProd catalog and resumed her run.

Claire's worries alternated between her mom and Lori. What could she do to help either of them? Her mother had finally found something to fill up her days, and she wouldn't let go of it easily. And then there was the Brad-ford Clinic. How could Claire find out its secrets? Her thoughts circled without making progress.

Claire turned onto Thirty-fifth Avenue. Less than three blocks from home, she picked up the pace. Suddenly, a dog came hurtling out the open door of a nondescript ranch house. As far as Claire knew, this house didn't even *have* a dog, an idea that was clearly erroneous because a black blur was shooting through a gap in the laurel hedge and streaking toward her like a bullet. The harsh hum of a growl was caught deep in its throat. Before she even had time to think, its shoulder collided with her knees. Hot breath grazed her left thigh, but the force of the dog's effort carried it past her and into the street. Tires squealed, but Claire didn't turn. She only had eyes for the dog as it whirled to face her. Already she knew this wasn't the kind of dog that would only bark and bark at a passing runner, its woo-woo-woof adding a note of triumph as the interloper ran down the street.

Claire balled her hands into fists and stamped her foot. "No! Go away!" she yelled. Her voice came out higher than she had intended, less definite. She stamped her foot again. Her mind was mesmerized by the sight of the dog's wet, open mouth, all sides lined with long, pointed teeth. Its narrow black-and-tan muzzle revealed a Doberman as a recent ancestor. She made a shooing gesture with her closed fists, and yelled, "No!" again, but the dog didn't budge, watching her with yellow eyes.

Where was the dog's owner? Claire cast a quick look back at the house from which it had come. The dog took that moment to leap at her. Her world narrowed to sharp ivory fangs set in wet pink gums. She scrambled backward, raising her forearm to shelter her jugular, already imagining the snick of teeth as they caught on bone.

Her left foot landed on something soft, a pothole filled with pine needles at the side of the road. The spongy footing sank beneath her. With an audible pop, Claire's ankle gave way.

The sprained ankle saved her. The dog had angled its leap to meet her chest. Instead it soared over her as she fell. It landed in the yard, paws already scrabbling to turn around, but by that time its owner was upon it. He was a scruffy-looking guy, small and wiry, his hair still rooster-tailed from a nap. The stub of a hand-rolled cigarette was clenched between his lips. He almost fell out of his rubber flip-flops as he grabbed the snarling dog's collar and began to pull it away.

"You okay, lady?" He threw the question over his shoulder as he dragged the dog through the dirt and back to the house.

Claire said yes as she got to her feet and limped away as fast as possible. She did not want to be anywhere near those teeth.

BAD DOG

● ● ●

"Wake up! Wake up! It's time to wake up and have a happy day!" The persistently cheerful voice was accompanied by the hollow sound of someone knocking on glass. Claire groaned, then rolled over to hit the button of her Tom Peterson alarm clock.

She swung her feet out of bed, ready to stumble to the bathroom and from there to her first cup of coffee. When she stood up, her left ankle buckled. As a lightning bolt of pain ran up her leg, she collapsed in a heap on the floor.

Gingerly, she examined her injured ankle. Before she had gone to bed, Claire had used her bathrobe sash to wrap an ice pack around her ankle, but sometime in the night it must have come loose. Her ankle was now streaked with purple and swollen to twice its normal size. Sucking in her breath, Claire probed the worst of the swelling. There wasn't even the slightest dimple to show where her ankle was. Maybe she had broken it. She tentatively tried wiggling her toes, then rotating her foot. Everything seemed to be working, albeit reluctantly. Somewhere, though, she remembered reading that the ability to wiggle something didn't necessarily mean you hadn't broken it.

Claire scooted over to the bottom bedpost and pulled herself upright, standing on just her right foot. Slowly, she tried to transfer some of her weight to her left foot, but it hurt too much. It was clear that she wasn't going to be walking out of her room anytime soon. She sat down on the floor again.

"Charlie?" Claire waited a minute, then called out again, louder this time. "Charlie?" Then she remembered. Twice a week, Charlie took private lessons at Valley Ice. Claire occasionally accompanied her for the simple pleasure of watching her roommate practice. Dressed in a black unitard worn under a sheer black skirt, Charlie would stroke calmly down the ice, her hands clasped behind her back. One foot spoke and the other answered, the sound like a knife on a whetstone. If Charlie stopped for breakfast at Marcos Café afterward, as she liked to do, it might be several hours before she came home. Claire looked down at her ankle again. Was it her imagination, or was it even puffier than it had been a few minutes before?

It was clear she needed a doctor. Doctor. That gave her an idea. Maybe she could kill two birds with one stone. After all, who would be more likely to know about the Bradford Clinic than another doctor? Claire reached for her backpack, which was hooked over the bedpost. She'd started carrying a backpack when she rode the bus. It held more and kept her hands free. People teased her about it, but they always came to her for what they needed—moist towelettes, a sewing kit, Band-Aids, aspirin. Her hand closed around her little red address book. With a slow series of hitches, she scooted backward until she could reach the phone on the bedside table.

It was answered on the fourth ring. "Hello?" The voice was draggy with sleep. Claire looked at her watch and realized it wasn't even eight yet.

"Dr. Gregory?"

"Yes." He wasn't sounding any more cheerful.

"This is Claire Montrose. I'm sorry to be calling you at home, but I remembered that you gave me your number and said I could call anytime . . ." She was talking too fast.

"Claire Montrose? You should have said so in the beginning." His voice had warmed up. "What's up? You know I always enjoy a call from a famous sleuth."

"Oh, my fifteen minutes of fame are long over." Claire's discovery of the long-lost painting had been just the kind of thing the tabloid TV shows loved—especially when her efforts to find its rightful owner had inadvertently resulted in further thievery as well as kidnapping and murder. "Anyway, the reason I'm calling you is kind of embarrassing. . . ."

"It can't be as bad as some of those license plate requests you used to ask me about. All those slang words for body parts. Or is that what you are calling about? Have you gone back to work at Specialty Plates?"

Michael Gregory, MD, was Claire's doctor. To take her mind off her Pap smear a few years back, Claire had cast about for a source of conversation. On the counter she caught sight of the *New York Times* crossword puzzle— completed in ink. Dr. Gregory revealed that his avocation was all kinds of word puzzles: crosswords, puns, Scrabble. He also told Claire that he collected heteronyms, which were, he explained, words that were spelled the same, pronounced differently, and had a different meaning. *Sow* as in pig and *sow* as in plant. Claire thought for a minute, then asked if *wound* was on the list—and made a friend for life.

In return, Claire had asked if she could add Dr. Gregory's name to her Rolodex. Vanity license plate requests often contained what turned out to be slang or Latin for various bodily parts, functions, or secretions. More than a few words and phrases had been added to the department's Vulgar List after Claire had found out from Dr. Gregory exactly what they meant.

"No, I'll never go back to Specialty Plates," Claire said. "This is more in your capacity as my physician."

"Is that all I am to you?" Dr. Gregory was a consummate flirt, but since he seemed to treat any female between sixteen and ninety-six the same way, Claire didn't take it personally. He gave a mock-tragic sigh. "Ask away."

"I sprained my ankle running yesterday afternoon, and it seems that it's gotten a lot worse overnight. In fact"— Claire looked at her ankle dubiously—"it seems to be getting more swollen by the minute. I can't put any weight on that foot, and my toes feel sort of tingly. I'm beginning to wonder if I might have broken something. Charlie's not going to be back for a couple of hours. Do you think I should call an ambulance—or can it wait until she gets back? I don't know how much more give my skin has in it."

"Don't call an ambulance. You don't want to have to pay seven hundred dollars out of your own pocket. I'll come by and take a look at it. If it looks broken, I'll take you in for an X ray."

After some protesting, Claire agreed. Even though he wasn't much over forty, Dr. Gregory was the last of the old-time physicians, the ones who made house calls and treated three generations of one family. He probably even accepted sacks of potatoes and live chickens in payment. He was like a modern Dr. Welby—only instead of a graying man with a fatherly smile, he had warm green eyes and tightly curled honey blond hair. He kept a small office in the Multnomah Village neighborhood, with only a part-time nurse. "Sure, I could work myself into the ground and make four hundred thousand dollars a year, but for what?" he had told Claire once. "This way I get to make a decent living, be my own boss, and still have time to go hiking."

Only after she had hung up the phone did Claire realize she was still wearing what she had worn to bed—nothing.

Pulling herself upright, Claire began to hop slowly toward her closet. Hopping was an even more ridiculous mode of transportation than she had imagined. She was able to advance only a few inches with each hop, and every time she landed it sent a thrill of pain through her dangling injured ankle. Normally, she enjoyed the long narrow expanse of her bedroom—it ran the full width of the house—but now it seemed endless. And when had her room gotten to be such a mess? She had to maneuver around a pair of Birkenstocks, a mystery novel she had started a few days ago, and a pile of clothes she had been meaning to take down to the basement laundry room.

By the time she made it to her closet, Claire was exhausted. Leaning against the doorframe, she pulled a black cotton-knit dress from the hanger. It was the dress version of a T-shirt, with long sleeves and a hem that ended just above her ankles. Her dresser—and underwear drawer—was about a hundred hops away. Then Claire imagined Dr. Gregory kneeling before her, assessing her ankle, and then noticing he had a clear shot of her crotch. Maybe she could skip the bra, but panties were a must. She had just finished struggling into a pair when the doorbell rang.

Claire hopped over to the window and pulled aside the curtain. There was Dr. Gregory's little red Mazda Miata parked in the driveway, behind Claire's infinitely less eye-catching ten-year-old tan Mazda 323 econo-box. And there was Dr. Gregory himself, holding a black doctor's bag. He waved up at her.

"Come on in!" Claire shouted after she had opened the window.

He motioned toward the door. "The door's locked."

Claire made a face. How long would it take her to hop down the stairs? "This may take a minute."

He cupped his hands around his mouth. "Don't you have a key hidden under the welcome mat or anything?"

She shook her head. And then remembered the backpack that was still looped over the bedpost. "Wait—I forgot. I do have a key up here."

He fumbled the ring when she tossed it down, then recovered it. "I'll be up in just a second."

When she heard Dr. Gregory's footsteps on the stairs, Claire called out, "I'm in here." He opened the door, and she saw that his hair was still a little damp in back from his shower. Claire ran into Dr. Gregory outside his office all the time—lifting weights next to her at the MJCC, getting a latte from Village Coffee, petting the resident black cat at Annie Bloom's Books—but still, it felt oddly intimate to have him in her bedroom. He was dressed in an expensive outdoorsy way that would never actually work in the real outdoors. His Hilfiger jeans were too snug, and his moss green long-sleeved polo shirt was made of pima cotton too light to keep out even a faint breeze.

"Let's have a look, then." He knelt at her feet, and Claire was glad she had remembered to put on panties. His cool fingers stroked her ankle and calf as he talked to her, reinforcing the oddly personal nature of his profession. On Claire's last birthday, Charlie had given her a gift certificate for a massage. It had been the same sort of thing, professional hands paid to touch in places and ways that you would normally slap a stranger for.

"I thought of the best heteronym yet," she said, as he flexed her foot.

His eyes were on her ankle, evaluating its range of motion. "Does this hurt?" He pushed until her toes pointed back at her. His nails were perfect, capped in white new moons and buffed to a discreet shine. It probably didn't pay to be a doctor with dirty fingernails.

"No more than anything else."

"How about this?"

Claire shook her head. From this angle she could see that Dr. Gregory must have grown up poor. His top teeth were white, even, and shining—and certainly capped, Claire realized, as she glimpsed the jumble of gray and yellow lower teeth, normally hidden by their spiffed-up brethren and his lower lip.

"What was the word you thought of?"

"Slough as in slough of despond, and slough, as in this loofah will slough off dead skin cells." She pronounced the first word *slau* and the second one *sluff*.

The skin around his green eyes crinkled as he smiled. "That's great. And I don't have it on my list." Dr. Gregory sat back on his heels and cradled her foot in his hands. "Well, what we have here is pretty simple. You've sprained your ankle. You've torn and twisted a lot of ligaments right here"—he trailed a finger across the puffiest part—"but nothing is broken. You won't need a cast, but you will need to take it easy for a while." He picked up his black bag, unzipped it, and pulled out an Ace bandage. "Now watch how I wrap this."

"What about running? I've been running five miles nearly every day."

"This is going to put a crimp in it, I'm afraid."

Running was the only reason Claire was still able to eat Doritos and not have the thighs to show for it. "For how long?"

"Take it easy for a day or two, and then after that you can gradually start running again." He saw the frown cross her face. "The better you take care of your ankle now, the sooner you'll be lacing up your Nikes. You can speed the healing by keeping your foot elevated for the rest of the day. In fact, let's get that foot elevated right now." He stood up and helped Claire to her feet—or foot. Before she knew what he was doing, he had bent down, hooked one arm under her knees, and hoisted her in his arms.

"Hey!" Claire protested. "You don't need to do this."

Underneath the cotton of his polo shirt she could feel the hard muscles in his chest. Was that the real reason he had picked her up, to sneak in a little physical contact?

A little huff of exertion brushed past her ear as Dr. Gregory settled her down on the bed. Claire pulled her dress back over her knees as he sat down at the foot of the bed. "I want you to take it easy, not be hopping all over your bedroom. I'm going to put an ice pack on your ankle, and I want you to promise you won't stir for the rest of the day. If I know Charlie, she will want to wait on you hand and foot. And if I know you, you won't want to let her. You're hereby under doctor's orders to let her. Here," he said as he bent down to retrieve the mystery novel from the floor, then handed it to her, "this should help you stay entertained until she gets back. Why don't you spend the next couple of hours seeing if you can figure out the solution before the main character does?"

The mystery novel gave Claire just the in she was looking for. "Speaking of solving mysteries, have you ever heard of the Bradford Clinic?"

Dr. Gregory didn't answer her right away. Instead, he took an instant ice pack from his bag, broke it open, and draped it over her ankle. When he looked over at her, his green eyes were thoughtful. "Why do you want to know? Are you pregnant, Claire?"

Claire was surprised to feel herself flush. "No, no, I'm not asking for me. So you have heard of it?"

"In my line of work, everyone knows the good doctor Bradford. Do you know someone who wants to adopt? I'll warn you, he's not cheap. But he can come through for parents who may not otherwise qualify."

"Look, I'm not pregnant, and I don't know anyone who wants to adopt. It's kind of an unusual problem. About ten years ago, my friend had a baby at that clinic. You know how it works, right? You give up all rights to contact the child." He nodded. "But see, now she has another child, Zach, and he's got leukemia. He may need a bone-marrow transplant, but there's no match in the national registry."

Dr. Gregory's reply was carefully phrased. "Does she know that even if she does find the child, the chances of a half sibling matching aren't much better than an unrelated donor?"

"That's the thing. The baby she gave up and Zach—the child she has now—both have the same father. Lori and Havi broke up around the time she got pregnant and then got back together a few years later. They have another child, too, a little older than Zach, but he doesn't match. They've thought about trying to conceive another child as a possible match, but the doctor says there's no time."

"Who's the pediatric oncologist?"

"Dr. Preston."

"I've heard he's a good man. I'm sure he's doing everything he can. But as for Dr. Bradford, that's a tricky one." Dr. Gregory seemed to be thinking something over. His voice dropped. "This is all off the record, right?"

"Record, what record? This is just me, Claire Montrose, talking in my"—she was about to say bedroom, but switched it to— "house."

"I've heard that he's been up before the board several times, but ultimately nothing ever came of it."

"The board?"

"Of medical examiners. There's been a few complaints about his clinic over the years. Not as many as you might think, even though he runs a fairly unorthodox setup. But there's so much money involved that all the parties have some incentive to look the other way."

"If there's a lot of money involved, isn't that getting pretty close to buying a baby? And isn't that illegal?"

"Tell that to the person who pays fifteen thousand dollars for an adoption."

"Fifteen thousand?" Claire echoed.

"That's how much one of my patients just paid for a

one-year-old girl in an open adoption. The child's mother was a stripper with a taste for meth, so my patient is paying a lot of money for a baby that may or may not have been born drug-addicted, and quite probably spent her first formative months in a less than ideal environment. And my patient got that baby through a strictly legitimate agency. Now just imagine how much someone would be willing to pay for a brand-spanking-new—excuse the pun—white baby, certified drug-free, whose birth parents are guaranteed to be college students with above average IQs. And on top of that, the baby comes with absolutely no strings attached, no birth mother who's going to want to stay in the picture. How much would that be worth to someone?" He answered his own question. "I think Dr. Bradford's prices *start* at one hundred thousand dollars."

Claire realized there was something wrong with his scenario. "But my friend's husband wasn't in college. Havi's smart, but he never went past high school. When the baby was born, he was in the army."

"And maybe the good doctor told the adoptive parents that. And maybe he didn't. There have been rumors around for years that Dr. Bradford might play a little fast and loose with the truth, especially when it's to his benefit. One thing nobody doubts, though, is that he cuts all ties between the biological parents and the adoptive parents. Nobody knows except Dr. Bradford, and he's not telling."

"Is that legal?"

"I think in this state that women have three months after the birth to change their minds about giving up a baby, but I don't know how well he explains that to them. And with the kind of money he has to hand out, a lot of these girls probably don't care. Whatever goes on at Dr. Bradford's clinic might be what libertarians like to call victimless crimes. The parents get the baby they always wanted. The girl gets a free education and the knowledge that her child is getting a better life than she could ever give it. And Dr. Bradford gets some money. So everyone's happy."

"How come you know so much?"

Dr. Gregory looked away from Claire. He pinched the end of his nose. "I may have referred a girl or two to him. Say a good Catholic girl comes in, wondering how come she hasn't had her period in three months. A little girl from Burns, Oregon, never been in the big city before, now she's a wide-eyed freshman at Portland State who forgot to say her Hail Marys and keep her legs crossed."

"And a girl like that probably wouldn't believe in abortion," Claire continued for him, although it went against her personal beliefs to call anyone over the age of sixteen a girl.

"Exactly. Dr. Bradford offers her a way out besides choosing between an abortion or quitting school to raise her kid." Dr. Gregory leaned over to pick up his bag, then stood up. "Let me know if there is anything else I can do for you."

"There is one more thing, Doctor."

He shook his head in mock irritation. "Michael, Michael, I've told you to call me Michael."

"This is something I wanted to ask you in your official capacity as a doctor."

"You name it."

"Can you tell me how to fake a pregnancy?"

There was a long pause while he considered her question. He finally cocked his head to one side. "Although I probably shouldn't be, I am willing to discuss this matter with you." Claire opened her mouth to thank him, but he raised a cautioning hand. "On one condition. You must allow me to take you out to dinner."

5● "I feel like a magazine ad for tampons," Claire complained. She was gratified when Lori smiled at her in the tall mirror that hung on the door of Lori's walk-in closet. Claire had called Lori the day before, while she reluctantly rested in bed. Hearing the news that Claire hoped to persuade Dr. Gregory to help her pose as a pregnant woman, Lori had insisted that Claire come over to plan what to wear. Lori was convinced that Claire lacked the appropriate outfit that would both guarantee Dr. Gregory's help and that wouldn't look out of place in Sinq, Northwest Portland's hottest restaurant. Claire, who mostly dressed in jeans and T-shirts, had to admit she was right.

"You don't like all white?" Looking in the mirror next to Claire's shoulder, Lori twitched the lapel of an antique white-silk jacquard vest into place. The vest was layered over a lightweight ivory-wool turtleneck and paired with matching wool pants.

Discarded clothes were heaped on the bed and scattered on the floor. Even though she was three inches shorter and currently fifteen pounds heavier, many of Lori's clothes from thinner phases in her life fit Claire.

"You know what will happen if I wear this within a ten-foot radius of any food or beverage?" Claire stepped back from the mirror, unbuttoned the pants, and let them drop to her knees. She sat down on a dark green velvet overstuffed chair to finish taking them off. After a day draped with an ice pack, her ankle had begun to heal, but it was still unable to support her weight by itself. In the shower that morning, her foot had looked bloated and shapeless, green near the ankle and purple along the bottom edge where the skin gathered to smooth out into the sole. "If I wear this, I'll guarantee you that I'm doomed to spill something on it that even *my* dry cleaner can't get out. She scolds me enough already. You know what she told me last time I brought something in?" Wagging her finger, Claire did her best approximation of the dry cleaner's Korean accent. "'You messy eater! Many spot!'" She slipped off the vest, pulled the sweater over her head, and handed everything back to Lori.

"I wore that outfit to a New Year's Eve party with Havi," Lori said, her eyes unfocused. "We had a wonderful time. We didn't get home until three." She sighed and shook her head. "Let me see what else I have back here." She disappeared again into the walk-in closet. The yellow halter dress she emerged with was splashed with bright orange sunflowers.

"Have you told him yet?" Claire asked.

Without looking at Claire, Lori shook her head. "How can I? You know how they say people either see the glass as half-full or half-empty? In Havi's case, he wants to know who in the hell drank his water." Claire smiled, but Lori didn't. "He's so angry right now, but there's no one to be angry at. If I tell him, then I'll just be giving him a place to put his anger, and I can't deal with that right now." Her tone hardened, as if Claire were arguing with her. "If you find her, then I'll tell." She let her breath out in a sigh, then amended it to, "When you find her." She sat on the bed and looked at Claire. There were shadows under her brown eyes. "What will you learn if you go to the Bradford Clinic posing as a pregnant woman?"

Claire was still figuring out the answer to that question herself. "The only way I can find out who adopted your daughter is to go to the clinic. We already know they won't talk to you, so they wouldn't talk to me, at least not as Claire Montrose. The minute I showed up asking questions they would show me the door. But if I go as a pregnant woman who is considering adoption, I might have the opportunity to beg, borrow, or steal the information we need." Claire hoped she sounded more confident than she felt. "Do you think I can get away with saying I'm a college student?"

Leaning forward, Lori put a finger under Claire's chin and examined her face with narrowed eyes. "Maybe. If you said you were twenty-five, you could probably get away with it. A lot of students at PSU are in their mid-twenties. It's a good thing you don't have many lines."

"Redheads don't tan, especially in Oregon. I gave up and started wearing sunscreen a long time ago."

Lori held the sunflower dress against herself. "Well, what do you think? This always looks good on me when I'm a redhead."

"It might be a little . . ." *Loud* didn't seem like a polite term. "Colorful?"

"Okay. I can take a hint. No big-flower prints." Lori disappeared again into the closet. Claire could hear hangers sliding back and forth as she sought another selection. "How about this?" She came out with a red cocktail dress, cut low in the bosom and high on the legs, the kind of thing that would show off Lori's curves and would make Claire look as shapely as a clothespin.

"I don't think it's really me," Claire said. "You have to be you to carry off that dress."

"I guess it's just another dress I have good memories of. Let's see, let's see. Wait a minute, I might just have something in the back. I bought it at Nordstrom's Rack, but it's a little too long for me. I've only worn it once."

The dress Lori emerged with was still swathed in clear plastic from the dry cleaner, but right away Claire could see how striking it was—and how unlike anything Claire regularly wore. A floor-length black knit, it had a cutaway back crossed by two curving bands of satin. "Could I wear a bra in that?" she asked.

Lori snorted. "What are you, a B-cup? Honey, you don't need to worry. Go on, try it on. And if you absolutely decide you have to have a bra, just go down to Nordstrom and get yourself some of those glue-on cups. They'll give you a little bit of support and prevent that 'headlight' phenomenon." For a moment, Lori seemed nearly her old self, dispensing fashion advice with a smile and a wink. It was almost possible to forget about the desperately ill child sleeping downstairs.

"At Minor High, guys would say your high beams were on. Or they'd yell down the hall that they wanted to 'taste your chocolate chips.' High school is a much blunter place than the rest of the world."

"Yeah, that kind of talk would be grounds for a class-action suit nowadays," Lori agreed. "Go on, let's try it on."

Claire stood up and Lori helped lift the dress over her head, the fabric cool as it slid across her skin. She looked in the mirror. The dress fit her like a dream, the knit hugging her, but not too tightly. Turning to the side, she smoothed the dress over her abdomen. Was it her imagination, or did it already look poochy after two days without exercise?

Lori read her mind. "Just go buy some of those Perfect Silhouette panty hose. They've got a lot more than a control top—they also stop your thighs from jiggling and contour your butt."

Claire was curious. "Where does all that extra flab end up? Can I move it up to my chest and give myself cleavage for the night? I've always wanted cleavage."

Lori snorted. "It's overrated. I got to be a double-D when I was nursing, and I quickly found out that it's no fun when your breasts are bigger than your head."

At the thought of nursing, Lori started to look sad again, so Claire switched subjects. "This dress doesn't make me look too pale, does it?" Her skin seemed as ghostly white as the vanilla ice milk Jean used to buy by the half-gallon box when she was dieting (and then polish off in a single night).

"There are yellow-based blacks and blue-based blacks," Lori said with the air of a connoisseur. Claire had never noticed any such thing herself. "And while a yellow-based black would make you look sallow, a blue-based black actually complements the slightly rosy undertones in your skin and also sets off that apricot-colored hair of yours." She gathered up Claire's hair loosely and pulled it to the top of her head. Their eyes met in the mirror. "Wear it up like this. Not too tight. And not too many hairpins, either. You want some of these curls to spring up."

"I'm not trying to seduce the guy. This is a fact-finding mission." Claire regretted the words as soon as she said them, because they brought her friend back to reality. Lori's shoulders curled over, and her lips pressed together in a thin white line. "There is something else you could do to help me. I need to know everything you remember about the layout and the staffing of the clinic."

"It's been nearly ten years, but I'll tell you what I remember." Lori took a notepad and pencil from the drawer of a bedside table. "It's near Sylvan." She drew a thick line, then a narrower line that snaked up at a right angle to the first line. "Here's the highway, and up here there's a private drive. It's not really marked—you have to know what to look for. I remember that by the time you get to the top you don't even believe you're near a city anymore. The cedar and fir trees up there must be a couple of hundred years old."

"And what's the clinic like inside? Does the doctor have an office—and where is that in relationship to the exam rooms? Is everything visible from the nurses' station, or are there walls in between?"

"I was afraid you were going to ask me about stuff like that." Her teeth sank into her lower lip. "That's one part I just don't remember a lot about. There's a waiting area, and a nurses' station in the front, but I don't really remember where things were exactly."

Claire was beginning to feel frustrated, although she knew it wasn't Lori's fault. "How about the records? Do you remember where they kept the records?"

"All I remember is that they always had a big fat manila file in the room. But now that I think about it, I'm pretty sure it had a number on it, not a name."

A number. That meant even if Claire could find the records, they might not do her much good. Maybe a better bet was the people. "Okay, so there's the head nurse, Vi. Are there other staff?"

Lori sighed. "Another nurse or maybe two. I only really dealt with Vi. And Dr. Bradford."

"What's he like?"

Lori looked up at the ceiling as she searched her memory. "Tall. Thin. He seemed old to me then, but he was probably only in his mid-forties. And he has these pale eyes, like blue ice."

"He doesn't sound like the warm, fatherly type."

Lori nodded. "He was all business." Her smile was bitter. "I guess that's what it was, a business. He probably sold my daughter to the highest bidder."

"Mommy!" The wail was faint, but Lori was already halfway down the stairs by the time it was repeated. "Mommy!"

Claire followed her down more slowly, her ankle protesting at every step. Zach was in the hallway on his hands and knees, his small body seeming to convulse as he vomited on the oak floor. It was still a shock to see his completely bald head. Kneeling by him, Lori massaged his shoulders, as tears began to run down her face.

Panic hummed in Claire as she looked at the bright red spattered on the floor. "Is that blood?" Was Zach beginning to hemorrhage inside?

Without looking up, Lori shook her head. "He had SpaghettiOs for lunch. Could you start filling a tub for me?" She continued to pat and soothe him until his stomach was empty. While Lori gave Zach a bath, Claire found rubber gloves, a bucket, and a sponge under the kitchen sink. She scrubbed the floor clean as she listened to Lori hum while the water splashed. How hard it must be to be strong for him, not to scream or cry or curse God, but instead to hum him a lullaby.

After he was tucked back in bed, Claire asked, "Do you need to call the doctor's office? He seemed so sick."

Lori shrugged. "I know what they will say. 'It's normal.' 'It's to be expected.' 'Bring it up with the doctor next visit.' It's all normal, according to them. Vomiting is normal. He's so tired he can't hold his head up sometimes, but if I call they say that's okay. From the oncology nurses' point of view, it's all normal. Constipation, stomach cramps, headaches, pains in his jaw. These drugs they have him on, they can permanently screw up his liver, give him heart failure or diabetes, even make his bones so brittle I could break his arm if I'm not careful. I guess they figure that all those are in the future, and the cancer is killing Zach now." Lori's voice broke.

A hundred years from now they will pity us, Claire thought, *for how we tried to fight cancer by burning, poisoning, and cutting the patient. And what if these remedies, as awful as they are, don't work?* She had to find Zach's sister.

● ● ●

Dante's phone rang for the third time, which meant the answering machine was about to click on. Claire decided she didn't feel like talking to a machine, not when what she wanted was the real Dante. Part of her felt guilty about going out to dinner with Michael Gregory, even though she knew in her heart that it meant nothing. She was about to disconnect when the phone was picked up.

"Hello?" The breathless voice was a woman's, low and melodious.

"Oops. Sorry—I must have dialed the wrong number."

"Were you calling Dante? He's in the shower. This is sara."

sara, the woman who thought her ghost-written quickie celebrity autobiographies meant she shared both a profession and a spelling affectation with e.e. cummings; sara, the woman Dante had dated two years earlier; sara, who seemed to be on a one-woman mission to make Claire feel provincial, stupid, and plain.

"Is this Claire?" Her voice was as sickly sweet as cough syrup.

"Yes. Yes it is." With an effort, she kept the speed and pitch of her voice normal. Claire had felt this way once before, when her car had been rear-ended. The impact had snapped her forehead onto the edge of her steering wheel, opening up a section of her skin as neatly as a seam. She had stared at her blood-flecked dash with the same sensation of disbelief, layered over the knowledge that in another second she was going to be feeling great pain.

"We were just planning a surprise birthday party for Ant." Ant was sara's putative boyfriend. Claire wasn't going to give the woman the satisfaction of inquiring why such an activity required a shower. "Should I ask Dante to call you when he gets out? What time is it there anyway?"

How like sara not to know whether New York ran ahead or behind the rest of the country. For a minute, Claire imagined the map of the United States the other woman must carry in her head. It would be like one of those caricatured cartoon maps you sometimes saw in tourist spots. New York City—complete with the Empire State Building and the twin towers of the World Trade Center—would bulge out to cover most of the nation, nearly overlapping with the slightly smaller Los Angeles, reduced to the Hollywood sign. The rest of the map would be mostly blank, with an occasional cartoon sketch of a cow or a blade of wheat.

"You know, you're right. I think by the time he gets out of the shower it will be too late to call me back," Claire said. Then she broke the connection.

NSTIG8R

6 In the shadow of an oversize bouquet of tropical flowers, Claire waited in Sinq's lobby. The flowers seemed too big to be real, but when she tapped a petal with her finger it was cool to the touch. The restaurant was all glossy pale wood and walls covered in wheat-colored linen, but its look of quiet elegance was offset by the loud babble of voices. Many of the diners weren't talking to their companions but to their cell phones. From the nearest table she could hear a man arranging to sell six hundred shares of stock. A waiter went from table to table, dealing drinks like cards.

Claire walked over to the window, but it was too dark outside to pick out the faces of the people walking by. Her Perfect Silhouette panty hose seemed to have shifted downward in just the walk from the car. Discreetly, she tried to tug on the waistband, which was now level with her hipbones. It didn't budge.

A cool hand cupped her bare shoulder, startling her. Before Claire could even draw in a breath, Dr. Gregory was dropping a peppermint-scented kiss on her cheek.

"You're looking lovely. I don't think I've seen you in a dress before, just jeans or running shorts. I now know just how much I have been missing."

"Thank you," Claire said. His gaze made her uncomfortable, so she looked down at her shoes, plain black Aerosole flats, stretchy enough to accommodate the Ace bandage she still wore around her ankle. When she had opened the door to the restaurant, heads had turned, and she'd both enjoyed the feeling and been unnerved by it.

Dr. Gregory's compliment just served to remind Claire of her continual promises to herself that she was going to stop walking out the door looking like she just woke up. She was going to start wearing earrings, she was going to buy pretty sweater sets, she was going to put on makeup more than once a month, and she was going to start wearing shoes that weren't meant for hiking or running.

The hostess took them to their seats at a small table on the outskirts of the restaurant. When they sat down, Claire's knees grazed Dr. Gregory's under the table, and he gave her a private smile. She was going to have to be careful. There had always been a little hum of interest coming from his direction, but tonight it seemed more intense. She gave him a brief answering smile, then took shelter behind her menu.

Claire had spent enough time with Dante in New York City restaurants that she now knew basically how to eat at a place like Sinq, how to sit so the waiter could smoothly set the plate in front of her, how to deconstruct a dish that had been created to dazzle the eye as much as the palate, even how to imagine how truffle-infused roasted-garlic mashed potatoes with chanterelles might taste. The thought of Dante gave her a pang, but she pushed the thought away.

The menu was filled with the kinds of terms she associated more with New York than Portland: banana ketchup, shredded arugula, mango chutney, broccoli rabe. Every entrée seemed to have at least a dozen ingredients. The first entrée listed was a pan-seared tenderloin of beef sandwich stacked with phyllo, dried cherry, and fig bigarade, caramelized Fuji apples and sweet potato, accompanied by hazelnut dumplings, and finished with a tawny port reduction swirl. This was beyond even Claire's power of imagination. She settled for the simplest thing on the menu, pasta topped with roasted red peppers, pine nuts, and tiny quills of asparagus. Dr. Gregory ordered a steak smothered in sautéed shallots and shitakes, which surprised her. He didn't seem like the meat-and-potatoes kind of guy, even the truffle-infused kind. While they waited for their main course they dipped slices of bread into a plate of what the menu had described as unfiltered Umbrian olive oil. Claire had no idea where Umbria was, or even if it was a region or an entire country, but the end result was still good enough to make her lick her fingers.

"So is it fun being a doctor?" Claire asked. Dr. Gregory had ordered the same drink for both of them, and Claire took a cautious sip. It was sweet-tasting, but with a kick at the end.

He smiled to himself. "It was what I always wanted to be when I was growing up. You know, Dr. Kildare. Dr. Welby. All the good guys on TV were doctors. Of course, a sixties TV version of a doctor's life isn't exactly how it works today." He pinched the end of his nose and sniffed. "Dr. Welby never had to deal with managed care or capitation."

"What's capitation?"

"If this is any hint, it has the same Latin root as decapitate." His mouth smiled, but his eyes didn't. "The HMOs tell you they will only pay you so much per head. Of course, that only works if everyone stays healthy. You pray like heck that none of your patients gets really sick or needs a referral to a specialist." He took another long sip of his drink, then set the empty glass on the table. "Thank goodness there are still a few private-pay patients like you. You know, I wasn't exactly fantasizing about having to turn myself into a hustler when I put myself through school. I did enough of that when I was an undergrad majoring in English lit. Once I got hired by a temp agency to walk around at a doctors' convention dressed in a giant stomach costume and hand out samples of a new antacid. I saw these guys in their nice suits and with their clean hands. The next day I changed my major to premed. I thought being a doctor would mean I wouldn't have to figure out how to make money." He signaled with two fingers for the waiter. "Here, let me order you another one."

Claire realized she had finished her own drink without being aware of it. She was going to have to take it easy, especially when she was sitting across from a good-looking man and trying hard not to think about whether Dante had betrayed her. When Dr. Gregory excused himself to go to the bathroom, Claire pushed her drink away from her and vowed not to touch it. She was relieved when their food came.

"Do you realize you are about the only woman in here who's eating?" Dr. Gregory asked her after she had eaten a few mouthfuls. He gestured with his fork, his words coming fast, his face animated and happy. "Look around. In a place like this, the men eat and the women pick. I'll bet you half of them go home and make themselves throw up whatever they *did* eat." Claire's gaze followed his gesture. It was a room full of bare shoulders and studied rumpledness, and just as Dr. Gregory had noted, the women's plates of striped sea bass or crispy mango duck with mandarin coffee glaze sat virtually untouched.

"So, why did you ask me about how to fake a pregnancy? I take it that it's not just that you want to put a good scare into your boyfriend?"

Claire decided not to answer his half-framed question about whether she had a boyfriend. She was going to keep everything on a professional level. "You like puzzles so much, I'm sure you know why I asked. I figured I could make an appointment to see this Dr. Bradford, and see what I can find out about what happened to my friend's daughter. But I don't want to get booted out of the clinic after I fail a pregnancy test."

He gave her a sly grin. "Claire, don't tell me you're sleuthing." He reached across the table to pat her hand. "You should leave that kind of thing to the professionals."

Claire pulled her hand free. "My friend doesn't have the money to pay a private investigator. She's got one of those insurance policies that only pays eighty percent, and the hospital cost fifteen hundred a day. I just want to look around the clinic a little bit, check things out. So, say I'm a patient of yours and I come to you and say I'm pregnant. How do you—"

He interrupted her. "Is that what you're planning on doing at the Bradford Clinic? And then what? Are you going to bring a miniature camera disguised as a ball-point pen? Hide a cyanide capsule in a false tooth?" The skin by his eyes crinkled when he smiled over the edge of his glass. He was one of those people who seemed to have a year-round tan.

"I don't know what I am going to do. But I need to get in there. I figure the only way I can get in the door is if I'm a patient. But that's the tricky part, as I'm not willing to actually get pregnant to do this. I was hoping there might be some way to fool them. So tell me—if I came to you and said I was pregnant, how would you know if I were telling the truth?"

"I wouldn't. At least not in the beginning, not until I see the results of your urine sample. If you tell me that your menses are two weeks late, then I begin to think you may be pregnant. And then if you complain of nausea, particularly in the morning or after going a few hours without eating, and if you say that your breasts are tender when I do my clinical exam, then I am nearly certain." He lowered his voice and leaned toward her. "Now as your doctor, I happen to know you have a tipped uterus, which is good."

Claire could feel herself flushing. "Why is that good?"

"Early in a pregnancy it's nearly impossible to palpate a uterus and tell anything, especially if it's tipped. I would rely more on what you report to me. A positive urine test would just be the icing on the cake. So to speak."

She lowered her voice. "But how would I pass a urine test? Could I put someone else's pee in the cup?"

He raised an eyebrow. "Say, for example, if you carried a vial filled with a pregnant woman's urine in your purse? The only thing that might trip you up is if the nurse picks up the sample and realizes it's cold. Everyone's supposed to be following universal precautions these days, which means you wear gloves whenever you handle blood or body fluids. Wearing gloves, a person might not notice whether the sample is the right temperature. When they do drug testing, though, the first thing they do is drop a thermometer in the sample to make sure it actually belongs to the person it's supposed to. I heard of a guy once who bought some clean urine. Before he went in for the test, he tried to heat it up in the microwave. I guess he thought it would cool down on the way over to the test site, but still be warm by the time he poured it into the collection cup. Only his brain must have already been fried, because he set the timer for two minutes. The container exploded—and that was the end of the microwave's useful life."

Claire made a face. "Can you think of a way to keep a sample the right temperature without destroying it?"

Looking thoughtful, Dr. Gregory took a sip of his drink. "A real sample should be internal body temperature, which, you'll remember, is nearly one hundred degrees. What you could do is conceal the sample in your armpit."

"Armpit?" Tipped uteruses, exploding urine samples, hiding things in your armpits—Claire hoped that none of the other diners was eavesdropping on their conversation.

"Axillary temperature—that's armpit temperature in layman's terms—is only a degree cooler than internal. That's why I sometimes suggest that parents stick a thermometer under their kid's arm for a few minutes. It's a good alternative for babies too young to use an oral thermometer—or for parents too scared to use a rectal one."

"How would I get my hands on a real sample, though? I don't know anyone who's pregnant."

"Then you're in the wrong line of work. Every pregnant woman who walks through my door has her urine checked to make sure she's not spilling sugar or protein. After that, the sample goes right down the drain. If you're nice"—a dimple flashed on his chin as he smiled—"I could pass a sample your way." He set down his glass and signaled the waiter again.

Claire didn't want to explore what he meant by *nice*, so she didn't ask. "But what I need is the urine of someone who's just barely pregnant, right? You'll have to be careful not to give me urine from some woman who's nine months along, or the clinic will know I'm lying."

"Actually it won't matter. An in-office urine test only looks for the presence—or absence—of the pregnancy hormone HCG. It doesn't make any distinction about how much there is, just whether it's there or not," Dr. Gregory said. He raised a cautioning finger. "If I do help you out, though, you have to promise me two things."

"Sure. What?"

"You can't tell anyone about how I helped you. And most especially you can't tell Dr. Bradford. Even if he catches on as to what you're doing, you have to promise me you won't bring my name into it. He's a big man in this town, especially in medical circles. If he got mad at me, I could easily find my name being 'inadvertently' left off preferred provider panels."

Claire agreed, with a mental asterisk that exempted Lori and Charlie. After all, they already knew about this dinner tonight. And she could swear them to secrecy. "You said I had to promise two things."

He smiled. "'Curiosity killed the cat, but satisfaction brought him back.' You have to let me know what you find out."

"Of course." Their salads had come and gone. Claire excused herself to go to the bathroom. When she got up, she could feel that her panty hose had shrunk a little bit more, trying to regain the original doll size they had been when she pulled them from their package. No longer anchored over her hipbones, they slid perceptibly as she walked to the bathroom. They were beginning to tug her panties down, too.

After she peed, Claire wrestled her nylons back into place. The bathroom was perfectly PC, the kind that came with a changing table, a condom machine, and a couple of bottles of complimentary perfume that previous patrons had overenthusiastically used. A look in the mirror reassured Claire that the dress she had borrowed from Lori had been the right choice, and she grinned at her reflection. A piece of lettuce had wrapped itself around one of her top eyeteeth. Hot with embarrassment, she picked it off, praying that she had been refraining from smiling widely. Was she always doomed to look like a *Glamour* magazine's "Don't" and not a "Do"? As if to confirm her fears, Claire could feel her panty hose slide down a millimeter with each step as she walked back to the table.

Dr. Gregory sniffed as he caught the scent that still clung to her, but he didn't comment. "Once you get in the clinic's front door, how will you know what to look for?"

"I've talked to my friend Lori, but she doesn't remember a lot about the clinic's layout. I need to find out before I go up there. Have you ever been inside?"

Dr. Gregory shook his head. "No. But I might be able to help you out on that front as well. You know that hypothetical case I gave you?"

"You mean about the good Catholic girl you might have referred to the clinic?"

"Maybe it wasn't so hypothetical. I don't think she's had her baby yet. I still have her number in my records. If you want, I could call and ask if she would talk to you."

Claire nodded. "I would, very much. What's she like?" Dr. Gregory hesitated until she added, "I'm just trying to understand what kind of young woman goes to the Bradford Clinic."

The gossip in him won out. "She's young, like most of them. Barely nineteen. Blond hair, blue eyes." He waved his hand in front of his mouth. "She has these unfortunate buckteeth. She's from a farm family that lives east of the Cascades. Before she moved to Portland, going into the big city meant La Grande. If she hadn't gotten pregnant right at the end of her freshman year, I don't think she would have come back. Portland's too overwhelming for her, but at least her parents aren't here to notice how big her belly's getting. Before she figured out she was pregnant, she thought she had an ulcer. That's why she came to me."

Claire thought of cows, sheep, horses. "Didn't you say she grew up on a farm?"

He shrugged. "Denial's not just a river in Egypt. This girl didn't come to me until she was five months along. She was freaking out, telling me there was no way she could have an abortion, and at the same time telling me her parents would kill her if she had a baby. She liked the sound of the Bradford Clinic because she wanted to make sure her parents would never find out. They have a reputation for absolute secrecy. It's one reason their prices are so high. Of course, sometimes the money also helps grease the skids, gets a couple a baby they otherwise wouldn't get."

"What do you mean?"

"When you adopt through the Bradford Clinic, there's no paperwork involved, unless you count filling out the withdrawal slip at your bank. And no lawyer, and no nosy child-welfare agency asking you questions and wanting to do hours of home studies. All that's very attractive to some people. Also, in this country, if you are over forty-five, it's very difficult to adopt. The rumor is that the Bradford Clinic has no age limits. There's also a rumor that, for a little extra money, a couple can get a birth certificate that lists them as the birth parents. I hear that some women even time a fake pregnancy to coincide with the birth. So you wouldn't be the only woman associated with the Bradford Clinic who might be faking a pregnancy."

The waiter cleared their plates. "Would you like a dessert menu?"

Claire shook her head and answered for both of them before Dr. Gregory could. "No thanks, I think it's getting late." It was not only late, but she had had far too much to drink.

Claire wanted to pay for her half of the meal, or at least the tip, but Dr. Gregory wouldn't hear of it. After he had signed his name to the credit-card receipt, he insisted on walking her to her car. Against the cool air, Lori's borrowed satin raincoat offered little protection, and Claire shivered. Before she could protest, Dr. Gregory had shrugged off his jacket and put it over her shoulders. Claire didn't think she had worn a jacket in that way since high school, but it made her feel cared-for. The waist of her panty hose had slipped to the top of her thighs, forcing her to waddle, and she hoped Dr. Gregory didn't take it for a deliberate dawdle instead. When she reached her car, he took the keys from her hand, opened the door with an exaggerated flourish, then stepped closer to her. Claire stiffened, afraid he was going for a kiss, but instead he looked at her steadily and asked a question that slipped past her defenses. "How's that boyfriend of yours back in New York?"

As Claire tried to find an answer, she took a jerky breath. The sound was like that of a person who has been crying a long time, and it revealed far more than she ever would have told him willingly. His green eyes were steady, but Claire couldn't read his expression. They stood for long seconds, just looking at each other, then he broke the silence by saying, "There's another heteronym I like because the words seem related. Tear and tear." He slipped the jacket from her shoulders. "I'll call you if that girl agrees to talk to you. And you let me know when you want that urine, okay?"

As Claire drove home, she wondered why Dr. Gregory was being so helpful. She hoped he wasn't expecting her to sleep with him as a reward. But at the same time, she needed his help to get inside the Bradford Clinic. She would just have to walk a fine line.

UJUSTME

7 • A year and a half of attending college in the big city had not erased Ginny Sloop's underlying small-town trust in people. Dr. Gregory's request that she consider talking to Claire had been enough to make her unhesitatingly agree. When Claire phoned, the young woman didn't even ask her why she wanted to talk. And when Claire knocked on her door, Ginny Sloop opened it wide without first inquiring who was on the other side.

Claire introduced herself and put out her hand. "I really appreciate your seeing me."

Ginny hesitated a beat and held out her own narrow hand. The squeeze Claire gave it wasn't returned, and Claire realized the other woman was young enough not to have had much experience shaking hands. She had a pale oval face, light blue eyes that blinked nervously, and curly dishwater blond hair parted in the middle and tucked behind her ears. Her narrow mouth was crowded with teeth, so that the top two protruded slightly, giving her a rabbitty look. Before she had gotten pregnant, she must have been nearly invisible, with her soft features and thin frame. But now she was dominated by her huge belly. It was almost bigger than the rest of her put together. Her tentlike gray maternity smock was stretched so tightly that Claire could see that her navel had popped out from the pressure, like a cork protruding from a bottle.

"Come on in." Ginny motioned for Claire to follow her inside. Her apartment was like that of poor students everywhere. Brick and board bookshelves lined the walls, and the only places to sit were a sagging couch and a single chair tucked under a desk made of a door balanced on two metal filing cabinets. The one thing that gave her apartment personality was the photos. Framed photos cluttered the scratched blond coffee table and hung thickly on the walls.

"Are you due soon?" Claire asked.

"Not for a month, if you can believe it. It's twins, if you hadn't guessed." Ginny's face was drawn with sadness when she said the word "twins." Huffing with each move, she sat down on the couch and rested her feet on the coffee table.

Claire sat on the other end of the couch. The plaid bedspread that covered the old couch did nothing to soften the protruding springs. What was Ginny doing with Dr. Bradford's money? Then Claire remembered the bulk of it was only received after the woman relinquished her child. She turned her head to look at all the photos of a different Ginny. Ginny laughing, her eyes sun-squinted, her arms draped around the necks of two other girls. Ginny at twelve or thirteen, her fingers buried in the fur of a border collie that looked at the camera with its mouth open in a doggy smile. Ginny holding up a blue ribbon, her arm draped around the neck of a black-and-white cow. Directly behind where the real Ginny sat hung a picture of the old Ginny on the back of a bucking horse. Her back was slim and straight, her smile wide and unafraid. One hand gripped the pommel and the other raised her cowboy hat straight over her head. In all the photos, Ginny looked tanned and sturdy and nothing like the pale young woman who sat in front of Claire, grimacing as she leaned forward to rest her hands on the arch of her back.

"Dr. Gregory told me you grew up in a small town. Has it been hard making the transition to Portland?"

Ginny nodded. "My graduation class had twenty-two people in it. I'd known all of them since kindergarten. Here, there's thousands of people who go to school. It's kind of overwhelming. It's hard to make friends. I never thought about it, but I guess I didn't have to before. I already knew everyone." The words bubbled out of her. Claire realized that Ginny must have days when she never spoke to anyone. "I haven't told my parents about what it's been like. Neither of them went to college, so when I was accepted at PSU with a full scholarship they were thrilled. They don't want me working twenty-hour days for months on end only to lose everything if it doesn't rain or it rains too much. My mom does some waitressing in town, and there's been times that's the only money we've had coming in."

"Do they know about your"—Claire was going to say *babies*, but changed it to, "pregnancy?"

Unconsciously, Ginny rubbed her palms over her swollen belly. "This happened right before I went home for the summer. I didn't know myself for a long time. I've always been irregular. I just thought I was throwing up because I had an ulcer or something. Besides, I don't think my parents really look at me anymore. I'm just Ginny to them, their baby. At Christmas break, I told them I couldn't come home because I was working on a special project for extra credit. This term, I just kept wanting to sleep all the time. I finally had to drop out. They don't know that either. They think I'm doing really well." She sighed.

No wonder Ginny had opened the door so readily. There must be days when she didn't even leave this room, with its reminders of what her life had been like before she pursued her dreams. "What will you do about school?"

"I'm enrolled again next term, but I lost my PSU scholarship. I don't know if you know this, but the clinic does pay the girls some money." She watched Claire's face carefully, as if expecting an outcry of disgust, but seemed reassured by whatever she saw there. "If I'm careful, it will be enough for at least two years. I'm going to take twenty credit hours this spring, which is more than a full load. If I do that for a few terms, I'll catch up." She sounded like she was trying to convince herself.

Even though Claire was only about a dozen years older, she felt a wave of maternal feeling for Ginny. "What about the father? Does he know?"

Ginny snorted. "He knows. I made sure about that. By the end of last year, I thought that everyone was partying except me. I figured I was probably the only virgin on campus. I decided I was old enough to make my own decisions, even ones the Catholic Church or my parents don't approve of. There was this guy in my American history class, and one day he asked me to study for finals with him. It turned out he wanted to do a lot more than that. He told me he used a condom." A dimple moved across her belly, and Claire realized one of the babies inside her must be turning. "I don't know if he didn't use it right or what. After I got back to school, I went to his apartment to tell him what had happened. You know what he said to me?"

"What?" Claire asked, unnecessarily, for the words were already spilling out of Ginny.

"He just sat there for a moment, and then he just said, 'Oh, I kinda forgot about that.' That's how special I was to him. He offered me money for an abortion, and he didn't look too jazzed about even that. Up until then I didn't know what I was going to do, but I knew when he said that that I couldn't kill my baby. I told him I didn't want his money. That I was going to have the baby. That was before I knew it was twins. He went all white. I think he's afraid I'm going to sue him for child support for the next eighteen years. I haven't corrected his impression. I figured it was the least I could do."

She raised her hand to cover her smile, and Claire found herself smiling back.

"Dr. G. didn't really say what you needed, just that you wanted to ask me some questions about the clinic. So are you pregnant? Or thinking about adopting? I'm afraid they already have parents lined up for these two." Ginny looked at her with her tired, open face.

Claire found that she couldn't lie to Ginny. She shook her head. "Neither, I'm afraid. Ten years ago, my friend had her daughter at the Bradford Clinic. Now Lori's three-year-old son has leukemia. If she can find the girl, she might be a match for a bone-marrow transplant. But the clinic won't tell Lori anything. I need to find a way to look at their records."

Ginny straightened up. "I could help you. I could look around at my appointment this afternoon. It's not like it's a really busy place. I could just poke around." She looked excited, animated for the first time.

"No," Claire barked, her stomach giving a lurch. Why had she been seduced into telling the truth? This girl could ruin everything. "Absolutely not. If you go around asking questions, you could make it so that Lori never finds her daughter. Leave the sleuthing to someone with experience."

"What are you, like a private investigator?"

Deciding a lie only counted if you said it out loud, Claire nodded.

Her face still painted with two bright spots of color, Ginny sagged back on the couch. "All right, I won't. But I can keep my eyes open when I'm there, can't I?"

Claire knew there was no way she could stop her, but she had to try. "Don't even do that. I don't want you asking one question, no matter how innocent. If you made them suspicious, they might move the records completely out of the clinic." She took out the little map Lori had drawn for her in pencil. "Where I need your help is right here and now. My friend tried to tell me about how things were laid out, but that was ten years ago." Claire handed Ginny the pencil. "Can you show me where the exam rooms, bathrooms, doctor's office, and nurses' station are?"

Ginny did. Then she surprised Claire by sketching in another rectangle a few inches behind the clinic.

"What's that?"

"The doctor's house. He lives on the property. It's this old, beautiful, three-story house, you know, the kind with the stone pillars and the big deep porch. It's on the crest of a hill, so it must have a great view of the city."

● ● ●

From Ginny's house, Claire drove to the I Spy Shoppe, fretting the whole way. The girl was so palpably lonely. What would stop her from blurting everything out to someone at the clinic? They were the only people Ginny ever spoke to. She seemed especially attached to the head nurse, Vi, the same one who had cut Lori off the minute she started asking questions about her daughter.

The I Spy Shoppe was located in a strip mall on Barbur Boulevard, next to a space that held a new restaurant every month. Now it appeared to have morphed from a Pakistani restaurant into an Ethiopian one. When the lone waiter saw Claire's Mazda nose into the parking lot, he picked up a menu and stood at attention, then slumped as she limped past the LENTIL STEW MADE FRESH DAILY! sign. Claire made a mental note to take Charlie to the restaurant soon, although it would do little to stave off its inevitable demise.

With its cheap gray-felt carpeting and white-painted walls, the I Spy Shoppe also had an air of impermanence about it, even though it had been selling its own particular brand of paranoia for over ten years. The small store's half dozen glass cases held an odd mixture of gag gifts ("Instant Worms," "The Two-Headed Nickel—Wins Every Toss") side by side with more serious—and expensive—items like leg shackles, bomb detectors, and a briefcase booby-trapped to give any unauthorized user a nine-thousand-volt jolt.

The clerk, Jimmy, looked up from his *Soldier of Fortune* magazine. "What happened to your ankle?" he asked.

"A little escapade with a killer attack dog." Claire said it with a smile, but he apparently believed her.

"An ankle's not much to injure in that case. One trick is to remember to throw your forearm over your throat. Better to have your arm bitten than to have your throat torn out." Jimmy demonstrated, looking as if he were trying to strangle himself. "And if you get knocked off your feet, you assume the pill bug position." He laced his fingers together and put his hands over the back of his neck, with the fingers facing inside. He curled his body over so that his face was against his knees. He straightened up, his knees giving an audible pop. "Of course, you're better off if it never comes to that. I always advise clients to try our Dog B Gon." As Claire thought to herself that the name would make a good license plate, Jimmy tapped on the top of the glass case, indicating a small metal canister about the size of a bottle of correction fluid. "It's guaranteed to stop any dog in its tracks. And another thing to try is German. Most attack dogs are trained to ignore English commands. Say 'Halt' instead of 'Stop.'"

"I think this particular dog didn't understand any language, English or foreign."

"That's the problem. People go out of their way to train their dogs to be mean, but it's like leaving a loaded gun lying on top of the TV set. You don't know who's going to get hurt." Eyes narrowed, he gave her a little nod, then switched into his salesman mode. "So what can I do you for today?"

Jimmy had once sold Claire a stun gun the size of a beeper. When it came to planning a break-in, he was again happy to give her advice, just as long as she understood it was speculative. Jimmy spent his days fantasizing that he was really 007, while he sold "nannycams" hidden in teddy bears to suspicious parents—and telephone-tapping devices to even more suspicious spouses.

Leaning on the counter so that she could keep her weight off her left ankle, Claire laid out her problem for Jimmy. "Suppose there's a building I need to get into at night—but I don't happen to have a key. If I were able to get inside beforehand, do you have anything I could use to keep the lock from closing so I could come by later?" She paused, then added, "Of course this is all hypothetical."

"Of course." He gave her a wink. The thing about Jimmy was that he never asked why you wanted to do what you wanted to do. He narrowed his eyes and stroked the sparse goatee he had been attempting to grow for as long as Claire had known him. "You could try putty. Or tape. But that would only work with certain kinds of locks, and only if no one tries the door after they think they've locked it. What kind of lock will you be working with? Standard Yale? Disc tumbler? Your five-pin household?"

Claire was already beginning to feel overwhelmed. "I don't have any idea."

"Then what I would really recommend is a pick kit. I've got the basics for thirty-nine ninety-five, or a deluxe set for seventy-nine ninety-five." He was already unlocking one of the display cases.

"You mean, like to pick a lock? Can anybody do that?"

"Sure, if you practice a bit." He pulled a palm-sized folded leather case from the top glass shelf and flipped it open. Inside were a dozen black-metal tools, each about the size of a toothpick. He picked up one that had a ninety-degree bend at one end. "See, you slide this in where the key would go, and then put pressure on it. Then you take a pick or a rake"—he touched tools that had either a single hooked end or a series of waves, then picked up one to demonstrate—"slip it in, and just start working it and working it until the tumblers click home."

"Won't that take a long time?"

Jimmy shrugged. "My first one took an hour. Now I can do one in about five minutes. My advice is to practice at home first on as many different types of locks as you can find. You would probably be pretty good at it." He cleared his throat. "In my experience, women have more delicate, sensitive fingers."

This was Jimmy's version of flirting, but Claire ignored it. Instead, curiosity got the better of her. "Do you sell very many of these pick kits?"

"They're a steady mover."

"What do people buy them for?"

Jimmy narrowed his eyes and gave a warning shake of his head. "You know my motto. I don't know, and I don't want to know. Maybe"—he lifted his shoulders—"maybe some people get locked out of their houses a lot." *Or*, Claire thought, *they get locked out of other people's houses a lot*. He realized she was eyeing him skeptically. "Or maybe, you know, it's like a hobby."

In a country where shooting an AK-47 could be classified as a hobby, Claire supposed anything was possible. She bought the less expensive pick kit, as well as a nineteen ninety-five booklet that Jimmy promised would give her step-by-step instructions for all types of locks. And, remembering the sickening wash of terror when the dog had leaped at her, she had Jimmy throw in a bottle of Dog B Gon. It might come in handy the next time she went running.

As he was slipping her purchases into a bag, Claire asked him if he knew where she might be able to get some fake ID. "I'm not talking a driver's license, or anything like that. But what if I wanted to make someone think I was a college student?"

Despite the fact that they were the only two people in

the Shoppe, Jimmy whispered his recommendation from the side of his mouth. "Harry's Camera. Beaverton." He handed the bag to her, then added, "This building you're interested in. It doesn't have an alarm, does it?"

Claire noted that Jimmy hadn't brought up that possibility until after he had made his sale. "I hadn't thought about that." Her plan, such as it was, was already crumbling. "I don't know. Do you have anything that could circumvent one?"

Jimmy shook his head. "Probably not. There's two basic types. One monitors the perimeter—your doors, windows, transoms, vents, skylights. They're usually set to notice vibrations. Some sophisticated alarms are tuned to the frequency of breaking glass. The other type of alarm monitors the interior space with either heat or motion detectors. But both are prone to falsing."

"Falsing?" Claire echoed.

"Say a heavy truck goes by. Or a helium balloon left over from a party starts drifting around. Nine times out of ten, an alarm goes off for the wrong reason. That's why most of them aren't hooked up to police stations anymore—too many false alarms. Even the monitoring agencies don't take them too seriously. And a lot of alarms aren't monitored at all."

"Then what would be the point of having one?"

"The primary goal is to scare someone off. If some jerk is kicking in your back door and starts hearing a loud noise, he'll probably decide it's better to go someplace else. And even with an unmonitored alarm, usually someone will notice and eventually check it out, even if it's just a neighbor calling to complain about the noise."

"But I don't have any idea what kind of alarm system this building has, or if it even has an alarm system."

"You've got questions, Jimmy's got answers," Jimmy said. He paused and looked around the empty store. "Do you want my advice?"

"Of course I do, Jimmy."

"I think you should break out, not break in."

• • •

Evidently, Harry was a lot less secretive than Jimmy about his business, because his half-page ad in the Yellow Pages trumpeted "ID—all types!" in seventy-two-point type. Harry's turned out to be located in another anonymous suburban strip mall. Harry probably made most of his money, not off the few cameras in a dusty glass case, but through the sale of instant identification displayed on a Plexiglas divider in the middle of the room. The clerk behind the counter told Claire that the ID section was self-serve, and she could see that the woman had the same "I don't want to know" attitude as Jimmy. The cards bore official-looking headings like *Employee ID, College ID,* and *Student ID.* Some had spaces for height, weight, date of birth, and/or hair and eye colors. One version just said *Official Identification Card,* another showed a pseudogovernmental eagle with the words *United States Federal Service Employee.* As far as Claire could tell, none of the college ID cards available at Harry's Camera were for colleges that actually existed. Corona State sounded good, Claire decided as she looked over her choices. It seemed plausibly Californian. She could be a transfer student who hadn't gotten her Portland State ID yet.

To complete her makeover, Lori had loaned Claire an age-appropriate outfit of chunky shoes paired with a frankly polyester dress. For a day or two, Claire had even thought about wearing a wig to the doctor's office, until she'd realized that once she took off her underwear she would give the game away. And she wasn't brave or stupid enough to try dyeing her pubic hair. Before coming to

Harry's Camera, Claire had compromised by pulling her hair back in a bun so tight that it made her eyes hurt. At least it no longer looked curly, and thus perhaps not so much like Claire Montrose.

She used a touch-screen computer to enter the information she wanted to claim as hers. The result was printed out on card stock on a special color printer. Then Claire sat in one of the photo booths, pulled the wine red curtain, and snapped herself two times. Holding the still wet photos by their edges, she took her new Corona State ID to the laminating machine.

WHO RU

8 After obtaining the pick kit and the new ID, Claire stopped by John's Market in Multnomah Village. Part grocery store and part deli, it also housed a mail center that rented boxes with addresses that sounded like they belonged to apartments. Claire had realized that it wouldn't be a good idea for any mail the Bradford Clinic sent Lucy Bertrand to be returned to them marked NO SUCH ADDRESS.

The phone was ringing when she walked in the front door. "Claire—it's Lori." Her words tumbled over one another.

"What's up?"

"We got the results of Zach's last bone-marrow aspiration today. Dr. Preston said he's in remission."

"That's great news!" Lori was silent for so long that Claire finally added, "Isn't it?"

"Havi thinks so. I'm not so sure. It's not that hard to get a child into remission. The trick is getting him to stay there. Zach still looks so sick. And just because the bone marrow looks normal doesn't mean that the leukemia isn't hiding out someplace. Zach's still going to be on chemo, just lower doses. That's for two or three more *years*. We're not out of the woods yet, not by a long shot." Lori took a deep, shuddering breath. "Do you believe in a mother's intuition?"

Claire didn't, not any more than she believed in people's bringing bad luck down on themselves by voicing their fears. "Why?"

"Because part of me thinks he will need a transplant.

And if that happens, and you can't find his sister, then there isn't any hope."

• • •

As she drove to Susie and J.B.'s house, Claire couldn't stop thinking about Zach and Lori. Why couldn't her friend relax and accept the blessing of her son's remission? But Claire knew if she were Lori, she would be weighing the odds, too, and doing anything she could to make them be in her favor.

J.B., her semi-brother-in-law, was something of a shade-tree mechanic. He could be counted on to own a half dozen cars in various states of functionality, and he had agreed to lend one to Claire, her last step in her efforts to distinguish herself from Lucy. In addition to J.B.'s pickup, three cars were parked in the driveway, with another half dozen along the curb. Each was beat-up enough that it could plausibly belong to a college student.

"Hey, Big Sis," Susie said when she answered the door. She dropped a kiss on Claire's cheek. "J.B. will be out in a minute. He's just getting Eric ready for the day." Dressed for her job as a hairdresser, Susie wore a white-denim miniskirt and a green smock with her name embroidered over her heart. An ankle bracelet made a line under her nylons.

When the painting Claire had inherited had sold for millions at auction, she had offered part of the proceeds to her sister. After all, Susie was Aunt Cady's niece, too, even if she hadn't been named in the will. But all Susie would accept was enough to set up a trust fund for Eric's college education and to pay for her classes at the Portland Beauty Academy. Susie had dreamed of being a hairdresser since her eighth birthday and the gift of a Barbie Kut-N-Kurl set.

"Suse, I've been meaning to ask you—have you noticed that Mom's buying a lot of"—Claire veered away from the word junk in case Susie also shopped Qual-Prod—"stuff off TV?"

"You mean that QualProd crap? I tried to talk to her about it. I mean, she's got three different skin-care systems underneath the bathroom sink. Mom tried to tell me it was like she was the member of a special club!" Susie rolled her eyes, which were highlighted with blue shadow and rimmed with black eyeliner. "Yeah, a real *special* club that you can only join if you have a credit card with some money left on it. She says no matter what time of the night it is, when she wants to talk to someone, she can always talk to a QualProd operator. I told her if she feels lonely, she should just call me, but she wouldn't listen."

Or me, Claire thought. *Or Mom could call me.* It hurt a little that neither her mother or her sister seemed to have discussed calling Claire as an option. "I'm worried about her. It seems like we should do something."

A shrug of Susie's thin shoulders. She was whittled down to almost nothing by cigarettes. "I don't know that there's much that we can do. When was the last time either one of us successfully told Mom how to run her life? Until she gets tired of it, I think she's going to watch QualProd all day wearing her QualProd bathrobe and with her QualProd slippers on her feet and her QualProd throw across her lap."

Claire realized Susie was probably right. "How are things down at Curl Up and Dye?"

"Same old, same old. Everybody's always yakking at me, telling me stuff I don't really need to hear. Sometimes I think they just come to get their hair done because I'm cheaper than a therapist. The worst ones are the perms because they take so long. By the time you finish combing them out they've had time to get everything— and I mean every little thing—off their chests. Yesterday, I heard about"—Susie began to tick off on her long, yellow-stained fingers—"one, about how some lady's having an affair with her boss and both their spouses know and think it's okay, and two, about how some other lady's mother wasn't really dead but stuck away in an insane asylum, and three, then I got some girl who wanted me to help her figure out if her boyfriend's gay." A snort. "Like I'm gonna know. She wanted to know if it was bad sign he was getting all these dirty e-mail messages from people with names like Boy Toy." She shook her head. "I got this job so I could cut hair, not be a counselor. "

That was the difference between her and Susie, Claire thought. Susie didn't want to hear everyone's secrets, but Claire would love a job where people confided in her all day. Whenever she saw a movie showing a Catholic making a confession, she always found herself a little envious of the priest sitting on the other side of the screen.

A little body suddenly hit Claire from behind, almost knocking her over. Turning, she reached down and swung two-year-old Eric up into the air while he squealed.

"Hey, sweetness, how's it going?"

Eric's only answer was to squeeze her nose and make a honking sound. He was still laughing at his own joke when she set him down.

"I wish I had his energy," Claire said as she watched him zoom around the room.

"God got it mixed up," J.B. said as he came into the room wrapping a rubber band around his ponytail. His denim shirt had the sleeves ripped off, the better to show off muscular arms tattooed with a Harley and a dancing girl. Around his neck, a black beeper dangled from a leather thong. Claire hoped that the beeper didn't mean J.B. had gone back to his old sideline of selling a kilo of this and a kilo of that. "It should be the kids drinking coffee and complaining that they just want to go back to bed, and the adults should be the ones bouncing off the walls." He turned to Claire. "Let's go see what we have on the lot."

As they stepped outside, Claire turned to catch the

screen door before it could bang into Eric. She caught a glimpse of J.B. sneaking a kiss from Susie. When Susie was sixteen, she had dropped out of high school, moved out of their mom's apartment, and in with J.B. Claire had thought Susie would be lucky if the whole thing lasted six months, but here they were, still together: seventeen years, one baby, five or six motorcycles, and probably three hundred cars later.

J.B. waved his hand to indicate the ten or so cars parked in front of his house. "You can have anything except my pickup or the Chevette," J.B. said. "Susie uses that to get to work."

"Chevette!" crowed Eric. In the daylight, Claire could see that his blond hair was beginning to darken, but his eyes were still a bright, fierce blue. He ran to one of the cars in the driveway and banged on its door with his fist. "Pinto!"

Claire looked closer. It *was* a Pinto. "Eric can tell cars apart? I thought kids his age were into dinosaurs."

J.B. shrugged, setting his dangling skull-and-cross-bones earrings into motion. "Oh, he can also tell the difference between a T. rex and a brontosaurus. But he likes cars nearly as well."

Claire guessed that, in its own way, the Pinto could also be considered a dinosaur. It seemed to be held together primarily by gray primer. "A Pinto, huh? I didn't think those existed anymore."

"It's a '71, so it's probably a collectible. I got it for fifty bucks. It even runs. Do you want to borrow it?"

Claire had an image of having to come to a sudden stop at a red light, her car being bumped from behind, the sudden whoosh! of flames. She shook her head.

She came away with a twenty-year-old Firebird, British racing green except for one bright blue fender. On the way home it started to drizzle, and she discovered that the car's heater didn't work. It was also almost impossible to see out the rear window, which was slanted at such an extreme angle that the rain beaded up on it and didn't go anyplace. She wouldn't need the car for long, though, just for her visit to the clinic the next afternoon. The car completed Claire's transformation into Lucy Bertrand, a transfer from Corona State who had just figured out she might have a little problem on her hands.

YY4U

9 "Hi, this is Ginny. Leave me a message after the beep." Even Ginny's voice was tentative.

Claire took a breath, ready to ask the young woman to call her. She wanted to ask Ginny if she'd ever noticed any sign of an alarm during her visits to the Bradford Clinic. She still wasn't sure which plan would be best—the one Jimmy had suggested, or her original idea of using a pick kit. Although she had practiced for several hours each day, Claire hadn't gotten to the point where she could open a door in five minutes, like Jimmy. Still, she was fairly certain that she could do it in fifteen.

Instead of a beep, a mechanized voice followed Ginny's, saying, "This voice-mail box is full and not accepting any new messages." With that, there was an abrupt click and then the hum of a dial tone.

Lonely Ginny, seemingly friendless—how could she end up with a full voice-mail box? She had told Claire that since dropping out of school the only people she regularly spoke to were the clinic's staff. Claire felt a spurt of uneasiness.

Slowly, she put the phone down. She found Charlie in the kitchen and explained the situation to her. "I'm worried something's wrong. She doesn't seem to have any friends. How did she get a full voice-mail box unless she's been gone for a while?"

"Is she near her time? Perhaps she has just gone to the clinic to have her babies." With a wooden spoon, Charlie stirred the chopped onion she was slowly sautéing for

Zwiebelkuchen. The onion-topped yeasted flat bread was southern Germany's answer to focaccia.

Claire shook her head. "She's not due for another month. When I talked to her four days ago, she had an appointment at the clinic later in the day. What if she started asking questions about Lori's daughter?"

Charlie wiped her hands on her white apron, then took it off and hung it on the back of a chair. "Let's go, then."

"Go?"

"I have watched you practice with those picks on every lock in this house. If that girl doesn't answer the door, you can get us inside to see if she is okay."

In the half-empty parking lot in front of Ginny's building, they parked next to a Pizzicato Pizza delivery van with a vanity plate that read U8MYPY. They walked up the worn, rain-puddled stairs to Ginny's apartment, which was on the second floor of the three-story building. Light leaked through the cheap yellow fiberglass curtains, but no one answered the door when Claire knocked. Thinking of the man who had recently been convicted of murder on the basis of a telltale ear print, Claire pressed her ear against the door, but heard nothing.

Ginny's apartment complex was laid out like a budget motel, with the doors of two mirroring apartments grouped together, then a gap, then another pair of matching doors. There was no one in sight. Probably most of the tenants were in class, and the drizzly gray day offered nothing to entice those who weren't. "I will keep watch," Charlie whispered, so Claire slid the pick kit out of her pocket, knelt down, and began to work.

Compared to the locks at Claire's own house, the lock on Ginny's apartment door was so simple it could have been opened by someone with a butter knife and a little patience. Claire had just felt the last tumbler click home when Charlie hissed a warning. *"Hier kommt jemand!"* *Someone's coming.* Charlie had taught her a few phrases in German, but Claire had already heard the footsteps coming down the staircase. Quickly, she turned the handle and nudged the door a fraction so that it was barely ajar.

"*Jetzt!*" Charlie hissed. *Now.*

Looking up, Claire could see a pair of Nikes coming to the bottom of the stairs, ten feet from where she was. There was no time to get to her feet. Suddenly, Charlie dropped to her knees next to her. She tilted her head as if she were looking for something. "There it is," she said.

Claire stared at her blankly.

Charlie stabbed her finger near a tiny pebble that had worked its way loose from the concrete. "There is your contact."

The footsteps had stopped. Claire looked up and into the eyes of a pizza-delivery guy, a white guy with long blond fuzzy dreadlocks. In his hands was a square red insulated bag. His nose, eyebrow, and lower lip were pierced with silver rings, but that wasn't what bothered her. It was the way he was staring, not at her, but past her, in the direction of the door that now sat slightly ajar in its frame. And then she saw what had attracted his attention. Not the door itself, but the pick kit, resting on the doorsill and flipped open so that all the tiny tools were visible.

Charlie had given Claire an idea. Making a show of it, Claire used her index finger to pick up the imaginary contact, and then popped it in her mouth. She got to her feet, blocking the pizza-delivery guy's view of the door. Then she opened her mouth and ran her right index finger across the tip of her tongue, at the same time pulling the red inside of her eyelid down with her left hand. In went the imaginary contact.

"Ooh!" She squealed. "It's not in right." Blinking and grimacing, she swept her finger against her open eye, mimicking other contact wearers she had occasionally watched with fascinated disgust.

The pizza guy grimaced. Averting his gaze, he started down the second flight of steps, a murmured "Gross!" trailing back over his shoulder.

As soon as he was out of sight, they stepped into the apartment. Claire scooped up the pick kit and quickly closed the door behind them. "Ginny?" Claire called out, already knowing there would be no answer. As she walked through the small apartment, Charlie's gaze went from photograph to photograph, not realizing the Ginny in the pictures was different from the Ginny who lived in this place.

A half-eaten burrito sat on a paper plate in the middle of Ginny's makeshift table. Bending closer, Claire smiled as she recognized the sweet spicy smell of Macheezmo Mouse's famous boss sauce. Only then did she see that the chair had been overturned. A cold pulse of fear went through her.

"Come look at this," Charlie called. In the bathroom, a pale gray towel lay on the yellow linoleum floor. The center was blotched with a dark brown stain. Claire pressed a finger against the matted loops. The blood was slightly tacky, nearly dry.

Without speaking, they opened the only other door. In the tiny bedroom, the narrow bed was neatly made. There was nothing in the room to help them unravel the mystery of what had happened in the rest of the apartment.

They went back out into the main room, and Claire pressed the blinking light on the black answering machine. "Ginny, honey, it's Mom. Could you call me tonight? I wanted to talk to you about your dad's birthday this Sunday. I was hoping maybe you could take the Greyhound home and surprise him. I've got some tip money saved up, so I could pay you back. You don't even need to bring a present. Just bring yourself, that would be all the present he would ever wish for. Anyway, give me a call and tell me if you can swing it." After the beep, a mechanized voice gave the time and day. Ginny's mother had called only a few hours after Claire's visit.

The next five calls were also from Ginny's mother, her voice increasingly plaintive and the time between calls increasingly shorter. "Ginny, please call me!" she pleaded in the last call. "Are you all right, honey? It's okay if you call me collect. Please call and let me know you're"—and then the machine mercifully cut the call short.

"She's got Caller ID," Claire said as she looked down at the machine. "Maybe she saw it was her mother calling and decided not to answer." Had Ginny stood and looked at the pictures of her old self as she listened to her mother's voice and tried to formulate the lie she would use when she returned the call? "Do you think maybe she couldn't figure out how to avoid going home and got freaked out enough to run away from her own life?"

Charlie shook her head. "Perhaps that could explain the chair being on its side, but not the blood. Maybe she got a nosebleed while she was eating. She stood up fast so that it would not stain her clothes, then went in the bathroom and cleaned up with a towel."

"I wish I knew what time she'd been eating. If this was her lunch, then it was before she went to the clinic, and this can't have anything to do with my having come here, asking questions. If it was her dinner, then it was after."

"Let us consider the possibilities," Charlie said calmly. "These things could be signs of a struggle or a bloody nose. But they could also mean that she went into labor."

"But she wasn't due for another month," Claire protested.

"Twins often come early." Charlie gestured to the overturned chair. "And didn't you tell me the father of this child was unpleasantly surprised by her announcement?"

Claire nodded. "Ginny said he wanted her to have an abortion. She said he seemed afraid that she would sue him for child support."

"Then he would have a motive for being angry with her. Perhaps he came here and argued with her."

"I don't remember hearing a lock turn when she answered the door," Claire said. "I don't think she was the kind of person to lock her door. She still thought she was living out in the boonies, the kind of place where you keep your keys in the ignition." She thought of something that made her feel better. "Even if she did go to the Bradford Clinic and start asking a bunch of questions, who would attack a pregnant woman over something that happened ten years ago? Besides, if they were going to have that strong a reaction, strong enough that they would want to harm her, wouldn't they do it then and there?"

Charlie looked at Claire with faded blue eyes that had seen everything. "And draw suspicions to themselves? Better to wait until she got home."

TYMZUP

10 "Name, please," said the guy in the yellow-and-black-striped booth that sat at the top of the long, twisty private road that led from Highway 26 to the Bradford Clinic's parking lot.

Claire's brain was still in shock, but her mouth took over. "Lucy Bertrand." Damn! Damn! Damn! Why hadn't Lori or Ginny mentioned that there was a guard at the entrance to the parking lot? Maybe there hadn't been an attendant when Lori was pregnant years ago. Maybe Ginny hadn't thought he was important enough to mention, although surely she would have brought him up if Claire had managed to see her again.

While her thoughts chased themselves, Claire gathered herself together enough to offer a smile. This guy seemed really more of a parking-lot attendant than a security guard. He certainly didn't look like a wanna-be cop. Instead of a shiny white shirt and a black-polyester uniform, he wore a blue parka zipped to his neck. A dark wool cap pushed his long brown hair into his eyes, and his untrimmed beard and mustache covered most of what was left. Claire guessed the guy was about her own age—or at least the age she really was, not what it said on her new ID. His little booth must get very cold, Claire thought, noticing he kept his free hand in his coat pocket.

"Betrand's a real pretty name," he said, and checked it off on a list. "Is it French?"

Claire thought it probably was, although she had picked the name out of the air when she had gotten her fake ID. "Yeah, I guess. We're Heinz 57." She broadened her smile and hoped it didn't look forced. "How about you? Are you anything?"

He looked away. "Don't really know what I am, either. Guess I should let you get in to your appointment."

"Don't worry. I'm early. I was afraid I might get lost." Maybe she was looking at the guy all wrong. It must get lonely, sitting out in the booth day after day. Maybe there was some way he could prove useful. Sticking to the story she had memorized, Claire continued on with the lie she had begun when she gave him a name other than her own. "I just moved up here from California last term, and I still don't know my way around." Inspiration struck. "I've been hoping maybe I'd meet someone who could show me around, give me a little tour. Have you lived in Portland long?" She gave him a frankly inviting look, figuring that a woman who was daring or foolish enough to get herself knocked up in the age of AIDS might also try to hit on a parking-lot attendant.

He stared at her for a long moment before understanding broke. "I was born here, so I guess I know my way around town pretty good." He left the words lying there, and she could tell he wasn't brave enough for the follow-through.

Claire cocked her head flirtatiously and acted as though he had asked her what he only wished he had. "So you could show me around sometime?"

His dark eyes widened, and Claire felt mean for the hope she was raising in him. He ducked his head, and mumbled, "If you want."

"Sure. Give me your phone number."

Something shifted in his face, and Claire could see that with a haircut and the application of a razor, he might be good-looking. Then his mouth drew down again. "Except for I should tell you, I don't have a car." The tops of his cheeks, about the only part of his face that wasn't obscured by hair, reddened.

"That's okay. You could ride shotgun and tell me which way to turn."

He nodded eagerly. "Okay. Let me give you my number." He hunted for a scrap of paper, then scribbled his number down. When he leaned out of his booth again, his breath washed across Claire's face, a mix of spearmint and garlic. She looked down at what he had written. Doug Renfro. "Nice to meet you, Doug Renfro."

"You, too, Lucy Bertrand." Retreating into shyness, he was already pressing the button to raise the yellow-and-black-striped arm.

Claire kept her foot on the brake. "Say, what time do you get off?" She had asked for the last appointment of the day, and gotten a four-thirty. If Doug left at five, Jimmy's plan might still work.

"I live here on the property, so I'm here until the last scheduled patient leaves." Doug's flush deepened. "Which I guess in this case would be you."

Claire realized he thought she was asking him to go out that night. She faked a sigh. "Since it's midterms, I guess tonight I really need to concentrate on studying. But I'll definitely keep your number handy." Claire waved the paper as she drove forward, then tucked it into the backpack that sat on the Firebird's passenger seat. She figured college-student Lucy would also carry a backpack, although this morning Claire had stripped it of anything that might identify her as Claire Montrose.

Scanning the grounds, Claire pulled forward into the tiny kingdom Doug oversaw, a parking lot with spaces for ten cars. Four of them were already taken. The new silver Mercedes she tagged as the doctor's car, especially since it was parked closest to the door. From what Lori had said, the doctor wasn't the type to walk the three-hundred yards from his house to the clinic. Next to it stood a late-model purple Toyota and a few spaces over sat an aqua Geo. Claire parked next to the only other car, a blue Subaru station wagon.

For a minute, she sat lost in thought. Doug posed a real problem. Jimmy's idea for gaining access to the clinic had been simple. All she had to do, he had said, was find a place to hide during business hours, then just wait until after the building emptied out. "In other words, break out instead of break in. All you need to find is a rest room or utility closet. Maybe just the kneehole of an empty desk. And then you wait until everyone goes home. Even if you do set off an alarm, you'll have a good start because you're already inside," he had said, before adding, "Hypothetically speaking, of course."

After talking to Jimmy, Claire had decided to use this visit as a scouting mission. She would note any signs of an alarm system, as well as potential places to hide and filing cabinets that might hold the adoption records she needed. Then she would choose how and when to come back. She might return in the daytime, just a pregnant college girl making her weekly visit, so routine that no one would notice when she failed to leave. Or she might come back at night dressed in black and with her pick kit in hand. If Claire had decided the first alternative was best, then she had planned to have Charlie drop her off, so that no one would mark her car still standing in the parking lot. But that plan was now impossible, given Doug's presence. The only way in was going to have to be with her pick kit in the dead of the night. Good thing picking a lock relied on touch rather than sight.

Sighing, she shouldered her backpack and got out of the car. For a moment, she rested her hand on her abdomen, just in case Doug was watching. Dr. Gregory had told her that pregnant women touched their bellies a lot. But when she half turned, Doug's head was bent over a magazine.

Claire looked over the clinic and grounds. Aside from forgetting to mention the parking guy, Lori's and Ginny's descriptions had been good enough that everything looked somewhat familiar. The clinic must have been built sometime in the early seventies, with odd angles and tall, narrow windows that reminded Claire of arrow slits on a castle. To the left, a stand of huge cedar trees with reddish bark and gray-green branches completely cut off any glimpse of the highway below. On the right, the drive skirted a rising sweep of green lawn as long as a football field. It ended at an oversize three-car garage next to a remodeled farmhouse. A white sailboat sat between the garage and the farmhouse. The house was painted a traditional white with green trim, but over time skylights, solar panels, and a glassed-in sunporch had been added. Next to the garage sat a tiny, doll-sized outbuilding that looked as if it might have begun life as the original garage. She guessed it might be where Doug lived.

Claire walked toward the clinic's front door. There were no little signs stuck into the grounds advertising Brinks or another security firm. No keypad in the alcove to disable or arm a security device. Finally, she looked for foil-covered wires leading from the doorframes or window frames, but didn't see any. Maybe there wasn't an alarm. After all, why would the clinic need one, what with Doug in his booth? And it wasn't like an Ob/Gyn was a good place to go looking for drugs.

When she opened the door, the young woman behind the counter tucked away the magazine she was reading. Underneath an old-fashioned white nurse's cap, she had a heart-shaped face with a mole by her mouth. It had been so long since Claire had seen a nurse's cap that she wondered if the clinic had to order it from a costume shop rather than a uniform supplier. Claire's gaze swept over the empty waiting area. It was furnished with blue armchairs arranged in two groups: One circled a coffee table bearing a perfect fan of magazines, and the other faced a fireplace that was clearly never used.

The nurse arched one of her perfectly shaped black brows. "Your name?"

For a second, Claire drew a blank. "Oh, um. Lucy. Lucy Bertrand. My appointment's for four-thirty, but I'm a little early."

The nurse handed over a clipboard with an attached pen. "I'll need you to fill out these forms." Leaning down, she pressed a button on an intercom that sat on the counter. "Lucy Bertrand is here."

Claire chose a seat by the empty fireplace. The questionnaire wanted to know everything about her as well as the father of the child she was supposed to be carrying. Where did she go to school, and what were her GPA and major? What about high school GPA and SAT scores? Had she ever had an IQ test? What was her natural hair and eye color, as well as her weight? Then there were pages and pages asking about what diseases might run in the family: Was there autism? epilepsy? nearsightedness? migraine headaches? heart disease? breast cancer?

Following the principle that a good lie always contained as much truth as possible, Claire's only complete falsehood was her age. It helped that there weren't many relatives to think about. She'd never known her father, so that left only Jean and Susie for near relatives, plus a couple of uncles and aunts and a half dozen or so cousins. Under the column labeled "child's father" she marked NA and penned a series of ditto marks under it.

Claire handed in her completed questionnaire, again interrupting the nurse's pursuit of *People* magazine. In the bored tones of someone who uttered the same sentences day after day, the nurse said, "Next we'll need a urine sample. The bathroom's right over there, and the instructions are on the wall. When you're done, go into the exam room next door, get completely undressed, and put on the gown that's on top of the table. Put the opening in the front. I'll let the doctor know you're nearly ready."

In the bathroom, Claire carefully pulled off her loose

sweater and raised her left arm. With the edge of her fingernail, she loosened the edge of the white first-aid tape that held a sealed plastic bag under her arm. At the bottom of the bag was a half inch of yellow liquid, an unknowing donation from one of Dr. Gregory's other patients. She had been worried that the bag might leak, but it had proved as good as its own commercials that endlessly touted its superiority to other bags with fasteners that clicked, zipped, locked, or changed color when properly sealed. Opening the bag, Claire carefully poured the contents into a plastic cup that sat waiting on the edge of the sink. She rinsed the bag, wrapped it in a paper towel, and then tucked it and the discarded tape in her backpack. The page of framed instructions told her to leave her sample on the stainless-steel shelf above the toilet, so she did. Claire was careful to flush the toilet and wash her hands before she left.

As she opened the bathroom door, she heard a low moan from the end of the hall, then the soft murmur of a woman's reassuring voice. Claire realized that behind one of the closed doors a woman was in labor, ready to trade a child for fifteen thousand dollars. She wondered if Ginny had made it this far.

After Claire got undressed, she sat on the edge of the exam table and tried to hold the edges of the gown closed over her breasts. There were two soft raps on the door, then the doctor pushed it open without waiting for an answer. He wore an open white lab coat over a blue oxford shirt, red-striped tie, and dark blue wool pants, and in his hand he carried the clipboard that held Claire's—or rather, Lucy's—questionnaire. A little above average height and thin, the doctor appeared to be in his mid-fifties. Frost-colored hair swept back over his ears to curl just above his collar. His narrow, ruddy-skinned face was dominated by a long nose, hooked at the end. His eyes were his most striking feature, a pale ice blue. Wolf's eyes, Claire thought when she saw them.

"Lucy? I'm Dr. Bradford." He set the clipboard down on the counter, then reached out his hand, shaking hers with the lightest of grips. "Let's get your exam out of the way with, and then I'll ask you a few questions. Have you ever had a pelvic exam?" She nodded. "Good. I'll go ask my nurse to step in. While I'm doing that, I need you to put this drape over your lap, put your feet in the stirrups, and then slide your bottom down to the end of the table."

The doctor returned a few seconds later with another nurse, a woman in her late forties. Her dyed red hair contrasted strangely with her sallow skin. She had the same cap and uniform as the younger nurse, but completed her outfit with white high heels rather than sensible flats.

This, Claire realized, must be the Vi Lori remembered, although Lori had said she was a brunette. The nurse confirmed Claire's guess by introducing herself. Then she stood a half step behind Dr. Bradford and began to study the ceiling while the doctor quickly kneaded Claire's breasts. She remembered Dr. Gregory's advice to flinch away from his touch.

"Ouch!"

"Tenderness is common in early pregnancy," Dr. Bradford said, a little above it all, and Vi looked down long enough to tip Claire a wink behind his back. As the doctor conducted his equally efficient pelvic exam, Claire became aware of the harsh sound of Vi's breathing cutting through the silence. She glanced at the nurse's nicotine-stained fingers, so like Susie's, and hoped Susie wouldn't end up sounding like Vi in fifteen years.

In less than two minutes Dr. Bradford said, "You may sit up now." He turned to the nurse. "Okay, Vi, why don't you go check on our other patient?" With a nod, she slipped out the door.

Dr. Bradford slipped on a pair of half-glasses that hung from a chain around his neck and picked up the paperwork. "Now I see from the questionnaire you filled out that your last period began about six weeks ago, is that correct?" Claire nodded. From the pocket of his lab coat, he pulled a flat cardboard wheel and began to turn it. "So your estimated date of confinement would be about thirty-four weeks from now, or around the first part of December."

"Date of confinement? That makes it sound like I'm going to be locked up in a mental institution." As she heard her own words, Claire realized the comment was hers more than Lucy's. Earlier she had decided that Lucy would be more meek and deferential than Claire really was.

"It's an old term, probably left over from the days when women spent weeks lying in." Over the edge of his glasses, Dr. Bradford gave her a professionally fatherly look that was belied by his pale, calculating eyes. "And why were you interested in carrying this baby to term and then giving it up for adoption?"

"I believe in a woman's right to choose, but for me, I just can't do it."

"And what about the father of this child? I see that you've left the spaces for his information blank. What does he want?"

Claire looked down at her lap and twisted her hands. "He's just someone I met at a party right before I came up here from California. To be honest"—she paused for what she hoped was the right amount of time—"I don't even know his last name."

"Well, Lucy, let me tell you something about the way we work around here. We specialize in matching babies to the right families. We'll want to know everything about you in order to give your child a home that will best suit him or her." He lifted a page of the questionnaire. Now I see that under medications you've marked, 'None.' Does that also include what we call street drugs?"

Claire remembered to answer as the shyer Lucy. "No, sir. I mean, Doctor. I mean, I haven't used anything at all."

"Not even marijuana? I'm not so old that I don't remember my own youth on campus."

She shook her head and dropped her eyes.

"Now I need to ask, Lucy, if you have ever been tested for the virus that causes AIDS."

The thought of Dante suddenly threw Claire off-balance. In reality, she and Dante had been tested right after they met. The thought flashed through her mind that maybe she had been unwise to agree to their giving up condoms. "I gave blood about three months ago, and nobody said anything. Don't they test it then?"

"Yes, they do, although that probably shouldn't be a reason to give blood, since there is a window in which a blood test for AIDS could be negative. I need to ask how many sexual partners you've had in the past six months, including the father of this child?"

In response to Dr. Bradford's sterile question, her mind offered up another image of Dante, with his full mouth and smoothly muscled shoulders. Claire didn't need to fake a blush as she dropped her eyes to her lap and gave him Lucy's story. "Just the one guy I met at the party. I, I broke up with someone a little over a year ago, and I haven't really dated since then."

While she had been speaking, Dr. Bradford had been snapping on rubber gloves. Now he began to probe the crook of her arm for a vein. "We need to test a sample of your blood for syphilis, as well as the presence of HIV, the virus that causes AIDS. It's just a precaution, as any sexual activity that can cause pregnancy can also cause disease." He plunged the needle in swiftly while Claire averted her eyes. He continued talking as he capped the tube of blood and discarded the needle in a small red-plastic box mounted on the wall. "Assuming your tests are negative, which they most likely are, then there is a good possibility we would be interested in your assistance in providing a family with a child. Now, as you were told on the phone, the Bradford Clinic offers complete confidentiality. If you give your child up for adoption through us, it will be as if this pregnancy never happened."

Claire swallowed and nodded, wondering how Lori had felt when she had heard these same words. Dr. Bradford explained that at each weekly visit she could expect a two-hundred-dollar stipend ("to help defray living expenses") as well as a checkup and regular medical tests. She would deliver the baby at the clinic, but she wouldn't leave empty-handed—she'd go home with fifteen thousand dollars in cash.

"So are you still interested in our program?"

Trying to convey the right mixture of certainty and sadness, Claire said, "Yes. Yes, I am. It seems like the best way."

He gave a little nod. "I think you're making the right decision. Stop by the front desk and talk to Vi before you leave."

As Claire was getting dressed, she heard Vi's voice call out, "Bye, Jennifer. See you tomorrow." A glance at her watch showed it was a few minutes after five o'clock.

The front desk was empty when Claire came out. With no one observing her, she took a minute to scan the layout. Her target when she returned, she decided, would be the two tall file cabinets that stood on either side of a photocopier.

Her thoughts were interrupted when Vi came tapping down the hall. "Okay, we'll need to get you registered." She reached underneath the overhang of the counter and pulled out a thick green ledger. When she flipped it open, Claire saw that a tab separated the book into two sections. Vi found a page in the front that was half-full of handwritten entries. In blocky printing that was easy to read upside down, she wrote down a number, 98027D. Claire could see that the number directly above it was 98026D, and the one above that 98025D, so she figured she was probably the twenty-seventh woman to sign up in 1998.

Vi left the next column blank, then wrote in Lucy's name. "Your address?" she asked without looking up. She wrote it down, without seeming to notice the long pause before Claire recited it. Then again, college students probably moved frequently. "Phone number?" She wrote that number down, then stopped to cough into her fist, bending her head so that it blocked Claire's view of the ledger. Her loose rattling cough seemed to go on and on. Finally, Vi looked up at Claire with watery eyes, and said, "Do you have a beeper number or a cell phone?" Claire shook her head no. She was still straining to see the other entries when Vi finished her questions and closed the book.

Claire's heart was beating fast. Maybe all the information she needed was just a few inches from her nonpregnant belly. Information. With a guilty flash, she remembered Ginny. "You know, I think my friend is planning on having her baby here," she said, trying to keep her voice light. "Ginny Sloop. She recommended you guys. Do you know Ginny?" She kept her eyes on Vi's face.

Vi's blue eyes didn't blink or look away. "No. But even if I did, I wouldn't tell you. Complete confidentiality, remember?"

"Oh, yeah," Claire said in Lucy's embarrassed voice. "I forgot."

"Now just let me get you your prenatals." Vi leaned down to rummage under the desk. Claire risked leaning closer and squinting at the tabs on the edge of the closed ledger that still sat on the counter. One said "Parents" and the other "Donors." She straightened up just as Vi sat back up with a bottle of vitamins in one hand and an oversize paperback book in the other. She set a copy of *What to Expect When You're Expecting* on the counter and then handed Claire the vitamins. "These things are horse pills, so be sure to take them with a big glass of water. And if you're prone to morning sickness, try taking them at night." She patted the book. "This should answer most of your questions, but you need to call us right away if you experience any bleeding or cramping. Also, Dr. Bradford expects you to follow the diet that's listed toward the back of the book. I'll warn you, it's rather strict." Vi shot Claire an amused look, and Claire remembered how Lori had talked about the nurse sneaking her peanut butter cups.

"You'll also need to—" Vi didn't get a chance to finish her sentence. The intercom on her desk buzzed to life. "Vi, could you come back here for a minute, please?" Dr. Bradford's voice sounded strained. In the background was the sound of a woman breathing fast and shallow, with a little grunt of effort at the end of each pant.

"I should be back in a couple of minutes," Vi said. She tucked the ledger back underneath the overhang before she pushed her chair back. "Have a seat and look through *What to Expect* for a minute, see if you have any questions."

Claire smiled and nodded, but as soon as she heard the door close in the hall she darted around the desk and snagged the ledger with one trembling finger. Maybe she could solve Lori's problem now, without resorting to her pick kit. She could sneak a peek and then put the book away the minute she heard the door in the hall open. Quickly, she paged back through the pages of donors, lines and lines all filled up with women's names. As she had thought, the first two digits seemed to stand for a year, because she only had to go back three pages before the numbers began with 97. Partway through the numbers that began with 97, she found Ginny's name, address and phone numbers, plus a string of meaningless check marks and initials. But on the end there was one thing she did understand, "2/17/98, twin Bs." The date was the day after she had met with Ginny. Claire didn't have time to feel relief that she had at least partially solved the mystery of what had happened to Ginny. The important thing was to find out who had adopted Lori's daughter. But the ledger ended when 1996 began. Only then did Claire notice three other ledgers tucked behind the first. Her heart was beating so strongly that the pulse filled her eardrums. Alert to any sign that Vi was returning, Claire pulled out the next book and began to leaf through it faster and faster. Her fingers rifled the pages until she found some where the first number began with an 88. The year Lori had given birth. A few times Claire tensed, thinking she heard something, but it was never the sound of a door opening, of heels marching efficiently down the hall.

There. She had almost paged past it. Lori's name, listed as Lori Hesselwhite because that was what she had been before she married Havi. She was 88095D. At the end of the column was the notation, *G.* And in the second column, in the one that Vi had left blank when she entered Claire's information, there was another five-digit number that also began with 88.

Claire's hands were sweating so badly that she was leaving fingerprints on the page. She would bet any amount of money that that second number had its match in the section marked parents. In a few seconds, she would know who had adopted Lori's baby. *Hurry, hurry, hurry*, she thought as she thumbed through the pages. She found a page where the second column started with 88097D, very close to Lori's first number of 88095D. Or was that really Lori's number? Damn. Now she couldn't remember what Lori's number had been. She had to go back and look it up.

Vi's heels *tick-tocked* in the hall. Claire had been so intent on finding the record that she hadn't heard the door open. There was no chance she could put the book back and get back out into the waiting room in time. Besides, the answer must be right here, staring her square in the face.

Claire threw the open ledger on the photocopier, pushed the button, and then did the only thing she could think of to do.

ALLLII

11 ● That girl, the one who called herself Lucy, hadn't fooled Vi by throwing up on her shoes. Vi had been hinky about Lucy even before she asked about Ginny, and that had given the game away. They even looked something alike. Same pale oval face and wide blue eyes. This girl might be her sister, maybe, or a cousin.

Growing up in eastern Oregon, of course Ginny had been in 4-H, raised sheep and goats. She wasn't naive. She understood about birth. She even told Vi about how one time she'd had to reach her hand inside a cow straining over a breech birth. Again and again, she tried to slip a rope loop around a tiny hoof. Ginny had told Vi she would always remember how that felt, the hot wet muscles clamping down on her arm as strong as a vise. Kneeling in green shit and dark blood, she had thought that the cow bellowing and thrashing on the floor was going to wrench her arm off. Finally, when the cow got too exhausted to fight, Ginny had managed to haul out the calf. Alive.

Ginny had assured Vi she knew what birth would be like, but the way it turned out, she hadn't known anything at all.

And now here was this girl, sniffing around, claiming to be pregnant, asking about Ginny, and holding her breath while she waited for the answer. Vi didn't like to think about what that meant. And Vi was also pretty certain this girl had been at the ledger, although she was wasting her time if she had looked in there. The only per-

son who really knew what had happened was Dr. Bradford, and he wasn't telling.

She could get out a magazine and a pair of scissors, Vi
supposed, but that seemed kind of silly, not when they
could dust the paper for her fingerprints, maybe even find
an eyelash and analyze her DNA. Instead she simply sat
down and began to write.

And when Vi had finished the note, she sealed it up in
an envelope addressed to the person who called herself
Lucy Bertrand and hoped that it would find its way.

● ● ●

Charlie smoothed down the photocopy Claire had
made at the clinic, crumpled after its brief detour to her
bra. They were sitting at the heavy oak dining-room
table. A storm had blown in as Claire was driving home
from the Bradford Clinic, and now the rain was lashing at
the window so hard she couldn't see outside. There was
just a vague, smeary impression of the limbs of the poplar
whipping back and forth as the rain stripped the new
leaves from the branches.

"Are you sure that this is the page with the right number?" Charlie asked. "The one that belongs to the people
who adopted Lori's baby?"

"No," Claire said miserably. When she had first
slapped the page down on the photocopier, yes, she had
been sure that the number that matched Lori's was somewhere on that page. Or at least she thought she had been
sure. At that point her head had been jumbled with numbers—phone numbers, Social Security numbers, addresses, dates, reference numbers. There were all the
numbers that really belonged to her, the imaginary ones
she'd given to Lucy, the ones she'd seen as she flipped
through the ledger and the ones on the page they were
looking at now. "I'm pretty sure it was one of these num-

bers. At least I think I was sure." She had already given Charlie the news that the records showed Ginny had had her twins.

When she had heard Vi's heels clicking back down the hall, Claire had had only a second to throw the ledger onto the copier. As her right hand pressed the COPY button, she stuck the fingers of her left hand down her throat. She was so nervous and frantic that the first brush of her finger was enough to make herself gag. The nurse appeared just in time for Claire to throw up on her white pumps. Vi let out a squeal and ran to the bathroom for a handful of paper towels. The brief window of time was just long enough for Claire to quickly thrust the ledger back under the desk and stuff the photocopy in her bra. By the time Vi got back, Claire was kneeling with her head hanging over the wastebasket. She had muttered a pitiful explanation of how she hadn't been able to make it to the bathroom, hoping that Vi couldn't hear the faint crackle of the stolen paper in her bra.

Now what Charlie and Claire were looking at was a photocopy of a lined page filled with seven entries, each separated by a skipped line. The first entry looked like this:

88097P 88010D Teresa Marquette   555-2381   √ √ G
                8412 SW Arthur   555-99364
                Portland, OR 97201

The information marched along in columns, entered in what Claire recognized as Vi's neat, square handwriting. In the first column, each number began with an 88 and ended with a P. The number at the top of the column was 88097P, the next one was 88098P, and so on in consecutive order until the last number on the page, 88103P.

"The eighty-eight must be for the year, and the P on the end must be for parent or parents." Under pale pleated lids, Charlie's blue eyes snapped with excitement.

Claire ran her finger down the second column. All the numbers in this column began with an 88 and ended with a *D*. "Then these must be the tracking numbers the clinic gives to the pregnant women. *D* for donor. This was the column where I thought Lori's number was." The numbers came earlier in the series and hopscotched out of order. The first number was 88010D, the one at the bottom was 88009D. She frowned. "Except I don't understand why they're not in order. Shouldn't they just give the first baby that comes out to the first person on the list, the second to the second, and so on?"

Charlie shook her head. "I think I know the answer to that, Clairele. They must match up the babies with the parents. You know, a child whose real parents have brown eyes and brown hair is probably given to people who look like that, and so forth. And look at this column on the end." For each entry there was either a *G* or a *B* noted, for a total of four *G*s and three *B*s. "It is likely that all these people who are paying to be parents want to choose the sex of their child. I think that is what these *G*s and *B*s stand for. Girls and boys. And there are only four marked with a *G*. Four girls." A look of satisfaction crossed her face. "That cuts the work nearly in half for us already."

"Assuming I got the right page," Claire said. The more she looked at it, the more uncertain she became. "And what about all these check marks? What do they mean?"

"There's a *P* at the top of the first column and a *D* at the top of the second. So all of these children must have been *P*'ed and *D*'ed, whatever the *P* and *D* stand for."

"It can't be parents and donors all over again, can it?" Shaking her head, Claire answered her own question. "That wouldn't make any sense." The next *D* word that came to Claire's mind was dead, and even though she knew it couldn't be right, it gave her a chill. "*D* for denied wouldn't make sense, because all seven have it, and I doubt Dr. Bradford denies anyone."

"Delivered. It must be *D* for delivered." The furrows

around Charlie's mouth deepened as she spoke. Claire saw the older woman unconsciously rub her left index finger along the green ink tattooed on her right forearm, unfaded after fifty years. The numbers in the ledger must remind Charlie of her own number, Nazi Germany's solution to tracking human inventory even when it was naked, stripped of everything except its own skin. "What about *P*? *P* could be for pregnant, but that does not seem right either. Promised?" Click, click, click as Charlie tapped her manicured nail on the letter.

Claire thought of the only answer. "*P* must stand for paid. I have a feeling that would always be the most important thing to Dr. Bradford."

Charlie nodded. "I have been thinking about that ever since you told me that he charges one hundred thousand dollars for each child, and that the woman who has the baby gets about twenty thousand." Charlie scooted back her chair and went to the kitchen and took a calculator from the drawer where she kept the bills. "Let us see. Your number was 98027, so you were the twenty-seventh woman to register for this year. If we divide that by the number of weeks we have had this year, that is something more than three pregnant women per week. So, conservatively, three women a week times fifty-two weeks times eighty thousand dollars is"—she pressed buttons on the calculator and then said slowly—"a little bit less than twelve and one-half million dollars. Accounting for the other costs of running the clinic, let us say twelve million dollars, or perhaps eleven and a half."

The number called for a whistle, but Claire had never mastered the art. She blew a puff of air between her lips instead. "That's a lot of money. Especially when you think that he's been running the clinic for fifteen or twenty years. He's had a lot of time to get used to having that much money. And twelve million dollars would mean he had plenty to spread around to make sure people look the other way and keep looking. That's what Michael said he does."

"Michael? Who's Michael?"

"Dr. Gregory, I mean." Until Charlie asked, Claire hadn't realized that she had called him by his first name.

The old woman narrowed her eyes. "He's too smooth, that one."

"I'll admit he does look like he either takes a lot of vacations or has a frequent-flyer discount for the tanning booth at the JCC. But I saw a different side to him when he took me out to dinner." She didn't tell Charlie that she had her own reservations, that she was still unsure of Dr. Gregory's motives. The most likely possibility was that he liked her in a romantic way, and she already knew that no matter what was happening with Dante, she didn't return Dr. Gregory's feelings. At the same time, if it would help her find Lori's daughter, Claire wasn't above taking advantage.

Charlie didn't argue, but the expression on her face didn't change. Claire also hadn't found the words yet to tell her about Dante's probable betrayal. Nor did she know what to do about Dante himself. After fretting about it for several days, she had finally decided to wait. She wouldn't call him or write him, and see how he reacted. So far, he had left her one more voice mail message during the middle of the day, a time, she noted, when she was least likely to be at home. Did he have a reason not to really want to talk to her? With a sigh, Claire looked back down at the list. "Lori was counting on me to come back from the Bradford Clinic with one name, not four."

"But now it is only four. Before, we had no idea who had adopted Lori's child. And we have their addresses. We will go to them and look and see what we have. Do a stakeout." *Shteakout.*

Claire shook her head. "What's this 'we'? I don't want you getting involved, Charlie. This could be dangerous."

Charlie straightened up to her full four feet, ten inches. "Do you want me to sit in a rocker, knitting? And how dangerous can it be? This is only about finding a child, after all."

"It's more than that, Charlie. I'll guarantee you that it's more than that, especially if it involves twelve million dollars."

"The frightening thing is not dying." Charlie's mouth was set tight. "The frightening thing is not living."

Claire gave in. Charlie had been her own woman for seventy-eight years, and she wasn't going to change now.

"All right. But promise me you'll be careful." The last time Charlie had helped Claire, she had ended up kidnapped.

"Of course I will be," Charlie said, in a tone that didn't convince Claire at all. With a decisive nod, Charlie picked up her car keys from the hook by the door. "I will get the map of Portland from my car."

Claire knew she couldn't put off calling Lori any longer. She picked up the phone.

It was answered after one ring. "Hello?"

"It's me."

Lori yelled, "I've got it, Havi," so that Claire would understand she couldn't talk openly.

"I got in the clinic. I even managed to see the records for a second."

"And?" Claire could tell that Lori was holding her breath.

"It's kind of hard to explain, but I don't have just one name. I have four. All girls, all born around the same time your daughter was. And I'm sure one of them is your daughter," Claire said with a firmness she didn't feel. But sharing her uncertainty seemed cruel—and with any luck, unnecessary.

"Four." Lori's voice was flat.

Claire said hurriedly, "But we have all their addresses." As she was speaking, she thought that some of the addresses were bound to be out-of-date, but she didn't point

that out to Lori. "Tomorrow, Charlie and I will start looking at them. One thing that would be useful would be to
have photos of you and Havi at around the same age your
daughter is now. Can we meet someplace tomorrow?"

There was a long moment before Lori spoke. She
sighed, started to say something, then stopped. When she
spoke again, her voice was falsely bright. "Sure, I'd love
to get together with you, Claire. How about ten A.M. tomorrow at Custer Park?"

Weighed down by guilt, Claire slowly hung up the
phone. If she hadn't gotten confused at the last moment,
she would have been able to give Lori the answer she
needed now. Claire remembered the way Vi had looked at
her with narrowed eyes as she cleaned up the mess. She
was sure the nurse had suspected something. More than
likely, even if Claire did use her pick kit to break into the
Bradford Clinic, she would find that the ledgers had van-
ished. Had she ruined her only chance to find Lori's
baby?

She sighed, then got the white pages from the hall
closet and joined Charlie in the dining room where the
map was spread out over the dining room table.

"I thought of something," she told the older woman.
"After ten years, some of these people have probably
moved. Tell me the first name on the list and I'll look it
up."

There was a T. Marquette listed at the same address as
their Teresa. They found it on the map after searching the
grid for streets the size of threads, the names printed in
tiny agate type. While they looked, Claire ran through the
stretching exercises Dr. Gregory had recommended. Her
ankle was no longer swollen, and the bruises had faded to
ugly shades of yellow and green, but it was still painful to
put her full weight on it. Teresa Marquette lived in Southwest Portland, close to the downtown area, and only a
few miles from where they lived. Second on the list were

David and Monica Liebling, and again the phone book showed they hadn't moved from Irvington, a district of Portland filled with stately homes built a hundred years before by timber barons and department store tycoons.

The third name was harder to find. There were no Mandy Prices in the phone book, nor anyone listed as M. Price. The street from the clinic's records wasn't listed on Charlie's fifteen-year-old map either. In the yellow pages, they found the zip code and used that to roughly figure out where the house must be. It was located in an area that on Charlie's map had been just an expanse of white space bisected by the Tualatin River. And the fourth . . .

"Do you know them?" Charlie pointed at the name and raised an eyebrow. "Kevin and Cindy Sanchez?"

"Why would I know them?"

Charlie tapped a manicured fingernail two lines lower, on the words "Minor, Oregon." In her obsession with numbers, Claire hadn't paid much attention to the names and addresses. When Claire was five, Jean had moved them from Portland to Minor, a rural town twenty miles to the west. Minor had been founded by a miner who had been unable to spell or to find the gold he was convinced must lie just under the ground. When Claire had lived there, Minor had been a small town surrounded by fields. Now it had become a bedroom community for Portlanders.

"Sanchez doesn't sound familiar. But I haven't lived in Minor for nearly twenty years, and it's grown a lot since then." The phone book showed that Kevin and Cindy had moved since their visit to the Bradford Clinic and now lived at Fir Terrace. "Fir Terrace doesn't ring a bell either. I'll bet it's one of those new subdivisions where they name the streets after all the natural beauty that used to be there before they put up the houses. Pine Drive, Cedar Lane, Fir Terrace, and there aren't any trees left standing at all." Claire thought of something. "They might be a good possibility, though, especially if the clinic does try to match kids to adoptive parents. Someone with the last name of Sanchez would probably be a good fit for someone whose biological father is named Estrada."

1DRING

12• After Charlie left for skating practice the next morning, Claire made one phone call and didn't answer another. The phone call was to Dr. Gregory, to ask him if he'd heard from Ginny. He hadn't, but he reminded Claire of her promise, wanting to know all the details of Claire's visit to the clinic as well as Ginny's possible disappearance. He persuaded her to meet him at Village Coffee after she met with Lori.

Almost as soon as Claire had set the phone down, it rang again. The Caller ID box showed that the call was from the Metropolitan Museum of Art. Dante. Claire's hand hovered over the phone for a long moment, before she let it drop to her side. On the third ring, the answering machine picked up.

"Claire—it's me, Dante. What's up? Hanging the new Impressionists show has been keeping me so busy that I'm practically living here, but I finally realized last night that I haven't talked to you for over a week—and that's way too long. Give me a call and let me know what's happening with you. And tell me how things are with Lori and Zach. I miss you, and," he lowered his voice, "I love you. So please give me a call as soon as you get in. If you get my voice mail, just press zero-pound to opt out and ask the secretary to track me down."

He sounded sincere. But Claire could not shake the memory of sara's voice in her ear, sweetly explaining that Dante was in the shower. Claire and Dante were separated by more than just three thousand miles. They were different in every way, from their family backgrounds to their educations. Was it so unthinkable that he might have turned, even for a moment, to someone more like him?

IMAUMBN

URNNML

• • •

The clouds clustered on the horizon were the color of steel wool, but it wasn't raining. Yet. There were fewer than a dozen kids in Custer Park. A toddler clambered through a green-plastic tunnel in the infants' play structure. Three boys about Max's age ran back and forth between the swings and the battered merry-go-round, engrossed in some private game. Two preteen girls balanced on adjacent teeter-totters, arms outspread. A couple of moms sat at a picnic table, one drinking coffee from a paper cup bearing the ubiquitous Starbucks logo, and the other nursing a bundled-up baby under the drape of a pastel afghan. In the grassy bowl that earlier in the year had held soccer players and soon would hold softball games, a young girl and her dad took turns throwing a Frisbee to a black Labrador.

Claire walked up the muddy grass to where Lori sat on a park bench, Zach on her lap. There was a faint growth of dark fuzz on his head, reminding Claire of a baby bird. She took a seat beside Lori on the wooden bench scarred with generations of initials. Max was walking up a blue-plastic curlicue slide, his feet slipping on the wet plastic with every step. Claire worried he would fall and knock out his teeth, but Lori didn't seem concerned. Her restless hands kept touching her younger son. She plucked invisible lint off his blue Polartec jacket, stroked the dark down sprouting on his scalp, straightened his white socks.

Zach squirmed under her attentions, finally sliding

down to the ground. His head swiveled back and forth as he watched Max, who had joined the three other boys as they tore through the park. Each had picked up a fallen twig, which quickly became swords, guns, or baseball bats, whatever the moment called for. Zach turned to Lori, his dark eyes depthless in his still jaundiced face. Claire's chest ached to see him. Despite his remission, he still looked very ill to her.

"Can I go play, Mama?"

Lori hesitated. Earlier she had told Claire how hard it was to let him do anything for fear that he would be bruised or cut, and not stop bleeding. "All right—if you're careful. I don't want you to fall or bump into anything, so no running."

Zach gave a put-upon sigh. "O*kay*, Mama."

Lori raised her voice. "Max! I need you to look after your brother." Max didn't turn around, although by the way his shoulders stiffened it was clear that he had heard her. "Max!" Lori shouted. He threw his stick on the ground and began walking back toward Zach, dragging his feet at each step.

A smile rising on his face, Zach limped off to meet him. Even Max couldn't resist that smile, and he allowed the corners of his mouth to twitch upward before resuming his blank, put-upon expression.

"The chemotherapy has done something to Zach's coordination," Lori said. "They call it peripheral nerve toxicity. All they can say is that they hope it's not permanent. Sometimes I think it's like that saying—which is worse, the cure or the disease?" Claire noticed that her friend's skin look oddly naked. She had drawn a thick line of gray eyeliner around each eye, but the rest of her skin was bare. Had she stopped for a moment and forgotten to continue her normal routine? Or had she hoped that people would register the eyeliner and believe it represented the rest of the makeup she usually wore—foundation and blush and eye shadow and mascara and lipstick?

"But at least he's in remission, Lori. That's a big step." Claire looked around at the budding trees, the new blades of grass. Even though the calendar said February, icy weather had already left Portland. "And it's almost spring." Spring always made Claire feel hopeful, but she found the idea would not leave her mouth.

"Sometimes it's so hard not to think that this could be the last spring, the last Easter, the last birthday, the last Christmas, the last Arbor Day, for Godsakes!" The words burst out of Lori. "I'm tired of thinking like that. I'm tired of being a lesson to people that they should enjoy what they have or it might all turn to shit."

Claire didn't have a response for her friend. She handed her the stolen photocopy. Then she explained what had happened at the Bradford Clinic and what she and Charlie were planning. "There's no chance that you remember the number the clinic gave you, is there?"

Lori shook her head, her mouth twisting. She traced her fingers lightly down the list of names, the way a mother might stroke a newborn's tiny starfish hand. Claire had to look away. With a stiff, old man's gait, Zach was climbing the three stairs that led to the infants' play structure. The other child playing on it, a boy about half his age, watched him with a puzzled expression. Max stood off to the side with his arms crossed, his gaze following the boys his own age.

Claire was still watching Zach cautiously climb up the play structure. When she turned to Lori, she found her friend crying silently, the tears dripping off the end of her chin. Something about the set of Lori's face told her that she wanted no hugs, no reassurances. "I don't even know how old ten looks anymore," Claire said. "How old is that girl?" She gestured to the girl playing with her dog. "Is she ten?"

With a long, shuddering sigh, Lori wiped her eyes on her sleeve, then turned her head to look. She shook her head. "I'd say more like eight. Look at her chest. It's completely flat. Most girls have two little bumps by the time they're ten. Do you remember that? I remember begging my mom for a training bra when I was ten or eleven. A training bra! Like you could teach your breasts to do tricks. I remember how all the boys would walk by and run their fingers down your back, hoping to snag your bra strap and snap it. If their finger didn't catch, then they knew you were still wearing an undershirt and you were so humiliated because you knew that *they* knew." Lori was still staring in the direction of the girl and her dog, but her eyes had lost their focus. "Sometimes when I bring the kids to the park I look for her. It's not too hard to figure out what she might look like. I remember a little bit from biology about how genes work. Or really all I need to do is look at the boys. Dark hair, dark eyes, olive skin. Because dark is dominant."

Claire was looking in the other direction, so she saw how Zach was now limping after the three older, taller boys, who clearly wanted nothing to do with him. He had a stick in one hand and was waving it in their direction, but they looked at each other and then ran to the far edge of the park where there was a small pond surrounded by boulders. The boys began to climb them, crowing to each other about who was higher. Max took Zach by the hand and led him back to the infants' play structure. Claire had to concentrate on her breathing so she wouldn't cry.

Lost in thought, Lori continued, "For some reason in Oregon there are a lot of blue eyes. I used to sit in meetings at work and look around the room. And mostly I saw light eyes looking back at me. I guess maybe I don't understand genetics. It seems like three-fourths should be brown, but it's always less than half. Maybe all you pale-skinned Scandinavian types were attracted to Oregon because of the rain. You don't have to worry about getting sunburned."

"Oregonians don't tan, they rust," Claire said, repeating a joke that had been big when she was in grade school. "Did you bring pictures of you and Havi when you were kids? I'm thinking that we'll take pictures of any likely girl. Do you think you would know your daughter if you saw her?"

Lori didn't hesitate. "If I could look her square in the face, I would know. You know your own flesh and blood." Then she leaned down to rummage in her purse and handed Claire an unsealed envelope.

Inside were two twenty-year-old photographs. One was a black and white, now yellowed and dog-eared. In it, Havi's solemn eyes were framed by uneven bangs and slightly protuberant ears. The other was a school portrait of Lori, her hair held back by a white knitted headband, her eyes hidden by thick octagonal glasses set in tortoise-shell frames.

"Hey, now I know what color your hair really is," Claire exclaimed. "It's brown." She looked closer at the photo. It was hard to be exact about color when you were looking at a faded black-and-white photo. "Or maybe blond?" she ventured.

Lori gave Claire a lopsided smile and didn't answer. "If you ever show that to anyone, I'll kill you." Then she reached into her wallet and handed Claire a third photo, this one in color. In it, Zach wore a red waffle-weave shirt, a pair of well-worn OshKosh overalls and a smile that lit up his whole face. Claire looked from the photo to the real thing, from the boy with a sharp-edged face to one whose features had been blurred by prednisone, from a smiling child to one whose face seemed burdened and aged.

Lori saw what Claire was doing. "That photo was only taken last October," she said. "Five months ago. He was sick then, too, only we didn't know it."

"Did you give this to me so that I could compare it with the girls we find?"

Lori shook her head. "So you'll remember why this is important." Claire wondered if this was Lori's way of re-buking her for not finding the right record.

Walking back to her car, Claire tucked her hands into her coat pockets and discovered a fistful of change. Her fingers picked out at least three quarters, plus a half dozen smaller coins. Rather than putting change in her wallet, she liked to slip it into the pocket of whatever jacket or coat she was wearing, a little surprise for her future self. Fingering the coins, she remembered the other task she needed to accomplish before she met Dr. Gregory at Village Coffee. She would use the pay phone on the corner to call the Bradford Clinic. In case the clinic had Caller ID, as Lori thought they did, she didn't want to risk calling from her house. As Lucy, Claire planned to leave a message that she had changed her mind about giving up her baby.

● ● ●

Claire was waiting for her latte (or, as the guy behind the counter termed it, "a tall skinny," which was how she had felt about herself for most of her life) when Dr. Gregory walked in.

"Hey, Dr. G."

"What's with this Dr. G stuff? Can't you just call me Michael?"

Claire avoided answering directly. She wanted to stay on Dr. Gregory's good side without promising anything. "You should look at Dr. G as a step up, halfway between formality and informality."

He gave a mock sigh and shook his head. "If I need to wait, I will. How's your ankle holding up?"

For an answer, Claire held up her hand and tipped it from side to side. "The swelling's mostly gone. But this morning I went for what I thought would be a half walk, half run that ended up being all walk. It just didn't feel right."

"Come over to my office and I'll take a look-see. Just

let me feed my habit first." He gave a nod to the kid behind the counter. "The usual, Bodie."

Claire didn't know if she wanted to be alone with Dr. Gregory in his office, his cool fingers tracing the bones of her ankle. "No, that's okay, I'm sure it's fine. You've already been so helpful, first with my ankle and then by taking me out to dinner and answering my questions. I don't want to impose on you any further. I've never even gotten a bill for your house call." Her gaze was caught by a phrase from a magnetic poetry set stuck on the back of the espresso machine. A previous customer had pushed a string of words together to read, "scream stop crash blood smear never could drive."

"Buy me my coffee, and we'll call it even." Dr. Gregory dropped his voice. "As soon as you tell me what happened at the clinic." His grin crinkled the skin at the corners of his eyes. "You know I'm dying to hear all."

When they walked back into the street, the light had turned a watery green, and the sky seemed to come within inches of their heads. Then it was cracked by light, so unexpectedly that Claire questioned whether she had really seen it. A second later, thunder rolled, loud and round and very close.

Hail fell from the sky and bounced up again, like Styrofoam pellets released from a giant beanbag chair. Stinging hailstones snapped against their skin. Dr. Gregory grabbed Claire's hand and they began to run back to his office on the next block. Claire was hobbled by her ankle, though, and they were both dripping when they stumbled in the door. The place where she was used to seeing the reception desk had been filled by a freestanding shelf of supplements and water-purifying devices. Dr. Gregory grinned at her, hail glinting in his curls like pieces of broken glass. The room was filled with the oddly intimate sound of their panting. He was standing so close that she was afraid he would kiss her. She loosened her hand and stepped back.

Rummaging in a closet, he came up with some folded patient gowns, thin fabric printed with abstract blue flowers. He tossed one to her and began to dry his own clothes and hair, sniffing a couple of times as he did.

"I hope I haven't made you catch cold," Claire said, remembering how he had sniffed all through dinner.

"Don't tell me you still believe it's getting wet that does it. You know it's germs and nothing but. The nose sometimes reacts to abrupt temperature changes, such as going from indoors to outdoors to indoors again." He took both gowns and tossed them into a hamper. "Have a seat and let me have a look at your ankle. And I want you to tell me all about your visit with Ginny and what happened at the clinic."

While Dr. Gregory examined her ankle with his fingers as much as his eyes, Claire told him about how she had been worried that Ginny had disappeared until she had found the record about her having twins at the clinic.

Dr. Gregory had stopped examining her ankle and now held her foot cupped loosely in his hands. She was aware of the soft ribs of his corduroy pants underneath the sole of her foot, but she felt awkward pulling it away. He gave her another smile. "Now come on, tell me the good stuff. How did it go at the clinic? Did our little ruse work?"

Claire nodded. "I think they took me at face value until the end, and maybe even then." Dr. Gregory gave her his full attention while she told him the whole story, ending with, "So I've got a whole page of names instead of just one. Charlie figured out that only four of the kids on the list are girls, but that still means we might be a long way from finding Lori's daughter." She bit her lip. "I don't think the nurse completely bought my throwing up, though. She gave me a long look after she had cleaned up. But I only had a second to think of a reason that I might be behind the counter. Lucky for me, the waiting room was nothing but acres of beige carpet and no wastebasket in sight."

Dr. Gregory trailed a finger across her foot and stood up. "Before I forget, let me tell you that your ankle looks fine. In fact, I would say it's recovering nicely. But you should listen to it. If it tells you to stop running and walk for a while, then do it."

"But I already feel like my muscle is turning into fat," Claire protested.

"Muscle doesn't turn into fat. It just atrophies while you're simultaneously gaining weight."

"And that's supposed to make me feel better?"

"As your doctor, I know you would want to know the truth, Claire." He turned away and began washing his hands at the sink. "Where's the list now?"

Claire took the crumpled photocopy from her backpack. After drying his hands, Dr. Gregory spread it out on his desk and began to study it intently. Claire explained what Charlie and she thought all the notations meant. Then he interrupted her. "Will you look at that!" There was something like awe in his voice.

"What?" Claire responded. He tapped on the third name of a person who had acquired a baby girl in August of 1988, the one whose address they had been unable to find in the phone book or on Charlie's outdated map. Mandy Price. "What is it?" Claire repeated, but he was just staring at the list, his lips moving a little bit as he considered something.

He gave his head a little shake before answering her. "I'm pretty sure that's Mandy Price. You know, as in Amanda and Kurt Price."

"I've never heard anyone call her Mandy. Are you sure?" Amanda and Kurt Price were Portland's most famous residents, on paper at least. They were so reclusive that they might as well live in New York City or Los Angeles. No one Claire knew had actually ever seen either of them in person.

"Look at the address. I know where Parrot Road is, out by the Tualatin River, and that's the area they live in. Fifteen years ago it was all farms. Now it's two-million-dollar estates with gates and guards and security cameras. You can't exactly call it a neighborhood when each house comes with a minimum of ten acres. I think the Prices have about twenty acres along the river."

Amanda Price was a chameleon who could play a Jewish refugee, a drugged-out rock and roller, or a struggling survivor of a future apocalypse. Her hair color changed as often as Lori's, and she was famous for adopting a pitch-perfect accent for whatever part she chose. Kurt Price, Amanda's husband, was at least a dozen years older, but aging well, his bright green eyes still captivating in his now craggy face. He had made a career out of playing one pumped-up action hero after another, although lately his roles had been a little less frequent. A star for a quarter of a century, he had spent his career saving various shrieking starlets from serial killers, earthquakes, Mafia dons, and the occasional evil tentacled alien from outer space. Off-screen, his marriage to Amanda a dozen years before had been covered by all the tabloids, especially after one off-kilter fan killed herself upon hearing the news that someone had finally succeeded in getting Kurt to the altar.

Renowned for being reclusive, the Prices refused to shill for their films, and their private life was just that. News of Amanda's pregnancy had only leaked to the media after she grew too big to hide it. Now Claire understood the reason for their privacy. They didn't want the whole world to know that despite the few grainy tabloid photos published of Amanda, her designer maternity-smocked belly perched above those famously long legs, the actress had never been pregnant at all.

13 • That afternoon, Charlie and Claire set out, armed with the pictures of Havi and Lori as children. They decided to concentrate first on the two houses that lay within Portland's city limits, one in the Burlingame area in Southwest Portland, and the other in the Irvington neighborhood across the Willamette River in the northeast. Teresa Marquette, presumably a single mother, lived within three miles of Charlie and Claire, in a minisubdivision of long, low ranch houses that had been put up after World War II. In J.B.'s borrowed Firebird, Claire and Charlie drove slowly down the street, until they found a turquoise house with a number that matched the one on Claire's stolen photocopy. There was no car in the driveway, and the curtains were drawn.

"Look at that lawn," Claire remarked. It was unmarred by weeds or even a stray leaf. The flat green was as unvarying and perfect as a golf course.

Charlie shook her head. "It does not look like a house for children."

She was right. The house looked more like it belonged to an old man who would confiscate any ball that accidentally ended up on his property. But when they turned around and drove back past the house, they saw the gold letters on the mailbox that spelled out Marquette.

Six blocks later, Claire pulled over. Dressed in her black running tights and an old gray sweatshirt, she began to run slowly down the street. The plan called for her to run by the Marquette house, continue on for a few blocks, then turn around and run back. In case she did spy a likely candidate, she carried a small disposable camera in her sweatshirt pocket. Portland—home of the main US office for Adidas and with Nike headquartered in its suburbs—was a city of runners, so her presence should arouse no comment. It was slow going, but Claire remembered Dr. Gregory's comment that her muscles might be atrophying, and decided to keep pushing herself. After just two blocks she was out of breath. She walked one block, tried to start running again, and then gave up and walked. A few weeks before she could have knocked five miles off without much problem, and now here she was trying to psych herself up to run at least a few feet.

The neighborhood didn't offer much diversion. She quickly identified the four types of houses the developer had offered. One had the living room and one front bedroom on the right. The next was reversed, with everything on the left. The third and fourth types simply tacked a second bedroom next to the first. It must be confusing, Claire thought, to visit your neighbors, like walking through a looking glass.

She worked up to a slow, shuffling run as she started down Teresa Marquette's block. Many of the neighboring houses were showing their age, sagging a little bit, some in need of paint. Not the Marquette house. It looked freshly painted and in perfect repair. But something about its very neatness gave Claire a stunted feeling, and she realized that there were no flowers edging the house or the street, nothing but the emerald grass, oppressive in its perfection. After running another block and a half, she turned and ran back past the still closed-up house.

When she got back to the Firebird, Charlie was sitting in the driver's seat. Claire fell into the passenger seat, still panting even though she had walked most of the way back. She fastened her seat belt, which was so old it only went over her lap. "There was nothing to see. I don't think anyone was home, although it was hard to tell.

Whoever lives in that house does so behind closed doors."

The next address belonged to David and Monica Liebling. As they drove across the Fremont bridge, Charlie told Claire that Liebling was German for darling. Searching for the address, they drove slowly down the wide streets of the Irvington neighborhood, past hundred-year-old homes, square, boxy, and generous. Now no one had the free time to sit on the deep porches, and the maids' rooms had probably all been turned into home offices.

Two stories tall with a daylight basement, the Liebling house was painted a dark mossy green with cream-colored trim. There was a new red Beemer parked in the driveway, although they couldn't see anyone moving in the house as they drove by the first and second times. Charlie parked six blocks past the Liebling house, and Claire started out for her second brief run of the day.

Unlike Southwest Portland, this part of the city had sidewalks, so Claire could run without worrying about sharing the road with traffic. Her ankle was another matter. She had thought the idea of a running surveillance would give her the push she needed to start again, but the concrete was proving much less forgiving than macadam. Each step sent a little zip of pain up her leg.

Worse, though, was her endurance. How could she have lost so much in a little more than a week? She tried to find the same easy scissoring pace that had come naturally to her before. But after only two blocks, her breath caught in little wheezes and her side ached. She was reduced to walking again.

The garages and yards in this neighborhood were filled with expensive adult toys—Range Rovers, boats, elaborate barbecue grills, securely padlocked mountain bikes, a swimming pool (now shrouded in blue plastic), a pair of matching Weimaraners behind a chain-link fence. These last made Claire's heart beat even faster, although they only glanced at her with slow indifference and looked away again. She picked up her feet and started running again.

By the time she reached the Lieblings' block, she was convinced that she tasted blood in her mouth. Luckily, a telephone pole was conveniently located directly across the street. Bracing herself against it, Claire stopped and made a show of stretching her legs while keeping her eyes fastened on the house. No one moved behind the large windows.

Claire squinted. A stuffed toy that looked like a cross between a person and an animal was perched on a windowsill on the first floor. It wore a yellow jacket and blue pants. She recognized it as a character from a popular children's television show. Claire didn't know any ten-year-old girls, but it seemed like the kind of thing that would appeal to one.

Her breath quickened, but Claire tried to caution herself not to get too excited. After all, if she and Charlie had unscrambled the ledger's entries correctly, all the children on their list should be ten-year-old girls.

Claire half ran another two blocks, then turned around and began running back on the other side of the street. The room she was now sure was a child's drew her eyes, but she didn't see any more than the stuffed animal regarding the world through round plastic glasses. She and Charlie would have to come back.

Charlie and Claire went to a nearby Natures store to discuss their next move as well as pick up a few groceries. Natures had expanded from its original niche of organically grown vegetables to embrace every upscale consumer. Shoppers could now purchase St. John's wort, hand-made chocolates, veal, taro-root chips, expensive hearth-baked breads, and milk guaranteed to be free of bovine-growth hormone. About the only item Natures refused to stock was cigarettes, and anyone smoking at their deli seating would probably have been driven out with a whip hand-woven from organically grown hemp.

While Charlie selected fresh goat cheese and some Yellow Finn potatoes, a man walked slowly past them down the produce aisle, holding a black cellular phone the size of a credit card to his ear. He seemed to be coshopping with whoever was at the other end of the phone. "The radicchio seems a little wilted. But the arugula looks good. Want me to get some?"

When they walked past the deli case, Charlie spied a Linzer torte and decided that she must have a slice. To be companionable, Claire ordered a piece of something called *Death by Chocolate* for herself, as well as a cup of coffee.

"What are we going to do about the Prices?" Claire asked after they had found a seat upstairs.

"It does not sound as if it will be easy to see what their child looks like." With the side of her fork, Charlie cut a tiny shaving of torte. "Such a child would probably have private tutors, so she might not even leave for school."

"We also need to figure out what to do if"—Claire corrected herself—"I mean *when*—we do find a girl that might be Havi and Lori's. What if all four of them look like possibilities?" Her fork scraped against the heavy white china. Looking down, Claire was surprised to see that her entire slice of cake had already disappeared. "Lori thinks she could tell just from looking them in the face."

"But what if more than one of them appears right?"

"If we had a blood sample, we could have a DNA test done," Claire said. "I see that in the newspaper all the time now, where they test the supposed father to see if he is or is not."

"Lori and Havi's blood we could get. But a child's?" Charlie pushed away her half-eaten cake. After fifty years in America, she still ate like a European. Quality counted for far more than quantity. Just a taste of the perfect flavor trumped the family-sized generic brand any day. Claire stared longingly at what was left of her friend's dessert while promising herself that she wouldn't touch it.

"There must be some way we could get a sample without tipping our hand and directly asking the parents. I could dress as a nurse and, I don't know, go to their school and arrange to have them taken out of class . . ." The idea already seemed to be going no place. "I guess that won't work." Claire tried again. "Maybe you could offer your services as a baby-sitter. Any one who looks at you trusts you. And then you tell the girl you need to give her a shot. Or wait, wait, you don't need a scientific sample, all neat in a syringe. And you don't even need a lot. That's not how they get it at a crime scene. You just need a little bit of blood on something. Maybe you could talk the girl into becoming your blood sister, you know, where each person pricks their finger? Then you could help her clean up and smear a little bit of blood on a washcloth. It might well be the last time you baby-sit, but at least they probably wouldn't call the cops." Without even being aware that she had done it, Claire realized that she had pulled Charlie's discarded torte to her and eaten several bites of buttery pastry and raspberry jam. Well, too late now. She shrugged and continued eating as ideas popped into her mind. "Or does it have to be blood? What about spit?"

"Spit?"

"Remember that lady in Vancouver who disappeared and was last seen leaving a bar with an ex-con? They found blood in his truck, but since she was gone there was none of her DNA to compare it to. But then they thought of collecting DNA from the flap of an envelope they knew she had licked. It shouldn't be too hard to get the girl to lick something. And at least that way we wouldn't have to worry about how to get blood. You could just find a way to play mailman, give the kid some stamps and envelopes, then cart it all off to be analyzed."

Charlie raised an eyebrow, but otherwise didn't comment. In her heart, Claire knew that all of her plans would be difficult, if not impossible, to carry out. As she sucked the last bit of Linzer torte from her fork, she wished desperately that she had been able to remember Lori's number when she held the ledger in her hands.

One-fourth of their problem was solved on the way home as they drove past the Marquette house. A white Eagle station wagon now stood in the drive, its tailgate open to reveal a half dozen paper grocery bags from Fred Meyer. A girl came out of the house, lifted one of the bags into her thin arms, and carried it back inside. A girl who looked about ten years old. A tall, gangly girl with hair the color of corn silk, and skin the blue-white shade of skim milk. Charlie took a pen and made a thick black line through Teresa Marquette's name. "One down and three to go," she said.

●●●

Charlie and Claire had been parked outside the Liebling house since four in the morning. After weighing the pros and cons of sleepiness versus urgent calls of nature, Claire had reluctantly decided not to bring her insulated coffee mug with her. At five-thirty, they watched the light behind a small pebbled-glass window go on upstairs. "The bathroom," Claire whispered, and Charlie nodded. After about five minutes, the first light blinked out, then another light came on in a rectangular window set high in the wall of the ground floor. "The kitchen?" Charlie guessed. A glimpse of a dark head dipping down, then something round and silver that caught the light as it was lowered and then raised. Claire imagined a kettle be-

ing filled at the sink. At 6 A.M., another light blinked on in
the second story, this one staying on. Shadows moved behind curtains and blinds, and gradually more lights were
turned on in the house until they burned in nearly every
room.

Dressed in dark colors, Charlie and Claire sat in the
borrowed Firebird and watched the Liebling house, hoping for a glimpse of the girl who lived there. They had
rolled the windows down a crack to keep them from
steaming up. Anyone glancing out would only see a car,
not an obviously occupied car. A steady drizzle kept even
the most motivated joggers indoors. At six-thirty, a
woman in a baseball cap and raincoat appeared at the end
of the block. Whenever the wolfhound on the end of her
leash stopped to sniff a hydrant or bush, the woman
jerked it forward. As the pair crossed by on the other side
of the street, Claire and Charlie held themselves absolutely still, but neither the woman nor the dog noticed
them.

When both garage doors rattled upward, Claire realized she had almost dropped off to sleep. First a bright
red BMW, with the sharply angled styling of the latest
models, backed out. A dark-haired man was at the wheel,
and he pulled out onto the street without seeming even to
pause to check traffic. Then a second car began to back
down the driveway. Claire blinked. It was another BMW,
identical in color and style, down to its fancy wire-rim
wheels. The only difference was that a woman sat at the
wheel, her blond hair pulled back into a perfect French
twist. In the backseat sat a dark-haired child. The
woman's BMW was two blocks away by the time the
garage doors had finished closing. The camera was still
lying on Claire's lap.

The sun had finally struggled up above the horizon,
making any contrast between artificial light and daylight
less obvious. Still, Claire thought the Liebling house was
now dark. Lights out, nobody home. Charlie and Claire

stayed where they were for another hour, but no curtains moved, no lights went on, no doors were opened.

Finally, Charlie voiced the question that was hanging in the air. "If these people have a ten-year-old girl, then where is she?" Claire could only shake her head, as mystified as her friend. Because the child sitting behind the woman had looked closer to Max's age than ten. And he had definitely been a boy.

14● "Thanks for the loan of the car." Claire dropped the keys into J.B.'s hand. She had found him outside, a cigarette clenched between his teeth as he moved back and forth between a faded green Mercury in the driveway and a battered blue Dodge on the street, both with their hoods open. He appeared to be doing some sort of transplant. "I even filled the tank and took it through the car wash."

J.B. patted the Firebird's fender. "Been a while since this baby's seen the inside of one of those. Let's hope it didn't wash off the rust. I have a feeling that might be the only thing holding it together." He dropped his cigarette onto the driveway and ground it out with the square toe of his heavy black boot. Then he bent over, picked up the butt, and slid it into the pocket of his motorcycle jacket. Catching Claire's surprised look, he shrugged. "If you're not careful, kids will pick up anything and put it in their mouths." He walked up the cement stepping-stones to the front door and pushed it open. "Hey, Susie, look who's here."

Claire followed him inside. The house was scented with cinnamon and yeast, and her mouth began to water. Eric and Susie sat at the Formica table in the tiny dining room, each with an oversize cinnamon roll in front of them.

"Want a cinnamon roll, Big Sis? J.B. just took these out of the oven about an hour ago."

Normally, Claire didn't mind Susie calling her Big Sis, given that she *was* two years older. But that morning,

Claire had had to lie down on the floor to put on her jeans. Still, the cinnamon rolls smelled wonderful. "Sure," she said. J.B. went into the kitchen. She heard the sound of the sink running as he washed the grease from his hands.

Susie asked, "So how did it go at the clinic? Did you pass as a pregnant woman?"

Instead of answering, Claire pulled up a chair and asked a question of her own. "Suse, do you remember anyone from Minor named Kevin or Cindy Sanchez?"

Susie closed her eyes for a second, giving Claire an un-observed moment to study her sister. It was like seeing herself in a subtly warped mirror. Thanks to two packs a day, Suzy had cheekbones even more sharply defined than Claire's. Their hands were almost identical—long with squared-off fingertips—only Susie's were stained with nicotine. With just twenty-two months separating them, they should have shared a similar outlook as well as a general body type, but they did not. Ever since she had moved in with Charlie, Claire had been trying to dis-tance herself from the more embarrassing elements of her childhood. Sometimes Claire felt guilty for judging her sister, for being glad not to be her.

Susie blinked open her eyes, and Claire looked away. "Sanchez? No, I don't think I know anyone by those names. But I've never been back since I left."

"I didn't know that," Claire said. "I thought I was the only one who felt like that."

Susie shook her head. "Oh, I've been *past* it a lot of times. Anytime we go to the coast we drive past the exit. But why would I want to go there? The last time I saw Minor was in my rearview mirror. Or J.B.'s side-view mirror, to be exact." She gave J.B. a playful pat on the rear as he set a cinnamon roll and a glass of milk in front of Claire. "I never saw the point of going back, either. It's such a tacky little town." Claire found this last comment ironic, since Susie lived off Eighty-second Avenue, the armpit of Portland. Eighty-second was a long stretch of failing businesses, lesser-known fast-food franchises, used-car lots, and places where a man could pay one hundred dollars to have a woman "model" lingerie for him after handing him a box of Kleenex. Still, Claire had her own memories of Minor and knew what Susie meant.

"I think it *was* a tacky little town. I hear it's all new now."

"Yeah, but I'll bet that underneath it's still the same old Minor."

J.B. pulled up a chair. "So why are you asking Susie about those Sanchez people? Did you get the records from the clinic? Are they the ones who adopted Lori's baby?"

Claire spoke around a mouthful of cinnamon roll. It was amazing how something basically made out of sugar, butter, and flour could be so heavenly. "Maybe. Maybe not. I just don't know." With pauses to lick her fingers, she sketched out for them what had happened. "So now I've got the names and addresses of four families who adopted girls at the same time Lori's was born. Charlie and I already found one child. She's very pale and blond, so we know she's not Lori and Havi's. One girl is supposed to be with the Sanchezes. One family that's on the list doesn't seem to have a daughter at all, at least not that Charlie and I have seen. And one girl might be the daughter of some famous people."

Susie straightened up, her face becoming animated at the thought of fame, even second-hand. "Who?"

"Yeah, who, Claire, who?" J.B. waggled an eyebrow at Claire.

Claire hoped to put Susie's encyclopedic knowledge of celebrities to work, but she didn't want her sister telling the Prices' secret to every customer who came in for a perm. "I can only tell you guys if you promise not to tell. No gossiping at the Curl Up and Dye."

Susie shook her head. "That's kind of a moot point, since I'm not working there anymore. I got a new job."

"Doing what?" Claire asked.

"Same thing, only without the chatty clients. So you don't have to worry about me spilling the beans to anyone." Susie and J.B. exchanged a look that Claire couldn't quite interpret.

"What do you mean? Are you styling wigs or something?"

"Not exactly. I'm working at Moyter's."

"The funeral home? You're a hairdresser for the dead?" Claire couldn't help glancing at Susie's hands. Didn't it bother her to touch dead people? Didn't it bother J.B. when Susie came home and touched him with those same hands?

"Don't look at me like that. It's not like I'm embalming them or anything. I just go in and make them look nice. Brush their hair out, use a curling iron, put a little makeup on, maybe some fingernail polish. So people can see their mama looking the way they remember her, which is a lot better than the way she did before she died."

"That kind of thing gets done just for women, then?" Claire suddenly remembered how their grandmother had looked in her casket. At her request, she had been dressed in her faded Hormel Girl uniform, a reminder of her youth when she had risen from being Yakima's Dairy Princess to the big league, one of only a few dozen Hormel Girls in the nation. She had spent the best year of her life marching in parades and autographing cans of Spam. Thanks to cigarettes, Grandma had still been thin enough to fit into her old uniform the day she keeled over from a heart attack in front of a slot machine in Reno. In her casket, she had looked like a shrunken cheerleader, dressed in spangles and fringe, her cheeks rouged in harsh red ovals.

"I've only done a couple of men. There are kids sometimes, too, but I've already told them to call the other gal in town for that. I can't do a child." Claire guessed she must have still been staring at Susie's hands, because her sister abruptly put them under the table and changed the subject. "So who are the famous people?"

"There was a woman who signed in as Mandy Price." Susie and J.B. still looked blank. "I think it's really Amanda and Kurt Price."

"Ooh," Susie squealed, "I love her!" She lifted her chin haughtily and put on a bad British accent. "'I'm sorry, milord, but I cannot accept your offer of marriage. I would much prefer to hang.' I loved that scene! And her husband can still play a hunk, even if he has been doing it for twenty-five years. I'm always hoping I'll see one of them around Portland sometime, but I've never known anyone who has. J.B. and I even drove past their estate one time. All we did was slow down a little and then all of a sudden there was a cop behind us with his lights going." She twirled her index fingers in circles over her shoulders, mimicking the lights. "He asked us our business, and when we said we were out for a drive, he said then maybe we had better just keep on driving."

"What I need to do is find out more about their daughter," Claire said. "After all, if their kid's blond, then she's probably not going to be Lori and Havi's child. Do you know anything about her?"

Susie looked at the ceiling and began reciting facts. She reminded Claire of some of the men she knew, who could recite baseball or football stats for hours. "Amanda Price is either thirty-two, thirty-four, or thirty-eight, depending on whose information you want to believe. Looking at her neck, I would believe thirty-eight at a minimum. Plastic surgeons can do a lot these days, but it's very hard to hide an aging neck. Now as for Kurt, I have it on good authority that that hair of his is really a very, very good weave and that he is actually fifty-six.

Every time he makes a movie they subtract a few more years off his age. They don't want people thinking this buffed stud is ready to join the AARP."

"But what about their child?" Claire asked, a little impatient. She had a feeling her younger sister was padding, wanting to show off how much she knew without admitting what she didn't know.

"I don't think I've ever seen any pictures of the kid. In fact, the only thing I do remember is that one time Amanda decked that tabloid guy for trying to take her daughter's picture when they were leaving the airport. They got back at her by running the picture of her in mid-swing with this real ugly pissed-off look on her face. And judging by the photo, she has a mean right hook."

Claire had forgotten that little tidbit, which revealed how far Amanda would go to protect her daughter's privacy. "So you don't know what her daughter looks like?"

Susie was finally forced to admit defeat. "No." She pushed her chair back and began to clear the dishes.

"Pretty much everything's on the Internet now," J.B. said. "Have you tried looking there to see if there are any pictures of the daughter?"

"We don't have a computer. I've never even surfed the net." Claire felt silly using the words *surf* and *net*. She hoped J.B. couldn't hear the quotes her voice put around them.

"Come into my office," he said, "and let's see what we can find. We'll type Amanda's and Kurt's names into a search engine, let it dig around a little bit." Claire followed him to the back of the house, where he cleared a chair of catalogs offering stainless-steel sinks and other kitchen items.

The phrase *Amanda and Kurt Price* yielded thousands of hits, as J.B. told Claire they were called. When he refined his search to specify only sites that contained images, dozens of hits were still returned. On The Official Unauthorized Amanda and Kurt Price Home Page they watched as several photographs began to draw themselves on the screen line by line. "I need a faster modem," J.B. apologized. "Twenty-eight-point-eight crawls nowadays, especially if you want to do something that's graphically intensive."

J.B. spoke knowledgeably, and Claire smiled to herself at her biker semi-brother-in-law (or out-law, as Jean liked to call him), who was nothing like he seemed. The smile slid from her face when she realized that what the computer was reproducing for them were pictures of a nude man and woman. As a set of perky nipples appeared on the screen, J.B. said, "Oops," and hit the STOP button.

Susie overheard and came into the room to look over their shoulders. "She'd be getting a bit long in the tooth to do that, wouldn't she?" Claire was glad that Eric was otherwise occupied in the living room, building a block tower.

"I don't think it *can* be her," said J.B., clicking on the BACK button. Even though Amanda Price didn't shy away from wearing sweaters so tight that everyone knew her perfect breasts must be implants, she was famous for never baring them.

Claire and J.B. spent several hours methodically searching, but the nude photos, even if they weren't of Amanda Price, proved to be the most interesting. They surfed official sites written by PR flacks who didn't need to be constrained by the truth, as well as dozens put up by Amanda and/or Kurt Price groupies. But nearly all of the pictures proved to be publicity stills from their movies. Amanda in oversize dark glasses, a scarf wrapped around her dark hair, offering an enigmatic smile from behind the wheel of a Triumph roadster. Amanda in period costumes ranging from Elizabethan to punk. In his photos, Kurt brandished a knife, a huge handgun, a grenade launcher, or simply his meaty fists. In every shot, his clothing was strategically torn to display his bulky biceps or the chiseled lines of his abdomen. Every now and then a web site revealed a few blurry amateur photographs of a couple who could have been anyone, hiding behind base-ball caps and dark glasses, walking fast with their eyes focused on their feet. But only one showed what could have been the actors with their child. A man with his head down walking through an airport alongside a woman and a girl who were both dressed in sunglasses and scarves. But the three could have been any man, any woman, any girl.

● ● ●

Not having driven the Mazda for several days, Claire had new ears for her own car's eccentricities. Compared to the deep purr of the Firebird's engine, her ten-year-old Mazda 323 sounded like an asthmatic squirrel. Someone else seemed to have been driving it, too. There were two or three empty Skittles wrappers on the passenger seat that she didn't recognize. Whoever had eaten them had probably thought they would blend in with the empty Chee-tos bags, crumpled tissues, and gas-station receipts that Claire was always intending to clean up. But Claire wasn't a Skittles fan. After she parked behind Charlie's car, she spent a few minutes picking up all the litter from the Mazda, starting with the Skittles bags.

She found Charlie in the living room, needlepointing a cushion. The design was of Charlie's own devising—a spray of red, orange, and pink flowers that she made up as she went along. The older woman cocked an eyebrow. "Was your sister able to help?"

Claire shook her head. "Susie knew lots about the Prices, but nothing about what their daughter looks like. J.B. even helped me look them up on the Internet, but we didn't find anything useful."

The two women talked about what to do on and off throughout the evening, but they continued to be stymied

by the seclusion the two stars had surrounded themselves
with. It was Charlie who hit upon the obvious solution.
"The answer is on your photocopy. We will call them."

"Why would they want to talk to us?"

"Because we know a secret of theirs. And from what
you say, they are very private people. We could offer
them a trade—we will not reveal where their child came
from if they agree to have the girl tested for a possible
match. That is assuming she looks to be a likely child."

Claire couldn't think of a better solution. So finally she
picked up the phone and pressed the buttons for the number listed after Amanda Price's name. One, two, three
rings, and then there was a faint click.

"Leave a message." A woman's voice, but even hearing
just three words, Claire recognized the same voice she
had heard issuing from the speakers in two dozen movie
theaters when she heard the beep. Claire took a deep
breath.

"This is Claire Montrose. I am calling for Amanda or
Kurt Price. I would like to set up a meeting with you. I
don't want to harm you or intrude on your life in any way,
but I do need to talk to you about your daughter and how
you got her. Please call me at 555-2854." She put the
phone down, thinking that now all they had to do was
wait.

YW84NE1

● ● ●

When the phone rang the next morning, Claire picked
it up on the first ring, thinking it might be Amanda or
Kurt. Instead, she heard her sister's voice on the line.

"I didn't ask when you were over the other day—but
have you seen or talked to Mom lately?"

"Not really, Suse." For the past two weeks, she had been so caught up in finding Lori's daughter that she hadn't had time to worry that her mother seemed to be on a first-name basis with the UPS delivery guy.

"I think she's in trouble."

"Trouble? What has she done now?" Claire already knew the general outline, even if the details remained to be filled in. Jean was a sucker for Kirby vacuum-cleaner salespeople. She sent twenty-dollar "processing fees" to strangers who called claiming she had just won the Sri Lankan lottery and then spent months wondering why her winnings hadn't yet arrived in the mail. During Girl Scout cookie season, green-costumed girls were lined up at her door three deep, knowing that Jean could be counted on to buy one box of each kind, plus at least a half dozen of Samoans, her favorite kind.

"It's that damn QualProd shopping channel. J.B. had a business meeting yesterday, so I had to take Eric over to Mom's while I was at Moyter's." Claire was momentarily distracted by the idea of J.B. having a business meeting. The last "business" she had known J.B to be involved in had resulted in him and some of his biker friends serving eight months in jail, charged with possession of marijuana with intent to distribute. When she tuned in again, Susie was saying, "So I go to pick him up, and there's Mom watching the TV, but no Eric. I'm like, 'Mom,'" Susie's voice arced in a sarcastic singsong, "'where is your grandson?' Mom admitted to me that she wasn't too sure where he was. She told me she figured he was being good because she hadn't heard him. Well, she was a mom long before I was, so she should know that if your kid is quiet, it's because he's doing something you don't want him to do."

"Where was he?"

"I finally discovered him in the back bedroom. He'd found a pair of scissors and he'd cut out all these pictures from one of her QualProd catalogs. But I guess he must have gotten bored with that, because when I found him he'd chopped off a big hunk of his hair. Now he's got a bald spot right above his forehead."

"At least it will grow back." Claire thought this didn't seem like much of a crisis.

"Wait, it gets better. When I come back from yelling at Eric, I find Mom with her hand in my purse. She jumps about a mile, and I see she's got my Visa card in her hand!"

"What did she do when she saw you?"

"She starts in crying, saying that there was some temporary problem with her card and that she just needed to borrow *my* card until the next billing cycle began on *her* card. Of course my bullshit detector was going off big-time. You know what I think? I think she's an addict. I mean, I can live with her watching TV all the time, she's always been like that, but this QualProd business is something else. It's like that's all she's interested in. I opened up the fridge the other day to put Eric's sippy cup away, and all she had in there was a half-empty tub of margarine and some Cool Whip. She's not eating right, she's not taking care of herself, and I doubt she's even going outside all that often. And now she's maxed out her credit card buying junk."

"We have to do something," Claire said, feeling a wave of exhaustion. "I'll call the credit-card people. But even if I pay off her charges, that's not going to solve the underlying problem. She'll just keep buying more junk."

"J.B. downloaded a bunch of info off the Internet. I think we should do one of those interventions like they do for alcoholics. Stop by my work, and I'll give you a set of the materials he printed out."

Claire hesitated. "You mean meet you at the funeral home?"

"Don't go all girly on me. It's a business, not a house

of horrors. Plus I'm backed up here. I've got three heads to do before the end of the day."

• • •

The woman in the coffin wore a maroon-cotton house-dress and a black-cardigan sweater. Her face was like yellowed ivory, carved with the lines of years. On the white-satin pillow, her thin black hair, barely flecked with gray, lay straight and limp.

"She looks like she just got off the boat," Susie said. Her voice held a note of tenderness that Claire didn't remember hearing before. "I doubt she ever did her hair." She plucked a photo off the woman's chest, just above her folded hands, and handed it to Claire. "What do you think?"

At first Claire didn't even see the woman in the Polaroid picture, which showed a bride and groom who looked to be about sixteen grinning foolishly at the camera. Then she spotted the woman who now lay in front of them. She stood at the edge of the picture, her face caught in profile. Her expression was stern, her nose prominent, and on her head was what might have been her one concession to vanity, a black straw hat decorated with an improbably large cluster of red cherries.

"She looks like she didn't put much stock in gussying up," Claire said. Rather than place the photo back on the corpse's chest, she handed it to Susie.

"Still, I'll bet she was gorgeous when she was young. Judging by the picture, I'm guessing the only thing she did to her hair was wash it and comb it. So I'll just put it back with a few nice waves in it." Susie picked up a cordless curling iron.

"Did you have to get her dressed or anything?" Claire was gradually losing her fear of the corpse. The room was cold and sterile, all white and stainless steel, but Claire was relieved that there weren't any instruments, drains, or equipment visible. There was a sharp smell in the air, like bleach or chemicals.

Susie laughed. "No, by the time I get them, they're already embalmed, dressed, and have some basic thick makeup. These guys need me for the woman's touch. I curl the hair, maybe tease it to make it look like there's more than there is. It's pretty much what I tried to do at Curl Up and Dye, you know, make the best of things. The good thing here is that the customers here don't talk to me. The bad thing is that they can't move or turn their heads. Then again, when I was working with live customers I couldn't fix a bare spot in front by clipping hair from the back and gluing it on with mortician's wax."

"Where you'd learn all this?"

"Most of it is just common sense. Plus I replaced someone who retired, so she spent the first few days with me until I got the hang of it."

"Doesn't it give you the heebie-jeebies?"

Susie shrugged. "Not really. Death happens. The best thing you can hope for is to meet it with some dignity. And hair makes the body. Even if you're alive and especially when you're dead. At the very end, when a woman needs someone looking out after her, I can be here. If Mom died, wouldn't you want her to look good?" She didn't wait for an answer. "Speaking of Mom, I brought in the stuff you'll need to work on. It's all over on that counter."

"I don't understand what there is to prepare." Claire picked up the half-inch-thick stack of papers. The top sheet was headed, "So You're Going to Have an Intervention."

Susie had curled the hair that showed, and now she sprayed it to keep it fluffy against the pillow, gently shielding the dead woman's face with her free hand. "What, do you think Mom is going to come right out and agree with us that she needs to have the QualProd channel blocked? She's going to fight like a cornered rat. She'll come up with a dozen different reasons why she doesn't need to do it, and we'll have to have an answer for each one. And when that doesn't work, then she'll go on to attack us as individuals." She set down the hair spray and picked up a pink-plastic cosmetics case.

Claire was impressed. "Is that all information J.B. got off the Internet?"

"What? No, that's just common sense." Susie clicked open the cosmetics case. "What do you think I should do about makeup? I'm thinking just a touch of blush and leave everything else alone."

Claire tried to regard the older woman with the same detachment that seemed to come naturally to Susie. "Probably. She doesn't look like she ever wore makeup."

Susie nodded. "Sometimes the family leaves me special makeup that their mom used to wear, but there's nothing like that for her. Look at those eyebrows. They've never been plucked." She gently brushed a pale pink swath on each cheek. "Almost done. Just got to make sure the earrings are on straight." She paused, checking details. Her eyes stopped on the woman's hands, on her gold wedding band. Sighing, she closed her pink cosmetic case and set it down. Susie slid the wedding ring off the woman's right hand and onto her left.

UDY11

15 • BYRLVR

Down came Lori's REJECTED stamp on the application. After a week back at work she was finally getting the hang again of deciphering the peculiar shorthand of license plates.

GLF NUT

Lori checked the license plate request against the state's Vulgar List of words and alphanumeric combinations. Forbidden were obscenities, sex, or excretory-related words, the promotion of religion or drugs, and words that meant something dirty in another language. She even halfheartedly took it into the bathroom to check out the words in a mirror, but the letters said nothing when reversed. Clearly, the owner, a guy in his mid-fifties, was simply telling the world that he loved to play golf. And since the computer showed that no one else had the plate, Lori stamped the application APPROVED and put it in her out box.

Lori was still puzzling over IMAYSGY when her phone shrilled into life. "State of Oregon's Motor Vehicles Division, Specialty Plate Department. Good afternoon, this is Lori. How may I be of assistance to you today?" She had even gotten used again to the whole awkward string of phrases that Roland, after attending an expensive four-day seminar about delighting the customer, now insisted was essential for answering the phone. In Lori's limited experience, however, the listener tended to become impatient and annoyed long before she finished.

"Lori, it's Tessa at WeeCare."

"What's wrong with Zach?" She had the same feeling she had when she sometimes went down the stairs too quickly and then discovered, too late, that there was still one more step to go. The feeling of beginning to fall.

"When I woke Zach up from nap time he felt hot to me, so I took his temp. He has a fever of a hundred and one." *A fever*, Lori thought, *a fever doesn't have to mean anything. Kids are always getting sick.* "But it's not just that," Tessa continued. "Zach's got, like, a kind of rash on his face. Like little red spots. I don't think it's measles, but I don't know what it is."

On the fifteen-minute drive from work, Lori's hands began to hurt from clenching the steering wheel. The words *Jesus no please* ran through her mind over and over. It was a chant, a prayer, a dirge. *Jesus no please.* In the little office behind the front desk, Zach lay on a cot. His eyes were closed, and he looked pale and clammy. Tessa was sitting beside him. Leaning forward, she began to talk to Lori, but Lori couldn't pay attention to the other woman's words. She bent over her son.

Tiny red dots were scattered across Zach's face. It looked as if he had been pricked from the inside with needles. *Petechiae,* Lori thought. Dr. Preston had taught her the word that signaled a platelet count so low that the skin began to hemorrhage spontaneously. She tried to re-assure herself that it might not mean anything. Maybe it was just a side effect of his maintenance chemotherapy. Only that morning she'd had to admonish Zach for jumping on her and Havi's bed. He was too healthy, too full of life, for it to be anything serious. Lori stroked back his hair from his damp forehead.

Opening his eyes, he squinted up at her painfully. "Mama, I want to go home."

"Just let me make a phone call, sugar."

Lori used the phone in the outer office. While she waited as they paged the doctor, the day care's secretary gave her a shaky smile and turned away to wipe her eyes. Anger surged through Lori. She could tell that this plump woman with her poodle perm had already written Zach off, was even doing a little premourning for him. What she didn't understand was that Lori would never let Zach die. Never.

Dr. Preston said that Lori should bring Zach straight to the hospital to be admitted. About six, he would stop by to examine him. He offered no speculation and no reassurances.

After a deep breath, Lori dialed another number.

"Buzz's Transmissions."

"Havi, it's Lori." Like a swimmer braving icy water, she plunged in. "I'm at WeeCare. Zach's running a fever and has some skin hemorrhages. Dr. Preston says he should be admitted. He'll come by around six to do a bone marrow. I'll see if Claire can watch Max. Can you meet me at the hospital?"

"Sure." The word was as heavy as a sinking stone. "I'll be there." He hung up without saying good-bye.

● ● ●

When Dr. Preston came back with the results of the bone-marrow aspiration, he motioned Lori and Havi out into the hall. He suggested they go in the nurses' lounge, but Lori would not let even a sleeping Zach out of her sight. When he had realized they were going to the hospital, not home, he had come to life, screaming that he didn't want to go to the hospital again, that he hated her. He kicked the back of her seat and threw himself from side to side in his car seat. Tears had burned their way down her face, but Lori had not let them stop her from driving to the hospital as fast as possible.

"This is very difficult," Dr. Preston began. Lori's chest tightened. There was a weight like a boulder on her lungs. She put her spread fingers over her chest. "Zach has had a relapse." He forced a brighter tone. "Even so, our chances of getting him back into remission are still quite good. But we do need to—"

Havi's hoarse voice interrupted him. "Zach can still be cured, can't he?"

Lori turned to stare at him, her mouth half-open. How could he ask that? He had been there when the doctor had explained it the first time. She had given him all the booklets to read.

Dr. Preston began to stammer. "The outlook for a cure at this point is, is, is . . . not good. But we can probably get him into remission again." He swallowed and continued on, his voice getting softer and more mumbly. "Since Zach has already failed a fairly aggressive therapy, it's doubtful that a second round of chemotherapy could produce a cure. Some of his leukemia cells have developed resistance."

"What about a bone-marrow transplant?" Havi's dark eyes were full of pain. "I know you said there's not a perfect match on the list, but can't we do it with a less-than-perfect match?"

The doctor shook his head. "There's not even a close match on the national registry, Mr. Estrada. That's a dead end."

"Then why can't you just give him more drugs, enough to kill off those resistant cells?"

Dr. Preston's voice was careful. "If we gave him higher doses, we might kill Zach's leukemia. But we'd probably also kill Zach."

"If we get him back into remission, how long will it last?" Lori asked. She could see the truth was dawning on Havi, that this was the beginning of the end.

"Probably its duration will be shorter than this one has been." This one had only lasted a few weeks, Lori thought. "And then we would try for a third remission. However, each remission tends to be shorter than the one preceding it. Eventually . . ." Letting his words trail off, Dr. Preston looked down at his empty hands.

Havi turned to Lori. The skin on his face looked like it was cracking. Tiny muscles tightened and jerked in his cheeks and forehead. The muscles around his eyes spasmed. "Let's take him home. Now."

A startled Dr. Preston said, "You can't do that!"

"Why not? What's the use of more drugs that will only make him miserable while we postpone the inevitable?"

Lori laid a hand on Havi's arm, but he shook it off. She said, "As long as there is any hope, we have to keep Zach in treatment."

"You're gonna let them torture him more? For what?" He looked at her with hooded eyes. "Lately, he's been feeling okay. Maybe not like he used to—but . . . better. Let him enjoy what he has now. What you're suggesting, I wouldn't do to a dog. And certainly not my son. This, this"—he waved his arm at the antiseptic-smelling hallway, the dimly lit rooms, each with its still prone figure, the sickness and death that surrounded them—"this is cruel! Let's take Zach home and make him as happy as we can." His voice cracked on the word *happy*.

"Hav," Lori said as gently as she could, "we don't have a choice. Not when there's any chance left."

"You heard him." He jerked his chin at Dr. Preston, who looked as if he wished he could just disappear. "What chance is there?"

Lori's insides knotted up. She would have to tell Havi. There was no way around it now. She had imagined this moment in a hundred different ways. Maybe a grown woman would reappear in their lives when they were old and passions faded. Or Havi might see a child on the street who looked so much like both of them that he would just suddenly know. Someday she might get good and drunk and her secret would come tumbling out. But this, this she had never imagined.

"Dr. Preston, could you excuse us for a minute?" Without saying anything, he left, his silver head down so he wouldn't have to look at them. Lori pulled Havi into a little alcove at the end of the hall. For Zach, she would sacrifice all her secrets, risk fracturing her marriage, open herself up to his hatred and scorn when he learned that she had given away their child. She opened her mouth and took a deep breath.

"Havi, I have something to tell you."

● ● ●

The phone call interrupted the game of Monopoly Claire and Charlie were trying to teach Max. None of them was paying much attention. Presented with a dinner of homemade macaroni and cheese, Max had picked up his fork and pretended to eat. Instead he had only scraped the noodles into piles, a trick Claire remembered from her days as a reluctant eater. Now one of Charlie's rich homemade brownies lay untouched in front of him, next to a glass of milk and a stack of play money. It saddened Claire the way he hadn't asked any questions about what was wrong when she had picked him up at school after Lori called her. It was like he didn't want to know.

"Claire—is Havi there?" From the question it was clear it must be Lori on the other end of the phone, but her voice was nearly unrecognizable, strangled by tears.

"No, he hasn't come by yet. What's wrong?" To judge by the way Lori sounded, the news about Zach must be very bad indeed. Was he dying? Max was staring down at his brownie, but Claire could tell he was listening to every word. She got up and took the phone into the kitchen.

"He left, he just left. I have never seen him so angry. And so cold. I don't even know what he's going to do. I told him about," Lori's voice caught, "about our daughter. Because after Dr. Preston said the remission had failed,

Havi said we should just take Zach home, that we should sign him out against medical advice and just take him home. He said," Lori gasped out, "he said we were torturing him. Experimenting on him. So I told him. Everything. About how I couldn't make myself have an abortion, and about how I decided to give, give, give the baby away. And I told him that you are looking for her. I told him that we can't give up on Zach even though his remission has failed. That we can't stop fighting for him while there is still a chance. After a while I was just—babbling. I knew I was talking too much, but I was frightened by the way he was looking at me. I knew when I stopped talking he was going to do or say something awful, but finally I had to shut up. He just looked at me, and he didn't say anything. I put my hand on his arm and said his name, and he looked down at my hand like it was some kind of spider." Lori's words were coming between gulps of tears. "His face was like a rock. He didn't cry, he didn't yell, he just looked at me, and he left. I don't ever want to see him look that way at me again." There was a long moment where all Claire could hear were Lori's sobs. "But I don't think he ever will look at me again. In any way. I don't think he's leaving me. I think he's already left. It's over. And for what? Tell me for what? I have lost my marriage, and I am probably going to lose my son. Why?" Her voice was naked with pain.

"Maybe Havi just needs a day or two to cool off," Claire ventured after a moment. The idea was unconvincing even to her.

"I don't think so. The last time he had that look on his face I didn't see him for four years." Lori's breath came in jerks and sighs. "Anyway, I have to ask you a big favor. Can you keep watching Max? It will mean some work, I know. He can show you where we keep a key, so you can get his clothes and books and stuff. And you'll have to take him to school and pick him up. He's not a picky eater, and I won't expect you to make him lunches like I do. If you could just give him money for lunch, of course I will pay you back. . . ." Lori's voice cracked. "I know it's a lot. But I don't know who else I can ask."

"Of course," Claire said. "Don't even worry about it. It will be a pleasure having him here." She looked up to see Max standing in the doorway, watching her. Underneath black hair as short as fur, his eyes were dark and unreadable.

16 • Would an intervention really be enough to make her mother part from her beloved Qual-Prod channel? Should Claire call Dante back and try to find a way to ask if he had betrayed her? And, most importantly, could Claire find Zach's sister before time ran out?

Her thoughts helped keep Claire's mind off the hitch and strain of her body as she tried to at least run more than she walked. She had planned to be on the Lieblings' block at 8 A.M., the same time she and Charlie had seen the couple leaving for work, but her calculation had been based on an overly optimistic estimate of how fast she could still cover ground. Her breath came in gasps. Her legs were leaden, her feet barely clearing the ground. Her ankle didn't really hurt anymore, but it didn't feel right, either.

It was the kind of false spring morning that makes Oregonians decide to put away their raincoats and heavy sweaters. In another day or two, the skies would surely darken, the rain would sweep back in, and the coats would come out of the closet. But for now it was warm enough that Claire was already regretting wearing her long running tights.

Without consciously making a decision, Claire found that she had stopped and was leaning over her right shoe as if to tie the lace, although it was still tied. She imagined the eyes of passing commuters upon her, seeing through her strategy. To buy herself a few seconds to catch her breath, she pulled the lace loose and tied it again. Raising her fingers to her sweat-slick throat, she found her carotid artery, and began counting the beats. Even after her pulse had dropped from 160 to a more reasonable 130, Claire found she didn't want to start again. She looked at her watch. It was a good bet that in about five minutes the Lieblings would be backing out of their driveway in their matching BMWs. With a groan, she started running again.

Claire turned on the Lieblings' block just in time to see the two bright red BMWs, one after another, scoot backward down the drive and go off in opposite directions. She only caught a glimpse of David Liebling as he drove away, but she was sure he was the only occupant of his car. Monica Liebling drove right past Claire, but didn't seem to notice her at all. Her hands were in the ten and two o'clock position, her lips pressed together. The little boy sitting behind her looked directly into Claire's eyes as she stared at him. With his dark hair, almond-shaped eyes, and high cheekbones, he could have been Max and Zach's cousin, or even a brother. But he was too young to be ten, and he was definitely a boy. Claire stopped at the telephone pole in front of the Liebling house and pretended to stretch her legs for a few seconds, but it was clear just by looking at it that the house was empty.

She was about ready to give up and go back to her car when she caught sight of a young woman kneeling in a garden at the end of the block. With a little grunt, Claire forced herself to start running again, slowing when she came abreast of the young woman. On one side of her was a little girl in a stroller, on the other a coiled green garden hose.

"Could I trouble you for a drink of water from your hose?" Claire didn't need to fake her gasping. "I guess I've really let myself get out of shape."

"Oh, here, let me get you some water from the house." The woman stood up and pulled off her gardening gloves. She had straight blond hair cut in a shoulder-length bob and a spray of freckles across her nose. "Just keep an eye on Lily, would you?"

Claire looked down at the child, who gave her a wet-gummed grin. "Sure."

The woman left the front door open while she went inside, and Claire noticed that for all her neighborliness she was careful to keep an eye on Claire through the window. In a second, she was back with an unopened, chilled bottle of Cascadia and a tall glass. She twisted off the cap and offered both bottle and glass to Claire. The water was so cold that Claire's throat closed, and she choked a little. The baby flapped her hands and babbled as she swung her gaze between her mother and the stranger. She had huge blue eyes and sparse blond hair worn in the baby version of a comb-over.

"You have a beautiful child," Claire said sincerely. She made sure her bare left hand was hidden by the water glass. "My husband and I are thinking of having a baby. Is this a good neighborhood for raising kids? Right now, we just live in an apartment over in Northwest."

The woman nodded, her hair swinging forward in two wings. "Irvington's a great neighborhood for children. The streets are quiet. We keep an eye out for one another. There's a block party every summer, and we have a group rummage sale every fall. I get a lot of great toys that way." She stopped in the middle of her recitation and leaned closer to Claire. "You should, you know."

"Should what?" Claire had already forgotten her story.

"Have a child. It was the best decision we ever made. Lily has changed our lives. You do give up some things, but you gain so much more." She bent down and kissed the baby on the top of her head. Lily let out a trill, and the sound sent an unexpected pang through Claire. The woman straightened up and pointed down the street. "That house on the corner just went on the market for three twenty-five. It's a little dated inside, but if you're interested, you should move on it."

Claire nodded brightly. With the average salary under thirty thousand, the house was well out of reach of any but the most affluent Portlanders. "Are there any other children on this block?"

As Claire had hoped, the woman scanned the surrounding houses and began to recite their contents. "The Guinns have a little girl who's five and a half. The Averetts have a boy who's four and a girl who's seven. Let's see, the Andersons have a little girl about Lily's age, but she's still a bit too young for play dates. And there's the Lieblings, well." She paused, then went on, "They've had more than their share of troubles when it comes to children."

"Oh?" Claire lifted an eyebrow. After years of watching Charlie, she had learned the value of keeping silent and seeing what came in to fill the gap.

"About a dozen years ago, their first baby died of SIDS when she was just a few weeks old. And then they had another child, another girl, and *she* died of SIDS when she was ten months old." She looked down at her daughter. "That's how old Lily is. I can't even imagine what it would be like to lose your baby like that, not once, but twice. I'll bet they have a hard time not hovering over Craig, but he's been healthy, knock on wood. He's eight now."

"When did that happen?" Claire said, staring.

"When did what happen?"

"When exactly did their children die of SIDS?"

"Their first child's death, that happened before we moved here. The second little girl died right after we bought this house. That was around the Fourth of July, 1989. I remember because I didn't know the Lieblings very well, and I kept wondering if I should bring them over some food. Why did you want to know when it happened?"

"I think maybe I heard that story from someone once," Claire mumbled. "They were talking about what a tragedy it was." Her thoughts spinning, she handed back the half-empty bottle of water as well as the glass. "Guess I'd better hit the road again before I lose all motivation. Thanks for your advice."

She waved good-bye to Lily and her mother and began to trot back down the street. But inside, Claire was overwhelmed with grief. Here was the answer to the Lieblings' seeming dead end: a real death. After seeing Lily, it was all too easy to picture the loss the baby represented.

But something nagged at Claire about the story the neighbor had told her. And then she realized what it was. During her last visit to Dante, he had brought her breakfast in bed every morning—coffee lightened with skim milk, a toasted plain bagel spread with cream cheese, and the day's edition of the *New York Times*. Then they had spent a quiet hour interrupted by nothing but rustling pages and an occasional coffee-tasting kiss.

One of the articles she had read while lounging on Dante's white sheets had been about mothers who had lost more than one baby to SIDS. Once, doctors had shaken their heads and proclaimed that the tragedy of sudden infant death syndrome was sometimes horrifically compounded when it ran in families. Some parents, so the thinking had gone, just passed on defective genes. But new tests had shown that in families where more than one child had died, it was more likely that murder was involved. District attorneys were getting court orders to exhume long-buried children. One mother, Claire had read, had tearfully confessed to covering the faces of her babies with pillows, one after another. Of her seven children, none had lived to the age of two.

What if the *New York Times* article was right, and that families with multiple SIDS cases might really be hiding the dark secret of infanticide? Wasn't that even more likely to be the case if two children were unrelated? Because the two babies who had died in the Liebling house had had nothing in common but the people who were raising them.

Claire's mind was so busy that she had stopped paying attention to what her body was doing. She realized she was walking again, not running. The body had its own agenda, and the mind willingly disengaged.

Ahead of her, a yellow bike leaned against a bus-stop sign. It was all yellow—handlebars, frame, tires, spokes—looking as if it had been dipped into a vat of bright yellow paint. Claire had read about the yellow bike program in the *Oregonian*, but she had never actually seen one. The premise had been that yellow bikes would be left all around the downtown core. Riders would use one when they needed it for a brief jaunt, then leave it for the next person. Supposedly the idea had worked in some Dutch city. In Portland, however, the hundred or so donated bikes had disappeared after only a few months, stolen, stripped for parts, or ridden into the hinterland and abandoned. Like this one.

Claire threw her leg over the bright yellow seat and rode off.

OWTAHR

17 The clerk at John's Market didn't really focus on Claire, which was fine with her. After all, what was a woman wearing running tights and ninety-five-dollar Nikes doing buying a twelve-ounce package of chocolate chips and a horrendously overpriced can of salted cashews? The answer was that she hoped to try to relieve her stress with food, and it was too early for Sweets, Etc., to be open. Recently Claire had discovered that if she popped two or three salted cashews in her mouth at the same time as a half dozen chocolate chips, she could achieve much the same taste as a milk chocolate cashew cluster. In some ways it was even better, because the salted cashews meshed with chocolate better than plain ones did. The combination covered the four basic food groups: fat, sweet, salt, and chocolate.

After leaving the yellow bike leaning against a signpost near her car, Claire had driven back across the river to Multnomah Village. The drive had passed in a blur as she fought her conviction that Lori's daughter had died while living with the Lieblings, quite possibly at their own hands.

The clerk handed Claire back her change and her stash, appropriately packaged in a plain brown paper bag. As she was leaving, Claire caught sight of the brass mailboxes at the back of the market. Realizing she hadn't canceled the mailbox she had rented in Lucy's name, she turned in her key and got back her ten-dollar key deposit.

The clerk caught up with Claire on her way out the door.

"You still had mail in your box," he said, handing her a letter with no return address. It was addressed to Lucy Bertrand, with quotes around the name.

In the parking lot, Claire opened it. It wasn't too much of a mystery who it had come from, as only the Bradford Clinic thought there *was* a Lucy. Still, the message took her by surprise. On plain white paper, a few sentences were printed in a distinctive squarish hand.

"I know what you really wanted. There were problems afterwards." Next came two lines that had been crossed out so heavily that Claire couldn't read them even when she raised the paper to the light. *"Her babies came early. And afterward she began to bleed, worse than I have ever seen. I tried massaging her belly, but it didn't stop. It had been a hard birth, and it was three in the morning, and I was so tired that I was no longer thinking straight. Dr. B. was yelling at me, saying that I shouldn't worry, that he would take her to St. V's and with their equipment they could help her. Check with St. Vincent's. That's where he said he was going. I pray to God that that's what he did."*

The world seemed to have gone very still. Claire had imagined that Ginny had given birth and then resumed her life the way she had planned. Was she hospitalized now, IVs running into her arms to replace the blood she had lost? But Vi seemed to be implying that she didn't trust Dr. Bradford. Was she saying that maybe Ginny had never made it to St. Vincent's at all?

● ● ●

Instead of turning right off Multnomah Boulevard, Claire found herself turning left, going to see Dr. Gregory instead of heading back to her empty house. Charlie would still be taking Max to school. As a physician, Dr. Gregory could give her advice. He would understand the note's implications better than Claire. And he should also be able to shed some light on what really had happened to the Lieblings' first two children.

She knocked on his office door, then waited. No answer. She looked at her watch. It was about nine o'clock, perhaps too early to be office hours. Just as Claire was turning to leave, the door opened. A woman brushed past Claire, her head down, walking fast. And behind her was Dr. Gregory, guilt chasing surprise across his face at the sight of Claire. The woman must be one of his conquests, Claire realized, and was annoyed at herself for minding. And maybe not one he was particularly proud of, given her downmarket appearance. She had been wearing ratty jeans, a fake leather jacket, and a pair of moon boots. Moon boots! Claire hadn't seen moon boots since about the last time someone had walked on the moon.

Dr. Gregory adjusted his face so that it wore his usually welcoming smile. Still, he couldn't quite hide his agitated nervousness. "Come in, come in." He closed the door behind her. "What brings you by this way? Ankle acting up this morning?"

Claire had been so worried by the note that she had forgotten she was still wearing running clothes. "No, that's not it. I need your advice on a couple of medical matters. This is one of them." She handed him the note.

After he read it, he looked up. "Where did you get this?"

"I found it in the mailbox I rented for Lucy Bertrand." He looked blank. "My alter ego for the Bradford Clinic, remember? I'm pretty sure that's the head nurse's handwriting."

As he read the note again, Dr. Gregory took a tissue from a box on his desk and blew his nose. Even before he had thrown it away he was sniffling again. "Sorry. Seasonal allergies. Some new tree or bush someplace is putting out pollen, and it doesn't like me." He rubbed his nose with the back of his hand. "Well, I know one way to figure out if Dr. Bradford did what he said he was going to do," he commented, picking up the phone.

Why was he always sniffing, Claire wondered, suddenly remembering the other times she had been with him. As he dialed the phone, she rapidly recalculated things. Was he using drugs? The idea didn't seem so outlandish. She already had seen how he liked to drink.

"Bed control, please," Dr. Gregory said, then tucked the phone under his chin. "I'm calling St. Vincent's." He slipped the phone back to his mouth, and his voice assumed an imperious tone Claire had never heard him use before. "Yes, this is Dr. Gregory. Could you tell me if Ginny Sloop is still in the house? Probably med-surg, or maybe family nursing." There was a pause. "She's not? Well, then when was she discharged? My understanding was that she was admitted Friday with postpartum hemorrhaging." He listened a few seconds more, frowning. "You're sure? How about any Jane Does with a similar diagnosis?" After hearing the answer, he hung up without a thank-you or even a good-bye. "Wherever Dr. Bradford took Ginny, it wasn't there. They checked the records for two days before and two days after. No Ginny Sloop and no unidentified females. So he must have taken her someplace else."

"Why couldn't he treat her at the clinic? He's a doctor, after all."

"Sometimes the only cure for a woman who starts hemorrhaging after labor is a quick trip to surgery for a hysterectomy. And the clinic certainly isn't set up for that."

"But if he didn't go to St. V's—where did he take her?"

"Maybe Good Sam. Or Oregon Health Sciences University, especially if he was afraid she was going to bleed out in the car. They've got a Level One Trauma Center. Tell you what—I'll do some calling and get back to you."

Claire watched as Dr. Gregory rapidly tapped his pen on his desk, then he turned his attention to her again. "You said there were two things you wanted to ask me about?"

Claire had almost forgotten about what she had learned about the Lieblings. She quickly recapped what she had heard from their neighbor. "Don't you think it's too much of a coincidence that two of their children died from SIDS—especially since we know one of those children was adopted?"

Dr. Gregory rocked back and forth in his office chair. "Stranger things have happened. But if I were the DA or their doctor, I'd be very interested in ruling out other causes, such as a pillow across the face."

"So you think they really could have killed those two babies?" She thought of Monica Liebling, of the tight press of her lips as she drove past Claire.

"In my line of work, you quickly learn that everything is possible. I've seen bank presidents who beat their wives, and wives who beat their bank-president husbands. I told one woman she was terminally ill, with less than six months to get her affairs in order. That was eight years ago, and now her tests don't show any sign of cancer. On the other hand, I once treated a Hmong immigrant who was convinced that he had been cursed and was bound to die. He sat right where you are now, trembling with fear, while I explained through the interpreter that he was perfectly healthy. Two weeks later, he went to bed and didn't wake up in the morning."

"But what about the Lieblings?" Claire demanded, a little impatient with his doctor stories.

"From what I've read, what sometimes happens in these cases is that the first child dies of natural causes. And that death triggers something in the mother. She craves that attention and sympathy again. Or maybe she realizes deep inside herself that she doesn't want to be a mother, and that a dead child is much easier to deal with than a live one. And for one reason or another, maybe they're Catholic or maybe the husband really wants children, she keeps having more babies—and then killing them."

"Why do you keep saying 'the mother'?" Claire asked. "What about the father?" She thought about Monica's husband, the man she had seen twice now, but only behind the wheel of his car. David Liebling had sharp-edged features and straight dark hair slicked back with enough gel that it stood up in points.

"Because the mother is the one who's implicated in most of these cases. When men kill children, it's usually more violently. Men might be more likely to throw a kid down the staircase or drown it in the bathtub, even torture it"—Claire winced, but Dr. Gregory didn't seem to notice—"especially if they aren't the biological father of the child. But when it isn't a clear-cut case of abuse, from what I've seen and read, it's most often the mother who is the culprit. Traditionally, mothers are supposed to be the nurturers, but there are a number of women who can't deal with the huge demands of the role of selfless caregiver. Have you heard of Munchausen by Proxy?"

Claire shook her head.

"Basically, the mother makes her child sick over and over again, just so that *she* can get attention. The doctors are baffled, run dozens of tests, sometimes even hospitalize the kid. And all the while they are telling the mom, 'Aren't you a saint to put up with this uncertainty, with your child sick all the time?' Even health-care professionals—who should pick up on this sort of thing faster—can take a long time before they start suspecting that something is wrong. Last year, I saw a videotape where someone in a hospital finally got suspicious and had a hidden video camera installed. You can actually see the mom leaning over to put her hand over the kid's mouth and nose. Even though I knew that's what I was going to see when somebody played the tape for me, it was still shocking."

Claire thought of the dark-eyed little boy in the back-seat, the woman at the wheel with her perfect French braid and pinched mouth. "What if Monica Liebling did kill her two kids? What about the little boy they have now? Would he be in any danger?"

"How old did you say the child looked again?"

She hazarded a guess. "Six or seven."

"If someone in that household had a predilection for killing babies, then a seven-year-old is probably not in any grave danger. Currently." He got up and began pacing around the room. "So where are you now with the search? You had four little girls you wanted to look at, right?" He held out four fingers, then bent down his pinkie. "And one seems to have died. Whether by natural or unnatural causes, we don't know. What about the other three?"

Claire shook her head. "I don't think one of them can be Lori and Havi's daughter because her coloring is all wrong. She's got pale blond hair and skin as white as cotton."

"I guess nothing's impossible, but I'll admit, that certainly doesn't sound likely." He bent another finger down. "What about the people with the Hispanic last name? That sounded promising."

"I'm going to go see them this afternoon."

Only his index finger was left, and he pointed it at her. "That leaves Portland's most famous stars, Amanda and Kurt Price. What about them?"

"I haven't been able to think of any way to see their child without them knowing. Their estate is completely secluded. That means I have to talk to them face-to-face. Charlie pointed out to me that we did have their phone number. I called and left a message, but no one's called back. I feel bad invading their privacy, but I don't see any other way to figure out whether they have Lori's daughter. How they got their child is certainly one secret I'm sure they want to keep. And deserve to." Remembering the delight Dr. Gregory had taken in seeing the actors' names on the photocopy, Claire regarded him, narrowing her eyes only half in jest. "You haven't told anyone, have you?"

He drew an X on his chest. "Cross my heart and hope to die, thousand needles in my eye." He paused. "But there is one thing, Claire."

"What?"

"Promise me something?"

"Of course," Claire said, hiding her reservations.

"Promise that you'll go out with me again and tell me all about what happened."

She couldn't say no, not when she didn't know if she might need another favor from him. "I'd love to," she said, feeling cheap.

As Claire unlocked the car door, her thoughts were tangled. Was Dr. Gregory interested in her romantically—or just in what she knew? After all, the Prices' secret would be worth a lot to a man who might have a drug habit to feed. And what about what Dr. Gregory had said about the clinic? He had said that it wasn't set up for a hysterectomy. But how could he know what procedures Dr. Bradford could or couldn't do, since he had told her he had never been there? Maybe she was being paranoid. Maybe Dr. Gregory just had allergies. Maybe it was easy to guess what the clinic might have, given Dr. Bradford's focus on outpatient visits and uncomplicated births by young, healthy mothers.

Claire didn't know what was true and what she was imagining. One image, real or not, filled her mind as she pulled into her driveway and turned off the motor. She pictured Ginny lying still and pale in the backseat of a car, the life ebbing out of her with each pulse. And with only Dr. Bradford, with his cold wolf's eyes, to care for her.

18• There was still a stretch of farmlands and fields between Portland and Minor, a taste of the country life Claire had all but forgotten about. The drive reminded her that it was spring, the season of young things. All the sheep had lambs, all the cows had calves, and the tail-switching mares watched their foals chase each other back and forth across the meadows.

The world outside her window seemed full of life—but if Claire didn't find Lori's daughter soon, then Zach would surely die. And even though Lori hadn't reproached her, Claire knew that so far she hadn't proved to be much of a sleuth. Even if she did succeed in finding the girl, what then? There would only be more hurdles, one after another. The adoptive parents would have to consent to having the girl tested. And there was still only a one-in-four chance the child would match Zach. And even if all those nearly impossible things happened, what if Zach had the transplant and it failed? Tears pricked Claire's eyes, making it hard for her to see. The truth was, Zach was dying. And she didn't know if there was anything she could do to stop it.

As her thoughts twisted and tangled, a half-grown calico kitten, orange-and-black spots on white fur, darted across the road in front of her. Claire smoked her tires to avoid it, then watched as it disappeared into a mile-long stretch of green field. Suppressing the urge to get out of her car and try to save it, she put her foot back on the accelerator.

Minor now rated two exits from the highway, and in her confusion Claire took the one that hadn't existed when she lived there. Soon, she was completely lost. In her memory, Minor was still an ugly two-story false-front town. Two decades before, the sawmill had been the main employer, marked by golden heaps of sawdust a hundred feet high. The sweet smell competed with the sour stench of the paper mill a mile away. When she remembered Minor, Claire thought of Pancake Mills and Pie Shoppes, of wizened old men in ball caps and short-sleeved polyester shirts, of pickups held together by rust and their I LOVE SPOTTED OWLS . . . FRIED bumper stickers.

The year Claire graduated was the year the paper mill went belly-up, victim of laws that declared it illegal to dump untreated water directly into the river. Too expensive to retrofit, the owners said, and moved on, leaving two hundred people out of work. People complained, but Claire remembered how the stink of chlorine had hung over the dead gray stretch of Bear Creek long after the mill was gone.

Minor was now an uneasy mix of old and new, with just enough of the old to make Claire really confused. Those few places she recognized—a Mr. Steak restaurant, Bear Creek Park, Sam's Feed Store, a Mode O'Day that looked as if the same clothes had been on the same mannequins since the day she left—were now surrounded by businesses and homes that had sprouted up in the intervening years. The few pieces she recognized didn't fit into her mental map of the town. She began turning left and right at random, sometimes passing nothing familiar for a long stretch, a feeling that was oddly comforting. When she did recognize something, like a weathered barn now slanting sideways and surrounded by houses, Claire felt completely discombobulated.

She drove past a sprawling shopping mall that looked as if it had sprung up overnight, but then behind it she glimpsed the Pietro's she had worked at during high school. The first thing the manager had done after he hired her was to ask her to hem her red uniform skirt up six inches. She still hated to think how unquestioningly she had complied.

When it was her turn to count out her till, the manager had always insisted Claire climb the stairs ahead of him to his little cubbyhole of an office, located behind the false balcony decorated with listing mannequins dressed up in faded flapper costumes. Claire supposed she should be thankful he had contented himself with looking.

Minor had been changing even while she lived there. For years its economic base had been the huge stands of trees that surrounded it. Over time, the big logs got scarcer and more expensive, and the city people and the environmentalists began to complain about the clear-cuts scabbing the land. Some of the same people Minorites called *tree-huggers* even moved into town, and the old-timers said that they were simply trying to get their piece of heaven before closing the door to anyone who might follow. One of them heard a bullet whine past his ear while he stood in his own front yard during hunting season. Afterward, the town was divided by those who said it was because he was stupid enough to wear light-colored gloves (so much like the flick of a mule deer's tail) during hunting season, and those who believed he should heed the shot's warning and get out of town.

Now that it had been overrun by identical-looking housing developments and strip malls, Claire found herself somehow missing the old Minor. Still seeking someplace she recognized, she drove on. And suddenly there was Hubie's Market, right in front of her, looking as weather-beaten and unattractive as it had when she was growing up.

Claire parked the car in the empty lot and went inside. It smelled just the same, of damp and woodsmoke from the cast-iron stove that sat in the middle of the store. Under a dozen different names, Hubie's had been in operation for over a hundred years.

And Hubie still stood behind the counter with his arms crossed over his thick chest, looking as he probably had for the last quarter century. Built like a fire hydrant, he had steel gray hair combed sideways across his head.

Even the way he regarded Claire suspiciously through the square black-plastic frames of his thick glasses was comfortingly familiar.

The store even looked like it stocked the same items it had when she was a kid. It concentrated on the staples: cheap beer and wine, brightly colored junk food, and low-priced cigarettes. There was still room on the narrow wooden shelves for some of the other goods Hubie thought you might find necessary: plastic digital watches, fan belts, wrestling magazines, romance novels for the ladies, staple foods in tiny boxes (with outsize prices), brass belt buckles, ammo, fuses, dusty balls of twine, fireworks available year-round, thumbtacks, and, skewered inside a glass case, hot dogs that had been revolving since the beginning of the world.

"Good morning, Hubie. Do you remember me?"

He continued to stare at her, his expression unreadable. Claire hadn't thought of him in nearly two decades, but now it was like the years had rolled back and she was twelve again.

"I used to ride my bike here every Saturday"—she suddenly remembered it, a lime green Schwinn with a banana seat and kick-back brakes—"so I could spend my fifty-cent allowance. Sometimes on chips or candy, or sometimes on milk or bread if we didn't have any in the house. And after a while, you started giving me food, stuff you said you couldn't sell because it was past the pull date or not what you ordered."

He recognized her now, she could tell that, even if he didn't smile. But then Claire didn't think she had ever seen Hubie smile.

He grunted. "Skinny girl."

"Pardon?"

"You're that skinny girl used to come in my store, all hair and eyes and long skinny legs about as big around as a piece of string. You looked like the wind was about to blow you away."

Claire felt a mixture of nostalgia and embarrassment for her old self. "Yeah, that was me. I never told you how much I appreciated your giving us stuff." Hubie had given Claire more than just the bags of Doritos and boxes of Pizza Spins that she craved. He had also given her milk and half cartons of eggs and one-pound bags of flour. Sometimes it had been Hubie's generosity that had put food on the table at the end of the month. "I haven't really been back to Minor since my mom moved us out. Everything looks different, but you and the store still look the same."

"Times change, but people still got to have their smokes. I have to cut my margin pretty thin so I can still compete. But now they're talking about putting in a To-bacco Town franchise a half mile a way. Guaranteed low-est prices on beer and cigarettes. The minute they do, I'm closing this place down. I'll make my old dog move over on the porch and give me some room." It was the most Claire had ever heard Hubie say at one time. "What brings you back here now?"

"I'm trying to find someone who lives here now. You wouldn't know the Sanchezes would you, Cindy and Kevin Sanchez?"

He looked up at the ceiling, thinking, then shook his head.

"Well, how about Pine Terrace? Do you know where that is?"

Hubie ended up drawing her a map on a grocery sack. Before she left, Claire picked out a bag of neon red Ex-treme Chee-tos. She tried to give Hubie a twenty-dollar bill for it, no change necessary, but he wouldn't take her money at all.

● ● ●

Pine Terrace turned out to look more or less the way Claire had expected it to. The neighborhood was so new that many of the houses were surrounded by churned mud instead of lawn. On the edges of the development a handful of would-be houses were in the middle of being framed. Mud-splattered yellow bulldozers smoothed out spots for more construction.

To Claire's eye, the finished houses all looked alike, cookie-cutter construction painted in skin-tone mauves and beiges. As she drove down the street, the first impression was of a long row of two-car garages. The houses were so close that you could pass your neighbor the butter through your adjoining dining-room windows.

She found the Sanchez address with no problem. A pinkish tan, it had two stories and was set back from the street. The street itself *was* a problem. It was a cul-de-sac, meant for kids riding their bikes or an impromptu game of basketball. A stranger jogging by several times or an unknown car parked for an hour or two would be immediately marked as out of place.

Claire had to think of something. She had no more answers for Lori than when she had begun this search, and time was running out. She had to find out if the Sanchezes, with their Hispanic last name, had adopted Lori and Havi's daughter.

An idea occurred to her. After driving a few blocks away, she parked in another cul-de-sac. She scrabbled through the contents of her trunk, all gifts from her previous boyfriend. Evan was an insurance adjuster who believed in being prepared for any type of calamity. Her trunk held flares, a tire-pressure gauge, a fire extinguisher, a gray scratchy wool blanket, a tube of something called adhesive bond, extra fan belts, a red tool chest full of Sears Craftsman tools that she had no idea how to use, and a yellow banner that read CALL POLICE in foot-high letters. Evan's last Valentine's Day gift had been a roll of quarters in case she ever broke down by the side of the road conveniently within walking distance of a pay phone. It hadn't escaped Claire's notice that his gift had cost just ten dollars. Finally, Claire found what she half remembered from Christmas three years ago, a brown fiberboard clipboard with attached pen. On top was an accident report form dense with type.

Slipping in behind the wheel, she drove back to the Sanchez house and parked in front. Not giving herself time to think, Claire picked up her clipboard and walked to the door. The fake brass knocker gave a hollow *clunk* when she let it fall. Narrow plates of yellow smoked glass were set on either side of the door, and for a long minute she watched the empty hall. In a hidden recess she spotted a doorbell. She pressed that, too, but the chimes died away without anyone appearing.

Claire was about to leave when a woman opened the door. Her dark straight hair was feathered against her cheeks, and she was wiping her hands on the white apron she wore over navy blue leggings and a tunic. Cindy Sanchez, with an olive complexion that belied her white-bread first name.

"Hello," Claire began speaking rapidly, trying to get some forward momentum going. "I'm from Alliance Survey, and I'm asking homeowners in the neighborhood if they would be interested in supporting a bond measure to add a neighborhood playground for children. Could you tell me, ma'am, if you would vote for or against such a measure if it would add"—she pulled a figure from the air—"fifty-nine cents for every thousand dollars of your home's assessed value?"

"Pardon?" Her hands still twisted in the apron, the woman looked at Claire with wide eyes. "My English is not so good."

"Could I come in and explain it to you further, Mrs. Sanchez?"

The woman raised her hand to hide her smile. "'Mrs. Sanchez'? Mrs. Sanchez, she working. I am Josefina."

"Oh, well, perhaps you could help me," Claire said, and put her foot in the door.

Dropping her eyes, Josefina took a step back. With her toe, Claire nudged the door open wider.

"Can I come in for a moment? I really, really, really need to use," she lowered her voice, "the ladies' room. The *baño*?" she repeated, thankful to remember the word from her *Let's Learn Spanish* tape, detritus from just one of a thousand self-improvement schemes she had undertaken and then abandoned.

Not waiting for the woman to assent, Claire walked into the Sanchez home. It was decorated in pinks and blues. In front of an unused fireplace, a pair of three-foot-tall blue-painted wooden geese sat facing each other, each wearing a white ribbon around its neck. But Claire wasn't looking at the decor, with its emphasis on knick-knacks and manufactured cuteness. Instead she was hunting for family portraits. There wasn't one in the living room, which flowed into a dining area on the right. She began to walk down the hall on the left.

"Is it down here?" she asked Josefina, who was scurrying behind her, looking as if she wished she could find a way to retake control of the situation. There was a single photo in the hall, but it was an eighty-year-old hand-colored print of a woman holding an impossibly red-cheeked baby. Claire could see the bathroom at the end of the hall, but instead she opened one of the other doors.

"Is it in here?" she asked as she quickly the surveyed the room. A girl's room, for sure, a girl who wanted to be both a child and an adult. Claire sympathized. Sometimes she had the same problem. Above the bed, strewn with stuffed animals, was a poster of a boy-actor Claire barely recognized. But no photographs, not on the narrow study desk, not on the walls. Was this Zach's sister's room?

A hand touched her elbow. "Excuse me—this way?" Josefina said, and pointed toward the bathroom. She looked frightened but firm.

Sitting on the toilet, Claire let her head droop until her forehead touched the clipboard resting across her knees.

Josefina hadn't stirred from the other side of the door, and she had the feeling the woman was listening to make sure Claire didn't steal anything. Chances that Josefina would let her wander anyplace else were slim. Plan A and Plan B hadn't worked—but what was Claire going to do for an encore?

As she flushed the toilet and washed her hands, she realized that the clipboard still might help her. She came out of the bathroom, walked right past Josefina, and settled herself on the couch. "Now, I just have a few questions I need to ask," she said, looking down at the words *Other Driver's Ins. No.* "How many children are in the home?"

"Just one little girl. Alexa."

Claire made a check mark in the middle of the space for Date of Accident.

"And she is how old?"

"Ten years." Claire wrote this answer down under *Other Driver's Name.*

"And would she be interested in having a playground nearby?"

Looking uncomfortable, Josefina shrugged. Claire couldn't tell if it was because she didn't have the answer or didn't understand the question.

"What does she do in her free time?"

There was a long silence, then finally Josefina put her index fingers in her ears. Claire thought the woman was saying the questions were overwhelming her, until she realized that Josefina was miming something, the words coming haltingly. "Alexa, she all the time listens to the headphones."

Claire was trying to think of a way to find out what the girl looked like when the front door opened and a tall blond woman rushed in, followed more slowly by a short, plump, freckled girl. Her hair was a brilliant orange. With a sinking heart, Claire knew that this child must be Alexa.

The blond woman looked Claire up and down with a frown.

"Who is this, Josefina? Haven't I told you not to let anyone in when I'm not here?"

"Oh, ma'am, oh, it is, it is . . ." Josefina stuttered.

Tapping the pointed toe of her black-leather pump, the other woman drew herself up to her full height, her red-manicured hands on her hips.

"Cindy Weaver!" Claire cut in.

Cindy wheeled. "Do I know you?"

Minor had served as a feeder school for all the rural areas around it, so there had been about four hundred in Claire's graduating class. Including Cindy Weaver, head cheerleader, party girl, and general bitch.

Claire put out her hand. "Claire Montrose. We both went to Minor High."

Cindy cocked her head to one side, her frosty blue eyes regarding Claire. "I'm afraid I really don't remember you."

Claire had a hundred memories of Cindy. Cindy sauntering down the hall wearing a short black dress and black pumps with lace-edged white ankle socks, a half dozen boys vying to talk to her. Cindy leading a routine, her large breasts seemingly without benefit of a bra. Cindy pulling Claire's hair when she sat behind her in social studies, for no reason that Claire had ever figured out. Cindy showing up late for graduation rehearsal, her face pale and her eyes red. Later, Claire had heard that Cindy had spent the morning aborting the fullback's baby. All Claire said was, "We went to Minor High together. I remember you from the games."

Cindy flushed, and her face relaxed. "I do cheerleading consulting now for college sororities," she said, straightening her shoulders with pride.

"I'm going to my room," Alexa announced. Cindy gave an absent nod, her eyes still on Claire.

Josefina was easing her way back to the kitchen. Claire nodded in her direction. "When she answered the door, I thought she was Cindy Sanchez."

"What?" Cindy jerked her head back, affronted. "We're not *Mexican*. Kevin's family came over from *Spain* in the seventeen hundreds." She lowered her voice. "Although sometimes it comes in handy to let people think your looks match your name. I think Josefina was surprised that we didn't speak any Spanish. I have to explain everything to her in the simplest terms. Although I shouldn't complain. You can get these people for two dollars an hour, and they think you're paying them a fortune. They're happy, you're happy, and they never heard of Social Security." She cocked her head to one side. "Maybe I do remember you. Weren't you the one who used to walk down the hall reading a book?" Claire nodded, swamped with a sudden memory of how a foot had come out of nowhere to trip her once. Cindy had been one of the people on the sidelines, laughing. "What are you doing these days, anyway?"

Claire walked to the front door, wagging her clipboard. "IRS, at your service," she said, then closed the door on Cindy's round lipsticked *O* of a mouth.

TAXMAN

19● "Everybody ready?" Claire whispered, her hand ready to knock on Jean's door. From inside the apartment came the muffled sound of applause.

Claire seldom saw her mother in anything other than the soft light of the TV, so when Jean answered the door the sight of her face in the porch light was something of a shock. Only fifty-two, Jean looked at least ten years older. Foundation was caked in the wrinkles of her cheeks, and her eyes were outlined with black stripes a quarter inch wide. The calls of the QualProd pitchman streamed past them into the air.

Jean took in their presence. "What are you guys doing here?"

Claire took a deep breath. "Mom, we are here to talk to you about a serious problem."

Jean looked from one face to the next, seeking reassurance. "Is somebody sick? Does—does somebody have cancer or AIDS or something?" She noted who was missing and put her hand over her heart. "Where's Eric? Ohmigod, is something wrong with Eric?" On the screen behind her, a woman was using what appeared to be a vacuum cleaner attachment to style a man's hair.

Like the mother she was, Susie made a shushing sound. Claire said, "Nobody's sick. Nothing's wrong. With us, I mean," she hastily amended. "But there is something wrong, Mom. And I think you know what it is." She marched past her mother and picked up the remote. Pointing it at the TV, now topped with a collection of dolls from around the world, she pressed the OFF button. Jean gasped as the picture shrank down into a pinpoint of light that flickered and disappeared.

"I need you to listen to a letter we all wrote to you." Claire cleared her throat, and began to read, "Dear Mom"—

"What is this all about?" From the way Jean was shaking her head from side to side, Claire was sure she knew the answer.

Claire tried to find her place in the letter she, Susie, and J.B. had written, following the instructions J.B. had downloaded from the Internet about how to confront an addict. Claire had always thought the Internet was where kids got information about how to build pipe bombs or where men met chat-room virtual vixens who talked—or typed—dirty until the credit card ran dry. In the past week, she had realized the Internet had more uses than she had ever dreamed of.

"Mom, you can ask questions after I'm done, but for now I need you to listen." Claire began again. "Dear Mom, we are here tonight to tell you that you have a problem. You are addicted to the QualProd shopping channel. You—"

"What!" her mother shrieked. "I can't believe I am hearing this!"

Claire soldiered on. "Your addiction has caused you to cut yourself off from your family. For example, Susie and J.B. invited you to their house for a New Year's Eve party, but you told them you were busy."

"I was!"

"Busy?" With hooked fingers, Susie made quotes around the word. "I found out later that you were sitting here in front of the television set the whole time, watching some silly 'party' with Lawrence Silver bouncing around shilling exercise videos and motivational tapes."

"Those were good tapes!" Jean interjected, stung. "You should borrow them sometime, maybe learn about how to quit smoking. I don't know how you can lecture me when both you and J.B. still smoke. Shopping never killed anyone!" There was a long pause, and when she spoke again her voice had dropped to a near whisper. "Besides, I didn't want to be the only single person at your party."

In a gentle voice, J.B. said, "Jean, you're not going to meet anyone sitting here in front of the TV."

Jean gestured at the dark screen. "But these people are like my friends."

"Like is the operative word, Mom," Claire said. "They're sitting in a studio a thousand miles from here, not in your living room. And after they're off the air, they go home to their mansions that you helped them buy. You don't ever talk *with* them. All you do is listen to their sales pitch. What kind of friendship is that?"

"But they talk about their lives. I know all about their boyfriends and their children. Half of my clothes now are the same ones they wear. We laugh together, we cry together—"

"And you *buy* alone," Susie cut in. "Do you honestly think they have this crap in their own homes?" From the cluttered coffee table she picked up a wicker basket filled with fake flowers, in the process knocking over a candle shaped like a kitten.

Claire said, "The whole setup is designed to make you buy, Mom. They tell you that there are only a few left, so you'd better act fast. They tell you they will never offer it again. They tell you that you're getting a numbered, limited edition—and then when it comes, you find out you have number three thousand, nine hundred and seventy-eight."

"Are you saying I'm not worth it? That I don't deserve a treat?" In her mother's voice, Claire could hear the echoes of the QualProd mantra.

They had anticipated this response. Claire made the planned rebuttal. "Mom, let's face it. You're buying clothes you don't wear, fitness equipment you don't use, cookware you never cook in, and porcelain dolls that just sit in a box on the floor of the closet."

Susie waved her hands to indicate the envelopes spilling across the coffee table, the boxes heaped in the corner. "You used to hide the boxes and bills, but now you're so sucked in you don't even bother."

"Quit lecturing me! Remember, I am your mother, young lady!"

Claire realized things were getting off track. She found her place again in the letter and read on. "We are acting out of love and concern. This is an illness, Mom. You're sick. We're not saying you're bad. But we have to point out the consequences of your behavior. Your addiction to QualProd has caused an ethical deterioration in your behavior. For example, you have broken Susie's trust by trying to steal from her."

"I was borrowing," Jean interjected. "Borrowing, not stealing!"

Susie parried her objection. "If I hadn't caught you with your hand around my Visa card, you never would have told me what you were planning on doing."

Jean's face fell. Sensing her vulnerability, Susie thrust home with the point they had all agreed was the strongest. "I can no longer trust you with Eric. I am no longer going to bring him here. Not when you're like this."

"Like this?" Jean echoed. A flush was building underneath the layers of makeup. "Like what? You talk like I'm some alcoholic. I'm not off in the corner tipping a bottle into my mouth. All I'm doing is having a little fun—and getting a bunch of great bargains. At QualProd, you can buy things you can't get anywhere else. Look at this!" She shook her hand in their faces. On one finger was a gold-colored ring with a faceted stone as big as a dime. "This Dymand ring cost me less than a hundred dollars, and it's modeled directly on a ring Lady Di used to wear.

Now you show me a store where I could get a deal like that."

"But you are buying stuff you don't need, and in the process you are neglecting your other financial needs," Claire interjected. "Mom, this morning I checked with the electric people and the cable people and your landlord."

Jean's head snapped back as if she had been slapped. "You had no right to do that!"

Claire had to look away. "Maybe not, but they told me that your bills were at least three months behind. And the electric people told me that when they threatened to cut you off, you sent them a check you 'forgot' to sign. God knows what your credit-card bill is like."

Jean began to sob, putting her hands over her face. "I haven't opened it for a while. It's over five thousand, I know that."

Claire saw the shock register on Susie and J.B.'s faces. Jean got by on a small monthly disability check from a local grocery-store chain, the result of a fall years ago on a squashed Thompson grape. It would take dozens of those checks to pay back the credit card—and that was if Jean stopped buying anything at all.

Claire held out the phone. "You have to take the first step, Mom. Call the cable company and tell them you don't want the QualProd channel anymore."

"I can't do that. I won't! This is stupid. I can stop shopping at any time."

Susie said, "Mom, listen to yourself. It's bigger than you. You have to give yourself up to a higher power. If you don't take this step, then I won't be able to bring Eric here anymore."

Jean's head dropped so that her coarse blond hair hung in her eyes. She held out her empty hand for the phone.

CHK PLZ

20 ● With only her elongated shadow for company, Claire made her way up Forty-fifth Avenue, past parked cars and still sleeping houses. She was trying a new tack that she had read someone—was it the Australian Boy Scouts?—used to cover a lot of ground without growing fatigued: alternately walking fifty paces and then running fifty. In her case, the running portion was more like a slow jog, but still, it felt like progress. Claire welcomed the feeling of accomplishment, as slight as it was. If only she felt she were getting closer to finding Lori's daughter. The only avenue that remained unexplored was the Prices' child. But if their daughter turned out to be a dead end, too, then that meant the Lieblings' dead child was also Zach's sister.

And what about Ginny? Claire had called the girl's apartment again yesterday, but her voice mail was still full. She and Charlie had discussed whether it was worthwhile to break in again, but decided against it. Deep down, they both knew things would look the same as they had before. Her mother must be in a panic.

The fifty paces Claire was supposed to walk had gone by too quickly, and now it was time to run again. She shuffled along, enjoying the promise of an unusually clear February morning. Whoever had platted this part of Southwest Portland had laid it out on a perfect east-west grid. Her shadow was straight ahead of her, and when she turned the corner onto Pendleton it stayed close by her side. Charlie and Max had still been asleep when Claire slipped out the door. It was still too early for there to be many people up and about. From the buds of her ear-phones, Tori Amos sang to Claire, her voice beguiling and fierce. She turned the Walkman up a tick louder. This early in the morning, she figured there wasn't any traffic to worry about.

When black-gloved hands grabbed her from behind, Claire didn't even have time to scream. Her heart flop-ping like a fish, she stumbled and nearly fell. One hand was clamped over her mouth, while a muscular arm wrapped itself around her shoulders too tightly for her to move her arms. Claire gagged and twisted silently, the meaty taste of leather filling her mouth. She had started carrying the bottle of Dog B Gon in the Tune Belt that held her Walkman, but her attacker held her so tightly that there was no way she could reach it. Something raked over the back of her head and down, snagging sev-eral strands of her hair. She realized her attacker was pulling off her headphones with his teeth. Claire felt soft fabric and hot breath against her cheek, smelled the sharp scent of peppermint. So even rapists used mouthwash. Then a voice hissed into her ear.

"Be quiet and I won't hurt you, 'kay? But if you scream"—the hand pressed down harder across her mouth, and Claire stilled herself, thinking hard. The hand relaxed a bit. Charlie had shown Claire a few of the moves she had learned in her Self-Defense for Seniors class. Claire could gouge her heel down his shin and stomp it on his instep, a move that was, unfortunately, much more effective in high heels than in rubber-soled Nikes. Like a piston, she could drive her elbow back into his solar plexus—but he was pressed so close to her there would be little momentum. Or Claire could try to bite his palm as hard as she could through the leather, and hope to buy herself a second or two in which to scream. But the neighborhood lay so still around them. Would anyone even wake to hear before her attacker's broad hands tight-ened on her throat? Or would the sound be integrated seamlessly into a dream, only half-remembered when the police came to ask about the broken body found in the gutter next to the yellow recycling bins?

It only took a few seconds for Claire to consider and abandon her options. At the same time, she was sizing up her assailant. The harshness of his words was tempered by his Southern-tinged drawn-out vowels. He was about Claire's height, five-ten, but far bigger, pumped up, so he was probably her age or younger. In addition to the gloves and the knitted ski mask she could feel against her cheek, she'd caught a glimpse of Levi's and Nikes. Since this was the unisex casual outfit of Portlanders, it didn't serve as much of a clue. Even though she couldn't see his skin, she'd lay money that he was white.

"I'm just going to say this to you once. Don't go poking your nose where it don't belong. See that car coming toward us?" he asked, and he swung her around so that she was facing the direction of traffic. Obligingly, a deep maroon sports-utility vehicle appeared at the crest of the hill. The driver was a white man, that much Claire was certain of, wearing a Blazers ball cap pulled low. He drove toward them, fast, his headlights on bright. Claire braced herself as she felt the hands holding her shift. Was he going to launch her into the road? "Do you know how easy it'd be to arrange an accident for you?" The car blew past, then braked to a fast stop behind them. Realizing she was safe for the moment, Claire took a shaky breath through her nose. "Wouldn't it be a shame if that little stereo of yours got you killed? People would think you'd gotten so into the tunes that you forgot to look where you were going. Do you want that to happen to you?"

Under the restraining yoke of his hand, Claire shook her head.

"Then leave it be!"

And suddenly the pressure was gone and he was running away from her. She turned in time to see him jump into the car. She memorized its details even as it squealed away from her. A maroon Range Rover, brand-new by the looks of it. Clean all over—except where someone had smeared thick mud on the license plate.

Fueled by adrenaline, Claire ran the rest of the way home. She didn't notice her ankle, didn't notice anything at all, so eager was she to get in the house and lock the door behind her.

She found Charlie hand-squeezing orange juice for breakfast. Her friend calmly listened to Claire's story. Max was still asleep. Instead of looking frightened, Charlie looked fully alive. Claire realized that Charlie missed taking part in the hunt. "Who do you think hired these men to warn you?"

Claire had thought of nothing else while she ran the three miles home. "The best candidate has to be Dr. Bradford. There are at least two reasons he wouldn't want me looking into things. One, offering very private adoptions makes him a lot of money. If people started to get worried that he wouldn't be able to guarantee privacy, they would go someplace else. The second reason is Ginny. What happened to her? Maybe the reason St. Vincent's doesn't have a record is because she died. The Portland medical establishment is probably willing to look the other way as long as Dr. Bradford's meeting a need and greasing everyone's palms in the process—that old victimless-crime thing. But if it turns out that a woman died at his clinic—that's a different matter. They would probably come after him, if only to save face with the public."

"Don't forget that there are other candidates, Claire. What if the Lieblings found out that you were asking about what happened to their children, and they really did kill one or both of those little babies? Or what about that woman you attended high school with?"

"Cindy? But her kid's not Lori's. Why would she bother with me?"

Charlie shook her head gently. "Remember what you told me you said to her as you were leaving?"

Claire flashed back to Cindy, shocked into silence. "You mean when I told her I was with the IRS? Wouldn't hiring two guys to threaten me be overreacting?"

"I understand that real IRS agents do not even use their true names, for fear of retaliation."

Claire considered it, then shook her head. "I can't seriously picture Cindy having someone come gunning for me. And how would the Lieblings even know who I am? My car wasn't parked in their neighborhood, and I never gave their neighbor my name. I still think it was Dr. Bradford." A shiver drew up her shoulders as she remembered his ice-blue eyes. If Ginny were dead, then he would stop at nothing to cover that up.

"Will you do what the man asked? Leave things be?"

Claire looked at her friend and shook her head. "How can you ask me that? If we don't find Zach's sister, he will die. I can't give up until I see if the Prices' daughter is Lori's child."

Charlie patted her hand gently. "Don't forget, even if we do find his sister, there is only a one-in-four chance they will match."

"But it's the only chance Zach has." Claire said. She went into the other room, picked up the phone, and dialed the Prices' number. Again, she got nothing but the answering machine. Frustrated, she left a brief message begging them to call her about a matter of life and death. But as she hung up the phone, she had the feeling it was all for nothing.

21 • The phone rang just as Claire was quietly closing the door to the guest room. Max had just fallen asleep, and needed to stay that way, so she pounced on the phone even before the first ring was over.

"Claire, it's Dante. Why haven't you called me back? I've been worried about you."

The sound of his voice touched her, but she refused to acknowledge that it did. Instead of answering him, she asked a question of her own. "How was Ant's birthday party? Did all your planning pay off?" Her tone underlined the word *planning*.

"How did you know about—" Dante interrupted himself. "You've been talking to sara, haven't you?" What did Claire hear in his voice? Was it a sudden understanding that sara had worked to undermine Claire's confidence— or was he hesitating simply because he had been caught?

"Only while you were in the shower." Claire had meant to make a matter-of-fact statement, but she knew her voice betrayed her.

"She answered my phone?" Dante's tone was annoyed now. "What have you been thinking? Claire, she showed up at my door right after I'd run six miles. I didn't want to sit there *shvitzing*."

"Shvitzing?"

"Sometimes I forget you're not from around here. *Shvitz* is Yiddish for sweat." As if Claire needed another reminder that she and Dante were from totally different backgrounds. "Don't tell me you're feeling threatened by sara, of all people."

Claire stated the obvious. "You used to date her."

"That was over three years ago, and we only went out for about a month. We've known each other since we were teenagers, but it was clear once we started seeing each other that we had different priorities in life." Dante sighed. "I'm going to have to talk to her. It's been pretty obvious that she's jealous of you, but this is going too far."

Claire softened a bit. "You sound like my mom when kids used to tease me in high school. She tried to tell me they weren't really mean. They were just jealous."

"Well, maybe they were. Have you considered that? A beautiful girl with red-gold hair like an angel's and a mind as smart as the devil's? That would be enough to make most people jealous—or nervous."

Claire was surprised to find that she believed Dante far more than she ever had her mother. "And what do I make you?" she asked.

"Nervous, definitely nervous. Especially when you get that frosty tone in your voice." There was a seductive pitch to his own voice that made Claire's bones melt, even if part of her still had trouble trusting his version of her. "You're a woman to be reckoned with, Claire Montrose."

Claire ended up telling Dante everything that had happened in her search for Lori's daughter. The only part she left out was the threat from that morning. If she told him, she was afraid he would insist that she heed her assailant's threat and stop looking for Lori's daughter. And there was no way she could do that, not when one possibility still remained, not when she still might be able to save Zach.

As soon as she hung up the phone, she dialed Amanda's number again. This time Claire got a live voice, not a recording.

"Yes?" The voice was distinctive, husky and slow. The kind of voice that some women were blessed with, and others acquired through copious amounts of whiskey and cigarettes. Claire was willing to bet this voice was the real thing in all senses of the term.

"Amanda Price? Mandy Price?"

"Who's calling, please?" The woman's voice had grown guarded.

"My name is Claire Montrose. I've left two messages with you, but you haven't returned my calls."

"I'm sorry, but I'm afraid I don't know what you're talking about." Amanda sounded genuinely in the dark, but then again, she was an actress, wasn't she?

"I need to meet with you to discuss a matter of great personal importance. It concerns your daughter."

"Exactly what do you mean?" Each word was clearly enunciated, separated by a beat of time.

"I know the truth about your daughter and how you got her. I need to talk to you about her."

"How did you get this number?" Her voice was sharper now, angry—but was she also afraid?

"That doesn't really matter, does it?" Claire said. "I don't want to harm you in any way, or reveal your secret, but I do need to talk to you."

"If you want to talk to someone so badly, you can talk to my lawyer."

"I'm sure you would rather this be kept between us," Claire said. "Does your lawyer know that Dr. Bradford *sold* you a baby?"

There was a hesitation, then Amanda rapped out, "How much do you want?"

Claire found herself shaking her head, even though the other woman couldn't see her. "I'm not looking for money. I just need to talk to you."

"No. It's simply not possible."

No talk of lawyers now, Claire noted. "If you force me to, I could go to *Stop the Presses*. I know the main reporter there." Claire really did, having given the woman the big break that had catapulted her into a Lucite anchor's chair. "I'm sure she'd be very interested in your story."

There was a long pause that Claire made no rush to fill.

When Amanda's reply finally came, it was so soft that Claire had to strain to hear it. "If you came tomorrow, I could see you."

22• Claire stopped her Mazda in front of the ten-foot-high metal gate that separated the Prices from the hoi polloi. It was topped with sharp spikes that looked more practical than decorative. The estate was hidden behind high stone walls, and Claire had seen the glitter of broken glass along the top of the wall as she crested Parrot Road. Clearly, the Prices did not welcome uninvited guests. Getting out of her car, Claire gave a tentative push to the heavy metal gate, which was locked. There was a whirring sound, and she looked up into the lens of a black surveillance camera set high on the gatepost. Then she saw the plain white buzzer set into the wall just above a small metal grille. She pushed it.

A crackle, then a man's voice issued from the tiny speaker. "Yes?"

"This is Claire Montrose. I'm here to see Ms. Price."

No answer, but there was the sound of a lock clicking. The gates began to swing open toward the road—and her idling car. Claire hurriedly jumped behind the wheel and backed up, then drove forward through the gates. In her rearview mirror, she saw them silently close behind her.

The narrow drive wound through a stretch of century-old cedar and fir. She rounded a curve, and the woods gave way to an open meadow that sloped gently down to the calm expanse of the Tualatin River. The house lay cradled in a river bend. Although house wasn't the right word, since Claire guessed it encompassed at least five thousand square feet. A sleek two-story contemporary made of sandstone and granite, it mimicked the undulating shape of the river. Floor-to-ceiling windows and a series of balconies ensured that its owners would have every chance to enjoy the babble of the water and the crisp profiles of the mountains.

When the drive reached the house it split in two—one portion curling in front of the main door, the other leading behind the house to a long garage. Claire counted bays for seven cars. She slowed, uncertain of where to go next.

And there she was, Amanda Price, recognizable even at a distance, standing on the cedar deck that ran the length of the house. Claire parked the car at the edge of the drive, then walked over to her, hand outstretched. The actress wore black leggings and an oversize steel gray velvet shirt, and she behaved as if she didn't see Claire's hand at all. She simply turned and went inside.

Together, they walked rapidly down a wide hallway. They passed ranks of closed doors on either side, then a kitchen that looked like it belonged in a five-star restaurant, with outsize brushed-aluminum appliances. Over the eight-burner stove, a long line of graduated copper pans dangled. Claire noted that there was nothing out of place, nothing left on the counter, but that was all she had time to observe because by then Amanda was striding past an open atrium. Two stories overhead, the ceiling sparkled. It was made of tiny panes of glass that shone in the morning sun like the facets of a diamond. Facing each other across the great open space were two ten-foot-square abstract paintings, slashes and drips of color. Claire hadn't seen anything like them outside the Museum of Modern Art.

At the end of the hall, Amanda opened the door to a room where the scale was a little more human. Still silent, she settled down onto the leather cushions of a mission-style couch. She kicked off her silver-linen mules and tucked her feet under her long legs. Claire sat down on the chair opposite, her back to the door. Faced with Amanda's velvet-framed cleavage and carefully made-up face, Claire felt underdressed and unisex in her denim shirt, khakis, and single swipe of mascara.

"So, how much do you want?" Amanda said without preamble.

Claire had the strangest feeling, as if she had seen this scene before. But of course she had. Amanda Price had made her living portraying women who asked for the truth without blinking.

Shaking her head, Claire said, "I told you on the phone that this isn't about money. What it *is* about is saving a child's life. I'm looking for a girl who was adopted through the Bradford Clinic in August of 1988—and I have reason to believe that that girl is your daughter."

Amanda's low voice was steely. "Emily is *our* daughter."

Claire chose her next words carefully. "Yes, she's your daughter now. I'm not arguing that. But you and I both know that she didn't come from your body. Your daughter was born at the Bradford Clinic around the same time that my friend had *her* baby at the Bradford Clinic. Now my friend's youngest son is dying from leukemia. Zach's only hope is a bone-marrow transplant. There are no matches on any bone-marrow registry in the world. If Emily is my friend's biological child, then there's a good chance she might be a match. My friend's not asking for the girl back. She just wants a chance to save her son's life. Zach is only three years old. Think of your daughter when she was three. If she were dying, wouldn't you do anything you could to save her? A bone-marrow donation would be nearly painless for your daughter—but it could save Zach's life."

Amanda shrugged her shoulders. "That's a sad story— if it's true. But our daughter is our child. No one else's."

"I have the record from the Bradford Clinic with your name on it." Claire decided it was politic not to mention that she actually had four records, not just Amanda's. "I understand why you would want to keep your adoption private. However, if you refuse to help me, I could go to the media."

"How do I know you haven't already? How do I know you don't have a little camera hidden in all that hair of yours?"

"But that wouldn't serve any purpose. I've kept this completely confidential," Claire said, lying only a little. After all, the people she had told had been sworn to secrecy. She just hoped Dr. Gregory would keep his word. "This is just between you and me."

A deep, nearly robotic voice came from behind Claire. "That's good. Because that's how it's going to stay."

Startled, Claire reared her head back. Kurt Price stood behind her, dressed all in black—black jeans, black cowboy boots, and a black T-shirt. Even the huge gun he held was black. Black fur poked above the neck of his T-shirt, which was so tight that the hills and valleys of his muscles stood out like a relief map. The actor had what serious bodybuilders called a *six-pack*, not a reference to a beer-fed spare tire, but instead muscles so defined that they cut the abdomen into six rectangles.

A snort from the other side of the room. Amanda threw up her hands in a deliberately theatrical gesture. "Acting!" she mocked in a dramatic tone, imitating a character who had been a popular fixture on *Saturday Night Live* a decade ago.

"Amanda!" Kurt snarled, but his wife just leaned back and crossed her arms. Her exquisitely expressive face did the talking for her, as she regarded her husband with mingled annoyance and boredom. But, Claire noted, there wasn't even a trace of fear, even though the gun he held seemed pointed someplace midway between her and Amanda.

Claire wished she felt as unflappable. "I don't want to violate your privacy," she stammered while slowly getting to her feet, an awkward movement, as she was holding her hands in the air. Claire figured once she was standing, she could keep the gun in her line of sight. She would also be able to move more quickly if she needed to. If only Kurt weren't standing between her and the door to the hall. And if only there weren't two hundred feet of hall separating her from the front door. Offering nothing but a straight shot, should Kurt be so inclined.

Once she stood up, Claire was surprised to find that she was taller than Kurt. As if she were reading Claire's mind, Amanda said, "Boxes," in a bored tone. "They have him stand on boxes if there's a close-up with another character. For the action shots he frequently wears lifts."

Kurt stuck out his chest. "I'm taller than Sly Stallone," he retorted. "Taller than Mister Tom Cruise." His voice was changing, the vowels drawn-out, the tone a little higher, less his trademark and often imitated clipped growl. There was something about his inflection that sounded familiar.

"And he's so muscle-bound you could pin him in a fight." Claire realized Amanda's comment wasn't addressed to Kurt, but her. "He has started *dyeing* his chest hair, did you know that?"

Before Amanda had begun taunting him, Kurt's gun had been aimed someplace in the direction of the fireplace, but now he pointed it squarely at Claire's chest. Claire hoped he wasn't going to use her dead body as proof of his manliness. "'Kay, Amanda, that's enough."

The last time Claire had heard anyone say "'Kay" in just that way, he had been wearing black gloves and a ski mask. She interrupted their bickering. "So you're the one who threatened me yesterday when I was running. But how did you figure out who I was?"

Kurt sneered. "Caller ID and a reverse directory. You're not much of a sleuth, are you, calling from your own home? I erased your messages before Amanda ever had a chance to hear them. You should have listened to me when I told you to stop asking questions. Now you've forced me to deal with you."

"Kurt!" Amanda's voice rapped out. "Get a grip! You're not in one of your own movies. This is not going to solve anything."

But the gun didn't move from where it was aimed at Claire's chest. Time seemed to slow down. Were his fingers beginning to tighten?

All three of them started at the sound of running feet in the hall. A girl bounced into the room. She was dressed in jeans, a heavy gray sweatshirt, and mud-spattered knee-high boots. In one quick motion, Kurt tucked the gun behind his back and into the waistband of his jeans. He managed to sidestep a hug.

"Mommy, Daddy! I did it! I jumped the high fence today! Dancer and me, we just sailed over it!" The girl was fine-boned, with huge dark eyes. An excited flush colored her skin. Her hair was very dark, nearly as black as her riding helmet. Her muddy boots were leaving smears on the polished oak floor, but neither parent seemed to mind as they both focused on her. Despite their acerbic bickering, it was clear that Kurt and Amanda had something in common. They both loved the girl.

Claire stared at her, remembering Lori's words. *It's not too hard to figure out what she might look like. . . . Dark hair, dark eyes, olive skin.* Were those almond-shaped eyes familiar? The proud way she held her head—was it Claire's imagination that let her see an echo of Havi in the girl?

Emily noticed Claire watching her, and she drew into herself a little. "I'm sorry to interrupt when you have company." She dropped her gaze and noticed the mess she had made of the floor. "I'll go get some paper towels."

"Just leave it, Emily," Amanda said. "I'll get Alice to clean up later."

The door was still closing behind the girl when Claire snatched the gun from Kurt's waistband. Raising it, she pointed it at Kurt. For all its size, it felt oddly light in her hands. But instead of being afraid, Kurt shrugged and turned away to look out the window.

"It's a prop, dear," Amanda said. "I don't know what he was planning to do with it. Probably *he* doesn't even know."

Claire thought she saw Kurt shrug, but she wasn't sure. She wasn't quite ready to believe the actress, not yet, but she did let her hand fall to her side. "I don't understand why he would point a gun—real or not—at me. I'm not asking for much. My friend truly doesn't want to take Emily from you. We just want to be able to test a tiny sample of her blood."

"Do you want the truth?"

"Of course I do." Claire was suddenly afraid of the answer. Was there some chance that the girl hadn't come from the Bradford clinic at all, but was Amanda's child by another man? That could account for Kurt's crazy behavior.

"This is Kurt's secret, not mine, so if I tell you, it can't go beyond this room. No one else can know. You have to promise me."

Claire gave a nod. "I promise."

Amanda let out a long sigh. "It's his image that Kurt's defending, not Emily. That's why he's always insisted on secrecy about her adoption. He doesn't want anyone to know why we had to adopt. He thinks his fans wouldn't accept it. I've tried telling him he could be a role model, a spokesperson, maybe even found a nonprofit research organization." Claire had the impression that Kurt was listening intently. "I keep telling him he needs to branch out a little. Show his fans he can be human."

Still feeling in the dark, Claire hazarded a guess. "He's, um, sterile?"

"Kurt's a diabetic." A pause, while Amanda let the implications sink in, but Claire continued to be confused. Finally, the actress took pity on her and spelled it out.

"Over time that can sometimes have a severe effect on some very important blood vessels."

Claire could finally read between the lines and Kurt's sagging shoulders. Amanda was saying Kurt—kick-boxing, weapon-wielding, snarling-in-the-face-of-death Kurt Price—was impotent, and had been for some time.

"I've told him over and over again that he can do other kinds of movies. Comedy, for example. He's naturally funny." Amanda addressed herself to her husband's back. "Or do a serious movie. Gain some weight and let every-one see you with a gut, like Sly did."

Kurt spoke without turning around. "And has Hasbro sold a toy action figure modeled on him since then?"

Amanda let out an exasperated sigh. "If you're still so set on shoot-'em-ups, then you could play the older friend, the one who doesn't get the girl. Maybe even the one who gets killed. Or go with your image, but parody it. Make fun of yourself before someone else does. If you're not careful, that's what your movies will be—parodies—without you planning it. You could stop talking about get-ting pec implants and just embrace the truth. You're not who you were. But you know what, Kurt? It doesn't mat-ter. How many times do I have to tell you that it doesn't matter to me? And it doesn't matter to your daughter. And she is your daughter, no one can take that away from you." She went up behind him and kissed the back of his neck, very softly, as if they were alone in the room. He al-lowed her to take his hand and lead him to the couch, but he wouldn't raise his head to look Claire in the eye.

"Let me show you a picture of Zach," Claire said. She wanted Amanda and Kurt to understand what they had traded their secret for. "Do you think he looks like your daughter?" Claire handed over the photo of Zach that Lori had given her, the one guaranteed to melt the heart of any parent, biological or otherwise.

Together, Amanda and Kurt regarded it for a long

while. Kurt looked sad and tired, but Amanda's expression was unreadable. "There may be a resemblance," she said finally. "Perhaps more than that." A tiny muscle flickered near her eye. So there were some things even an actress couldn't control. She looked up at Claire with the smoke-colored eyes that had been projected on a thousand movie screens. "If they took Emily's bone marrow, wouldn't it hurt her?"

Even though her heart was racing, Claire tried to keep her voice calm and reassuring. "First of all, they would just test to see if there was a match. And all that requires is a blood draw." This child of Amanda and Kurt's, this Emily, she was Lori's daughter, too, Claire was suddenly sure of it. And she would prove to be a match. Claire's bones lightened as she imagined Zach well again. "If she does match, it's not like a real surgery, where they open you up and take out an organ. They just suck out some bone marrow from the pelvic bone, under anesthesia. There's some soreness for two or three days afterward, but that's about it. In a couple of weeks, the body naturally replenishes the bone marrow that was taken, just like it would with a blood donation."

Amanda let her breath out in a sigh, and then was silent for a long time. She looked at Kurt, and he gave the smallest perceptible nod. She said, "We'll consent to a blood test. And if Emily is a match, and she agrees, we will also consent to her donating."

GONFSHN

● ● ●

Claire drove straight to the hospital. On the seat beside her was a small silver-framed photograph of Emily that Amanda had given her after Claire asked if she could take the girl's picture. The actors didn't want to tell their daughter anything until it was clear that she was who Claire knew she must be—Lori's daughter.

Claire walked quickly down the cancer ward's long corridor, scarcely taking in the sights and sounds of terribly ill children. When she reached Zach's room, she found him curled on his hospital bed, the IV lines running into the plug in his chest. His eyes were closed. Lori lay beside him, but started up when she saw Claire. She eased herself out of bed without speaking, and they walked into the hall.

"I think I've found her," Claire whispered.

With trembling fingers, Lori took the photograph. She studied it for a long time, then the picture fell to the floor with a clatter. "She is a beautiful girl. But she's not mine."

"How can you say that? You can't tell just by looking at a picture!"

Lori's mouth tightened. "I looked at her face, and I knew. I just knew." There was a finality in her words. "We can still have her blood tested. But I'm sure it won't be a match." She raised her hands to cover her face and began to cry without making a sound.

23 ● Was this it then? Claire wondered as she walked through the hospital parking lot. Amanda had promised to make arrangements for Emily's blood to be drawn tomorrow, but was it already over tonight? Claire tried to tell herself that Emily could still be Lori's daughter, that they still had to wait until the blood was typed. But somewhere inside, in a place deep past reasoning and logic, Claire found herself believing Lori. If Lori said Emily wasn't her daughter, then the girl wasn't. That meant that Lori's daughter had been adopted to the Lieblings and had been dead and buried for nine years. And with her was buried all hope of Zach surviving. Claire's chest ached. There was a river of tears dammed up inside her.

Driving home from the hospital, Claire realized she was only a couple of blocks from Ginny's apartment. What had happened to the young woman? Despite his promise, Dr. Gregory had never called to report if Ginny had been admitted to another hospital.

She parked in the lot and went up the worn cement stairs. An orange-and-black sign was taped to Ginny's door. "Apartment for rent. Inquire with manager in unit six." The yellow curtains to her apartment were open, but the apartment was empty. Every trace of Ginny was gone.

When Claire knocked on the door marked with a listing metal six, a frowzy woman with a bad perm and a cigarette perched on her lip answered the door.

"I'm a friend of Ginny Sloop's. Where is she? Did she go home?"

The woman shrugged. "That's what her father said."

"Her father?"

"He called me up and said the girl had decided to go home. He told me I could take all her stuff and sell it or give it to Goodwill, didn't make no difference to him."

Relief washed over Claire like a wave. "So she went back to eastern Oregon then."

"That's right. Her daddy said she decided to have those babies there and raise them up with the help of her family."

"He said she was still pregnant?" Claire asked, staring.

The woman exhaled a cloud of white smoke into Claire's face. "Little thing's not due for another month, now is she?"

● ● ●

Claire parked on Terwilliger Boulevard. For as long as Portland had had streets, Terwilliger, with its stands of tall trees and breathtaking views of the city, had been the preferred route for local runners and the favorite place to park for local lovers. Below them, the city lay cupped between the hills. The wide, dark ribbon of the Willamette River wove through the sparkle of hundreds of city lights.

Doug Renfro, the parking-lot attendant from the Bradford Clinic, sat still and silent beside her. She had called from a pay phone near Ginny's old apartment. They had arranged to meet at 8 P.M. at the foot of the long hill that led to the clinic. Before going home, she had stopped by the liquor store.

Claire had had to tell Charlie what had happened in fits and starts, waiting for moments when Max was occupied. Charlie's eyes filmed with tears when she learned that Lori was firm in her belief there was now no hope for Zach. Max seemed to make a point of not noticing the expressions on the faces of the adults around him. The three of them ate dinner together in silence. While Max watched a children's video in the living room, Claire told Charlie her plan to wrest the truth about Ginny from Doug. Charlie had her doubts that Claire would learn anything, but they both had agreed that they had to know what had happened.

"Are you cold?" Claire asked Doug now. His hands were stuffed in his coat pockets, even though the evening was warm enough that Claire had rolled down her window a couple of inches. "I could run the heater if you want."

Doug shook his head without answering. He hadn't said much on the phone, either, just agreed in monosyllables that he wouldn't mind seeing her again.

She had filled a fat thermos with a batch of Long Island Iced Tea, which through some miracle combination of five kinds of hard liquor resulted in something that could be sucked down as easily as a soft drink. Her plan, such as it was, was to get Doug good and drunk, so drunk that he might tell her all he knew about what had happened the night Ginny gave birth. Maybe he didn't know anything. She remembered that Vi had written it was three in the morning when Ginny started to bleed and wouldn't stop. Doug had probably been sound asleep.

Then again, maybe he knew a lot. A few days before, when Claire had pulled her keys from her backpack, a slip of paper had fluttered onto the floor. She had picked it up and stared at the strange handwriting for a minute, puzzled. It took her a while to remember who Doug Renfro was. Claire realized that was the thing about Doug. He was forgettable. He sat in his booth all day and watched people drive in and out. They might talk to him for a minute, or if there were two of them in the car, they might continue their conversation as if he wasn't there at all. Claire knew. She had had that kind of job before, cashiering at an all-you-could eat restaurant, where you didn't even need to eavesdrop to hear bitter arguments and protestations of desperate love.

Long Island Iced Tea might not be the best approach to loosening Doug's tongue, but at least it would be quick. And with luck she could get Doug drunk enough that he wouldn't be interested in exploring her body and discovering that her pregnancy was really a throw pillow she wore strapped across her belly.

She filled two paper cups to the brim and handed one to Doug, along with a straw. While she waited for the alcohol to have its effect, Claire told him stories she made up on the spot about growing up in California, basing them loosely on lyrics to Beach Boys' songs. She turned herself into a surfer girl with a tan, two things she could never hope for in a million years. Doug only grunted at her tales, but she thought there was a kind of approval or interest hidden in the guttural sounds.

"How about you—where did you grow up?"

"I'm local. There's not much to say about that." His straw sucked air. "Any more where that came from?" He turned in his seat and held out his cup, and she noticed his left hand was still in his pocket. At least he wasn't trying to slip it around her neck. Yet.

"Is it interesting, working at the clinic?" Claire asked.

"I could tell you some stories." He wiggled his eyebrows at her, and she hoped that meant he was loosening up.

"Oh?"

He leaned a little closer. "More than one famous woman has come in to Dr. Bradford with a flat belly and come out with a baby and a birth certificate that says she's the mother."

"Oh really? Like who?" She thought he might say Amanda Price, but evidently he wasn't loose enough yet to name specific names.

"Let's just say some pretty famous ones, including

some whose names you would definitely recognize. You get to see a lot where I sit. Pretty much everybody takes you for granted, you know, like they do the guy who cleans the floors. You're just an extension of the mop. Or in my case, the little striped arm that lets them get where they want to go. They only notice you if they need something. Like once a girl begged me to hide her and her baby. I'm sitting there reading a magazine and suddenly there she is in a hospital gown with no back and a little itty-bitty baby in her arms. There's still blood running down her legs and she is begging me to hide her. As if I had a way to do that."

Was Claire imagining sadness in Doug's voice? "What did you do?"

"Dr. Bradford was there about ten seconds later, so there wasn't much I could do, was there? Vi—that's the head nurse, did you meet her?—Vi told me all about how hormones will make a woman say things she doesn't mean."

"Do you think that was true? That she really didn't mean it?" Claire asked. She imagined what it would be like to be that girl with the baby and no place to hide.

He lifted one shoulder. "Who knows? Maybe Dr. Bradford talked her into doing something she decided she really didn't want to do. Maybe he didn't even talk her into something, just took the baby. I learned a long time ago that Dr. Bradford is all secrets; he is layers and layers of secrets. Maybe some I know, maybe some Mrs. Bradford—the first Mrs. Bradford—knew, maybe some nobody but him knows."

"The first Mrs. Bradford?" Claire echoed.

"The real one. Two years ago last month, she died of a heart attack. Six weeks later, Dr. Bradford married one of the nurses from the clinic. He expects me to call *her* Mrs. Bradford now. But she didn't like me when she was working there, and she for sure doesn't like me now that I'm living two hundred feet away."

"You said only Dr. Bradford knows all the secrets. Do you know any secrets, Doug?"

"What kind of a question is that, Lucy?" He was definitely warming up now. He had turned to face her in his seat, and now he leaned forward and tucked a curl behind her ear. "I like your hair like this." Aside from the pillow, Claire had come more or less as herself—with her hair down and in her Mazda. He had commented on the change in cars when he got in. She should have thought to borrow the Firebird again from J.B.—a parking-lot attendant probably had little to do all day but memorize cars. "I'll trade you," he said now. "I'll trade you a secret for a kiss."

His tongue was in her mouth, his teeth knocking against hers, before she could argue. He smelled like Ivory soap, and he tasted only of Long Island Iced Tea and what Claire thought was Crest, so at least she had that to be thankful for. With his right hand, he tried to pull her toward him. Maybe Mata Hari had done this willingly, but Claire was having a hard time staying in character. Unbidden, she thought of Dante, of his dark curls and the way one of his front teeth had been broken and then mended with a flash of white. Claire remembered the last time she had been with Dante, and without planning to, she tore her mouth away. Humming with desire, Doug leaned over her. Reflexively, she put both hands on his chest. Putting his arm around her waist, he tried to pull her closer, but instead his hand grabbed the pillow. Claire pushed him so hard that he fell halfway back across the seat, his right hand still holding the pillow. His left hand came out of his coat pocket. Claire jerked back when she saw it.

Gray and shiny with scar tissue, it was half the size of a normal hand. It retained enough of the look of a hand so that it was eerily familiar, like a monkey's paw or a raccoon's humanlike hand.

They spoke at the same time.

"You're not pregnant?"

"What happened to your hand?"

Only then did Doug notice his shriveled hand was still on display. He quickly thrust it back into his pocket, his expression unreadable. "My first *mother*"—his voice lilted sarcastically—"got herself pregnant in college and decided to make some money off the deal. She got her thirty pieces of silver off Dr. Bradford, who sold me to my second mother. Then when I was two my second so-called mother was doing her ironing while I played on the floor. The phone rang. She left me alone while she went to answer it, and while she was gone I pulled on this long dangly cord to see what was on the end."

"Oh, no," Claire breathed.

"The iron fell flat on my hand. They say you can't remember anything that happened when you were that little, but I do. By the time she heard me screaming, it had burned right down, through the skin and the tendons and the muscles. Down to the bones." His words were matter-of-fact, but Claire could hear the pain that underlay each one.

"After my second mother ruined me, she decided she didn't want me, either. She just drove up to the clinic and left me on his doorstep and drove off. It's like I was some toy that she broke the wheel off of. Since she couldn't put me in the trash, she did the next best thing and tossed me on Dr. Bradford's doorstep. He didn't want a little two-year-old boy-child with a crippled hand either. But putting me out on the street might have led to too many questions. So he got his wife to raise me. The first Mrs. Bradford. The real one. She was like the only mom I ever had." Doug's low voice was full of bitterness. "Except for Mrs. Bradford, Vi was the only one there who was nice to me. After she got her daughter, I told her about what happened to me. She understood, you know. And now she's dying, too."

"Dying?" Claire interjected, surprised. It was hard to

think of Vi, with her impractical high heels and bright intelligent eyes, as dying.

"She's got lung cancer. Dr. Bradford's new wife has been filling in for her again, just like the old days when she used to work there."

"I got a note from Vi," Claire said. "At least I think it was from her. She might have guessed I had another reason for being at the clinic. See, I want to find out about what happened to my friend Ginny Sloop. I think she went to the clinic to have her babies, but no one has seen her since. Vi wrote about how something went wrong with the birth, about how it was three in the morning and Dr. Bradford told her he would take Ginny to St. Vincent's, but she didn't believe him."

Doug shrugged. His hand was back in his pocket now. "Things go south sometimes."

"I checked with St. Vincent's. She never got there."

"He thinks I don't notice things. I do." Doug was talking to himself more than Claire. "I woke up and heard them yelling in the parking lot. He told Vi to take care of her end and not to worry about it. I decided it was better for me to go back to sleep. But the next day I noticed that the dirt had been dug up between the roots of that big cedar that stands halfway between my place and my booth."

"What do you think it was?"

"What do you think?" He leveled a long look at her, and she knew they were both thinking the same thing. Dr. Bradford had dug a grave.

"I need to see what's buried under that tree, Doug. I need to see."

He dropped his gaze. "So that's what this"—he waved his hand in the direction of the city lights, the thermos of Long Island Iced Tea, the sofa pillow, Claire herself— "that's what this was all about, then?" he asked. "This is why you called?" His voice was rough.

She nodded, but wasn't sure if he saw her.

"I can't help you. I dropped out of school when I was fourteen. What chance do I have out here, on my own?"

"Could you look the other way, though? Could you just not tell him if you hear something out there tonight?"

His head jerked back as if Claire had struck him. "Of course I wouldn't tell him. How can you ask me something like that?"

They didn't speak as she drove him to the foot of the private drive that led to the Bradford Clinic. As she nosed the car in, Doug said, "If someone were going to come up after hours, they should know that there's a sensor in the road up ahead about thirty feet that registers a car's weight."

"Thanks, Doug." She leaned over and kissed him on the cheek, his beard coarse beneath her lips. There was a single intake of breath, and then he held himself still until she leaned back. Her heart was flooded with sorrow for the child he had been and the man he had become.

"Oh, and you should watch out for the dog. Sometimes he lets her loose on the grounds," Doug said as he opened the car door.

"A dog?" Claire felt a twinge in her ankle as she remembered the terrible sight of long yellow teeth.

"A real mean bitch named Pansy. She even snaps at me sometimes. Chow mix. They're the worst." And with that piece of advice Doug slammed the door, then gave her a short wave before walking away.

1MORTNG

24• After leaving Doug, Claire drove without paying attention to where she was. Tears streamed down her face, but she made no attempt to wipe them away. Since she had begun trying to help Lori, she had found nothing but death. The Lieblings' two dead babies. Zach was doomed to die, if not immediately, then in a handful of weeks. And now this news about Ginny.

Was Ginny's body cradled between the roots of a tree? Claire had to find out. Not just for Ginny's family, but for all the other Ginnys out there. A body—even if Ginny hadn't been intentionally killed—would be enough evidence to put Dr. Bradford out of business forever. He must have had his suspicions about the Lieblings, whose children died with alarming regularity, but Claire was sure that their current child, the boy she had seen in the car, had still come from him. He sold babies to the highest bidder, the kind of people who didn't want social workers examining their lives too closely. And now because of the secret way he ran his clinic, a young woman might have died. If Ginny was dead—which seemed likely—and Claire could prove it, then she could save other women, other babies.

She had to put a stop to Dr. Bradford. But if she tried calling the police, Doug would deny everything he had told her. And the police couldn't search without a warrant, and they couldn't get a warrant without probable cause. Dr. Bradford would get his lawyers to stall. If Ginny's body were up there, he would be sure she got moved well before anyone set foot on the property.

Claire drove to a nearby Fred Meyer store. It was ten-forty-five, fifteen minutes until closing, so she zipped her cart up and down the aisles. Freddies—Oregon's own one-stop shopping emporium, where you could pick up anything from a gallon of milk to a drill bit—had the items Claire needed, but they were spread out all over the store. As she wheeled up to the checkout, she was a little nervous, thinking her purchases looked like a starter kit for a burglar. But the clerk scanned and bagged the items—a black sweatshirt, a black knit cap, a can of black shoe polish, and a folding camping shovel—without comment. The woman tucked the final item—a T-bone steak, the biggest one in the meat department—in a separate plastic bag. Back at her car, Claire put on the sweatshirt and tucked her hair under her new cap, then unzipped her backpack and stowed the rest of her purchases next to the stuff she always carried, including a flashlight and the canister of Dog B Gon Jimmy had sold her.

There was a pay phone twenty feet from her car. Should she call Charlie and tell her her plans? No, Claire decided. She would wait until morning. By the time Charlie woke up, Claire would be home safe and it would be too late to forbid her to go. Better to ask forgiveness than to beg permission.

She parked just off the highway, at the foot of the un-marked private road that led to the Bradford Clinic. As she smeared shoe polish over her face, cars zipped by without pausing. The noise was like the droning of a thousand giant mosquitoes. Even so, Claire was careful to close the car door quietly.

Keeping to the edge of the road, she began to climb the steep hill. In her left hand she held the handles of the plastic bag that contained the steak, and in her right palm she cupped the bottle of Dog B Gon. A half-moon offered a faint, filtered light. Her ankle began to ache. She wished she were wearing hiking boots instead of a pair of Nikes retired from running.

Finally, the parking booth came into view. Claire stood next to it for a long time, evaluating what she saw and heard. A faint breeze rustled the trees, but it was otherwise quiet. Up here, even the sound of the traffic was hushed. Doug's little cottage was dark, and only a single light burned in the big house.

It was harder than Claire had thought to locate the tree Doug had told her about. At least six trees could be described as "halfway" between his cottage and the parking booth. Claire walked back and forth, considering. She finally saw that one tree had a bare spot underneath, clear of the moss, needles, and twigs that littered the ground under the others. Putting down the steak, she opened her backpack, then unfolded her shovel and set the blade into the ground. The earth, loamy and loose, turned easily beneath her shovel, and she knew she had chosen correctly. In less than twenty minutes, the shovel caught on something and slid away from her, accompanied by the crinkling noise of plastic.

As her heart pounded in her ears, Claire knelt and gently began brushing away the dirt. Her fingers touched something smooth and slick, layered over something that yielded. She snatched her hand back, rubbing her fingers together. They were dry. This must be Ginny, or at least her earthly remains, wrapped in plastic. All Claire had to do was see her body with her own eyes, then she could race down the hill and go to the police.

Claire fished in her backpack for her flashlight and Swiss Army knife. The flashlight revealed a blue tarp. She plucked up a corner, cut a small slit, then flicked the knife closed. She didn't want to risk cutting Ginny, even if she was past feeling. With her fingers, Claire carefully enlarged the hole she had made. She saw enough to know that she had been right. Blond strands of hair lay across Ginny's open, dull eyes. The sweetly rotten smell of old blood made Claire gag.

A twig cracked behind her. Claire froze and prayed that she was imagining things. Another snap, this one closer. The skin crawled between her shoulder blades. At the sound of an indrawn breath, Claire pushed herself to her feet, still clutching the metal handle of the shovel. She turned to face Dr. Bradford.

And was met with a silent dark blur that hit her square on the knees. Pansy. She staggered backward into the trunk of the tree, which kept her from falling. Claire swore at herself for getting so caught up in finding Ginny that she had forgotten all about the dog. Pansy began to bark triumphantly. Claire had read about coon and fox hunts, about how the dogs howled when they found their prey, just before reducing it to a bloody scrap of fur.

The dog crouched on its haunches, gathering itself to launch at her again, and Claire found herself watching it as if everything were happening to someone else. *Move*, she commanded herself as she saw long teeth glinting in the moonlight, but she couldn't. As the dog leapt, Claire remembered the shovel, still in her hands. Swinging it like a baseball bat, she heard first a crack and then a whine as it connected with the dog's midsection. The shovel flew out of her hands, but the dog turned to rush toward her. Claire bent down and grabbed the steak. Raking the plastic open with her fingernails, she tossed it on the ground in front of Pansy.

The dog didn't even dip its head. The three-pound steak held no appeal, not compared with 140 pounds of living, breathing Claire. The dog circled Claire, its low growl throbbing on the edge of her hearing. Like a flat stone over still water, Claire's mind skipped over her choices. Everything was out of reach. The Dog B Gon and the shovel were six feet away—in opposite directions. Closest was her Swiss Army knife, but what good would the two-inch blade be against the dog's heavy muscles? As Claire tried to decide what to do, Pansy leapt.

Remembering Jimmy's advice, Claire swung her left forearm across her throat. Hot lines of pain scored her arm. She landed on her back, the dog on top of her, its eager breath foul in her face. Claire sent up a silent thank-you to Jimmy when she realized the dog's jaws were worrying the heavy fabric of the sweatshirt, not her arm. She swept her free hand along the ground, frantically trying to find a weapon. The dog loosed its teeth from her sweatshirt and lifted its head just as her hand closed on the little canister of Dog B Gon. She pointed it toward Pansy and pressed the button.

Her eyes caught fire. The smell of ammonia burned her nostrils. Damn! Claire realized she had sprayed herself, not the dog. And now she was blind. The weight of the dog was gone from her chest, but she knew that was only a temporary reprieve. Where was Pansy? She was as helpless as a bug caught in a web, just waiting for the spider to come along.

At least she could meet death on her feet. Claire rolled to her stomach to push herself upright. Something dented her cheek. The closed knife. She grabbed it and got to her feet. Feeling exposed and vulnerable, Claire was determined to find a tree to put her back against. She waved her arms in front of her. Her foot landed in the open grave and she stumbled and almost fell. Rough bark grazed her outstretched fingers, and Claire turned to press her back against the tree. She tried to force open her eyes, but they refused to obey. Tears and mucus washed across her face. The oily, nauseating taste of shoe polish filled her mouth.

Hadn't Claire always read that blind people developed heightened senses to make up for what they lacked? She wished that would happen to her in a hurry, because she couldn't hear the dog at all. The next thing she would feel would be its teeth in her throat. Her hands were shaking so hard that she couldn't open the knife. Instead, Claire put her arm over her throat and braced herself for the attack. If—or when—she was knocked off her feet again, she would try to get into what Jimmy had called the pill bug position. The rumble of a growl made her jump, but she could not tell what direction it came from.

Then Claire thought of something. What had Jimmy

told her? That attack dogs were trained to answer to German, not English? Claire wracked her brain for the words that Charlie had taught her. She shouted them out, trying to tamp down a quaver. *"Nein! Halt!"* No. Stop. What other words did she know? *"Schlechter Hund!"* Bad dog. Or since Pansy was a bitch, would she only respond to the female form of the word? Knowing it was hopeless, Claire screamed out, *"Schlechte Hündin!"*

But then the dog's growl changed to a whine, the sound of an overeager animal being commanded to stay and obeying only reluctantly. Hope electrified Claire. She had done it! Then she heard another sound and identified it. The cluck of a tongue. A human tongue.

"Well, well, well. Aren't you a pretty sight? You look like Al Jolson on a crying jag. And to think that our little Lucy Bertrand knows German. So sorry, but I'm afraid Pansy doesn't." Claire recognized the icy voice, and her mind conjured up what she couldn't see—Dr. Bradford regarding her with his wolf's eyes.

Through her swollen lids, Claire felt more than saw a beam of light being played over her. She heard herself panting with fear, and tried, without success, to still her breathing.

"Come along." As his hand closed around her left wrist, Claire gasped in surprise. He began to tow her along, saying, "Please do us both a favor and don't try anything. I have a gun."

Claire realized that she was still clutching the closed Swiss Army knife. Knowing Dr. Bradford would confiscate it as soon as he saw it, Claire staggered as if she were off-balance, using the second to tuck it in the waistband of her jeans. It slid down an inch but then stopped, and she was suddenly thankful for the little shelf of flesh she had recently added courtesy of her bum ankle and Safeway Select Chocolate Chunk Peanut Butter cookies. She stumbled along as Dr. Bradford jerked her across the uneven ground. Once she tripped over a tree root and nearly fell, but he just jerked her back to her feet. By the dog's low, continuous growl, Claire could tell that Pansy accompanied them.

Finally, Dr. Bradford stopped and let go of her hand. Claire heard the sound of a key turning in a lock. With his hand on the flat of her back, Dr. Bradford pushed her inside, and she stumbled over the doorsill. Grunting with exasperation, he maneuvered her until she felt the edge of a chair against the back of her legs. "Sit," he commanded, and she did. She heard the dog sigh as it also obeyed. Dr. Bradford snorted a laugh. "I've finally got you and Pansy both listening to me."

The closed knife pressed painfully into Claire's abdomen. She folded her hands meekly in her lap, where they were partly hidden by the folds of the oversize sweatshirt.

"So who are you really? Did that girl's family hire you?"

If he didn't know who she was, then it must have been Pansy, not Doug, who betrayed her. Claire didn't know whether it was better or worse to lie. Which would buy her more time? Would either buy her her life? Her eyes were finally beginning to open a bit, allowing her to see the white blur of Dr. Bradford's face and the silver blur of the gun he held in his hand.

"She has a name, you know. Ginny Sloop. And the only reason she died was because secrecy was so important to you. Her family will never rest until they find out what happened to her. And then they'll find you."

He shook his head. "No they won't. They didn't even know she was pregnant. If they weren't smart enough to figure out that something was really wrong with their daughter, they won't have the brains to connect the dots to me. The one thing I appreciate about your coming here is that it's made it clear to me that I was foolish to think I could keep her here for long. So later tonight I'm going to be taking a little drive to the coast. I'll hitch up my boat with a couple of oversize coolers stowed on board. And then I'll go sailing. Remember that lawyer who dumped his mistress's body into the ocean in a weighted cooler? They've never found her. It's a good thing you like Ginny so much, because you'll be keeping company with her forever."

Claire started as an engine rumbled into the parking lot, and then the night was quiet again except for the sound of a car door opening and closing. Squinting at Dr. Bradford, Claire tried to make out if the sound was a surprise. But as far as she could tell, he didn't take his eyes from her.

The clinic door opened. Even with her smeared vision, Claire recognized Dr. Gregory, only without his trademark smile.

His words were sadly chiding. "Oh, Claire, why did you have to come here?"

Something inside Claire crumbled. Dr. Gregory must have weighed whatever he felt for her against whatever he would get for helping Dr. Bradford. And it was clear which side had come up short.

"Take care of her!" Dr. Bradford commanded, then pressed the gun into Dr. Gregory's hand.

"What?" He bobbled it, then recovered. "But I don't—"

Dr. Bradford cut off his protest. "You're the one who sent me that stupid girl. I want you neck deep in this, like I am."

It was then that Claire made her move. She leaned forward so that the drape of the sweatshirt hid her hands. There was no time to fumble or make a mistake. She grabbed the knife, pinched it open, rolled to the side, and lunged at Dr. Gregory with her arm stiff before her.

And as she did, she saw what she held. Not the knife, but the corkscrew. It plunged into his right shoulder. What happened next was a blur—Pansy leaping, Claire diving, the gun going off so loud that she felt as if her eardrums had exploded. Hot blood spattered her face. Where had she been hit? she wondered, even as she scrambled to her feet and ran for the door. Only when Claire heard the odd high-pitched howl of the dog did she realize that Dr. Gregory's wild shot had hit Pansy, not her.

Claire wrenched open the door of the clinic. Darting past the little red Miata, she made a split-second decision to stay on the road. It was faster and at that point all she could hope for was to put as much distance between her and the two doctors as possible. As she was thinking this, a bullet whined into the ground in front of her. Bits of gravel pricked her face.

The sound of her own ragged breathing filled her ears. Her muscles burned. Claire was a distance runner, not a master of the anaerobic hundred-yard dash. Suddenly, the Miata drove up beside her. The passenger door was open, and Dr. Gregory was leaning out the driver's side window yelling, "Get in! Get in!"

Claire stared at him. For a second, he lifted his hands from the wheel to show her he no longer had the gun. There was no time to weigh what he was—an opportunist or a killer or an admirer—or some mixture of all three. Claire threw herself into the seat. Dr. Gregory shoved the accelerator to the floor, and the car began to fly over the last hundred yards toward the highway, so fast that her door closed on its own.

We're getting away, Claire had just enough time to think. Then a bullet shattered the back window, plowed through Dr. Gregory's back, and burst from his chest, burying itself in the dash. His mouth opened in a terrible silent scream. His hands tightened on the wheel as he fought to drive the last hundred yards. But his body was already betraying him, and the wheel slipped from his grasp. Instead of flying to freedom, they crashed into the trunk of a great cedar.

Before Claire could even form an impression of the impact, the airbag already lay like a deflated white balloon in her lap. The stench of powder hung in the air. Her chest burned, and her mouth filled with blood from where she had bitten her tongue. She turned to Dr. Gregory. He listed sideways against the door, his eyes half-open. Claire put her hand out to him, and saw that her ring finger crooked off from the rest of her hand. Gently, she touched his bloodied lips, and started when he whispered something. She leaned forward to hear him over the cars that sped past them, out of sight behind a scrim of trees.

"Man's laughter and manslaughter," was what she thought he said, but she didn't know what it meant. She reached for him, but his eyes rolled back in his head. His head fell forward, and she knew he was dead. Another shot sang past the car. Claire knew if she didn't move fast, she would be as dead as Dr. Gregory.

She wrenched open the car door and rolled out into the dirt. Crawling was noisy and inefficient, and her broken finger felt like someone was sawing it off with a knife, but she was afraid to stand up and make too much of a target. When she reached the shelter of the woods, she stood up and began to dart from tree to tree as she ran in the direction of the highway.

The problem was that she would soon run out of trees. She heard Dr. Bradford crashing along behind her, and ahead of her the noise of trucks and cars tearing past at sixty miles an hour. She sent up a swift prayer that someone might notice her once she scrambled up from the ditch, that a nice truck driver might fishtail to a stop before Dr. Bradford put a bullet through her head. The chances of her not being hit by one or the other seemed slim, but what other chance did she have?

Then Claire saw the lights. Revolving, red and blue, cutting into the darkness around her as they sped past, then the sound of brakes squealing as one, two, three police cars turned into Dr. Bradford's private drive.

2DRESQ

25● With his tongue protruding between his teeth, Max was trying to solve a sixty-four-piece jigsaw puzzle of jungle animals that Charlie had bought for him. Although the piece he held was half blue sky and half tree, he was stubbornly trying to fit it in underneath the lion that was missing a paw.

It had been two days since Doug had called the police when he heard the sound of gunfire. And yesterday the test results on Emily Price had come back. As Lori had already known, the child's blood shared so few markers with Zach's that the doctors had decided there was no way she could be his sister.

Sitting by Max's side at the dining-room table, Claire attempted to take the puzzle piece from his hand, but he resisted. Then she tried to show him how to approach the problem. "See how the piece you have has some sky on it? And where is the sky—down low or up at the top?" He was silent as he continued to try to force the piece into a space where it almost fit, even though it didn't match.

"You can't fit just anything into the holes, Max. Sometimes things will look like they fit, but they don't, not quite. You have to look for patterns and match them up." She tapped the top part of the puzzle again, and finally Max snapped the piece in where it really belonged. Absently, Claire answered his proud smile. Her own words echoed in her head. Something at the edge of consciousness nagged at her. What had she ignored because she thought she already knew the answers?

Today's *Oregonian* lay folded up neatly next to Claire's

bandaged arm and splinted finger. The story of Dr. Bradford's arrest for one count of first-degree murder, one of manslaughter, and one count of attempted murder was splashed all over the front page. The doctor himself was sitting in jail, too canny to admit anything. When they first hauled Dr. Bradford in, he had made his one phone call, not to a lawyer, but to his second wife. While the cops swarmed over the crime scene and the burial site, she slipped into the clinic. The clinic's records went into one of the big stainless-steel sinks and were doused with lighter fluid. By the time someone managed to put the fire out, all that remained was a heap of white-hot ashes. Paper burns down to nothing.

But people remember. Claire realized what had been nagging at her. Something Doug had told her. *"After Vi got her daughter, I told her what happened to me. She understood, you know."* Why had Vi understood? And why had Doug chosen to use the word *got* instead of *had*? A tiny flame of hope flickered within her. Had she fit together the pieces of the puzzle of Lori's missing daughter incorrectly?

There were only a dozen Trumbos in the phone book, and Claire picked up the phone, ready to call them all. But before the first one slammed down the phone on her questions, he had spit out Vi's husband's name. John, John Trumbo. The phone book gave the address in Southeast Portland.

Claire figured it was better to go without calling first. "I need to go talk to that nurse, Vi," she told Charlie. "Something Doug said made me think she might know more about what happened to the child the Lieblings had. The one who was Lori's daughter."

"You mean the one who is dead," Charlie said. It wasn't a question. Her faded blue eyes were filled with sadness.

● ● ●

The Trumbos lived on SE Henry. It took a bit of back-and-forthing before Claire figured out which house it was, a tan ranch house unremarkable in every way, except for the wooden wheelchair ramp out front. When she got to the door, there was a hand-made sign posted on the front, reminding her of the sign Lori had posted when Zach got sick. *"We will not talk to reporters."* Claire wasn't one, so she knocked.

She had just decided the door would never open when it did. Claire had to adjust her gaze, dropping it to the man in the wheelchair. "I need to talk to your wife," she said. She could already hear the harsh, wet sound of her breathing.

John Trumbo looked at her appraisingly. His hair had once been black but was now nearly silver. If he had been on his feet he would have been tall, and even sitting he still seemed powerful, his arms ropy with muscle.

John and Claire looked at each for a long time, but finally Vi called out, "Let her in." John rolled backward without speaking. He didn't take his eyes off Claire.

Walking through the doorway, Claire could see most of the house, even back to the kitchen and the refrigerator decorated with elaborate drawings of horses. The living-dining-room area had flat gold carpeting and worn furniture. Something seemed subtly off, and Claire realized what it was—all the furniture was spaced far enough apart that a man in a wheelchair could pass between. From the end of a short hall, she could hear the sound of a TV, turned up loud enough that Claire could make out every word of a *Simpsons* episode.

Vi was seated in a recliner, her back held straight by pillows. Claire almost didn't recognize her. Wrapped in a quilted pink robe, her frame looked as small as a child's. Her head was bald, but on a Styrofoam stand on the dining-room table, Claire saw the reddish wig Vi had been wearing when Claire visited the clinic. Oxygen ran from a tank on the floor through two clear tubes that hooked over Vi's ears and ran into her nose. In some ways, Vi reminded Claire of Zach, of the way that oncoming death began to pare down a person.

"You've come about Ginny? I'm sorry I didn't do more to help her." Between the two sentences, Vi had to pause to take a breath.

"That's not why I'm here. I'm here to ask you if you know what happened to Lori Hesslewhite's daughter."

Vi closed her eyes for a long moment, then opened them again and regarded Claire calmly. "So it was never about Ginny?" When Claire shook her head, Vi gave her a smile that was half-rueful, half some other emotion Claire couldn't name.

Claire said, "I started thinking about how you threatened to sue Lori when she called the clinic and asked about her daughter. Women must call the clinic from time to time. But what you did seemed like an overreaction. And then I started thinking about what Doug told me. He said you 'got' your daughter, and that you understood what it was like for him to be given back to the clinic. And I decided I had to come here. See, Lori has another child—and he's dying." Except for the hiss of the oxygen, there was complete silence as Claire explained the situation to them.

John turned to his wife. She had closed her eyes as Claire was speaking, and for a long time after Claire finished they remained closed. Finally, she said, in a voice so soft it was as if she were talking to herself, "For the longest time, I thought we were the only ones who wanted her. I still remember the day that woman called, saying that they wouldn't keep her. She was screaming, 'I didn't pay $100,000 for this!'" Her voice took on another woman's harshness.

"This was Monica Liebling?" Claire asked.

Vi opened her eyes and nodded. "They were both investment bankers, both used to getting what they wanted. Expensive cars. A house full of gadgets. Vacations in the

Caribbean. Even when their first child died of SIDS, they immediately made plans to move on. Have another child. Only Monica Liebling couldn't seem to get pregnant. So they came to us."

"And adopted Lori's daughter," Claire said.

Vi adjusted the clear plastic tubing behind her ears. Her hands had shrunk down to skinny bundles of tendons, bones, and blue veins. "Yes." The word was so faint that Claire barely heard it over the sound of the oxygen. "But everything changed when Diana was ten months old. Monica Liebling called me right after she left the pediatrician's office. She said Diana was defective and she wanted a replacement. I reminded her we weren't talking about a broken toaster. That we were talking about a child." Vi paused and pushed herself up higher on the couch. "She said we were talking about a *deal*. And that if I didn't see it that way, she would go to her lawyer." Vi smiled at the ghost of a memory. "And if there's one word Dr. Bradford never wanted to hear, it was the word *lawyer*."

And so, Vi explained, they had made a new deal. The Lieblings would be matched with one of the next pregnant girls that signed up, and eight months later, they would bring home a baby. In the meantime, the Lieblings would explain to their friends and neighbors that another tragedy had struck them, terrible in its random cruelty— their second child had died from SIDS, just as their first child had. They would claim to be too distraught to hold even a memorial service. And Dr. Bradford would supply them with a death certificate, in case the need ever arose.

That left only one loose end. A ten-month-old baby girl with a shock of black hair and fierce dark eyes. Vi's soft expression at the memory hardened as she talked about how the Lieblings left Diana at the clinic, still fastened in her car seat, along with a half-empty bag of disposable diapers, her Paddington Bear rattle, and all her clothes. This time, they had said, they wanted a boy.

"See, we couldn't have any children of our own. Some kid fiddling with a tape deck when he should have been driving took care of that right after we got married." She exchanged a glance with John that was so private in its pain and longing that Claire had to look away. When Vi looked back at Claire, her gaze was unblinking. "Maybe I shouldn't have stayed put at the Bradford Clinic once I figured out exactly how he ran things. But it was all those babies that kept me there. I loved holding them right after they were first born. I'd always figured we would have a big family."

"So you took in Diana," Claire finished for her. The other woman nodded. "And she has"—Claire hazarded the likeliest guess—"Down's Syndrome?"

"What?" The word came from both John and Vi's mouths. Then Vi looked at John, and said, "Can you go get her?" A pause for breath, a pause where he didn't move. "Please?" she added.

He looked at his wife for a long time, then he brought his arms back, put his hands on the wheels of his chair, and pushed himself down the hall. After opening the door, John flicked the light on and off several times, surprising Claire. Why was he resorting to such a drastic way to get his daughter's attention when he could just talk to her?

A slightly built girl followed him out into the living room. Her black eyes were wary. There were two slight bumps under her navy blue T-shirt. And nearly hidden by the wings of her dark hair, the flesh-colored buds of hearing aids nestled in her ears.

John signed and spoke at the same time. "This woman knows your other mother, the one who gave birth to you."

"Ask her," Claire said, "ask Diana if I can call her biological mom and say I've found her."

John did as she asked, and they all waited a long moment, eyes on Diana.

Who gave a nearly imperceptible nod.

An hour later, when Lori walked in the door, she was transfixed by the sight of her daughter. Diana stared at her for a long moment, then suddenly flew at Lori and began flailing her with her fists. Her eyes were fierce and black and just like Havi's. Strange, wordless, nasal screams flew out of her mouth, past sharp teeth. Lori offered no defense, did nothing to shield herself, even as the blows rained down on the face that had never watched her daughter grow up, the arms that never carried her. A stray punch to the abdomen left Lori doubled over and breathless, but as soon as she could she straightened up again to face the girl's pain. Diana's fists gradually slowed until her blows were like soft, cupping slaps as they continued to stare into each other's eyes.

Finally, Diana began to cry, tears leaking down her face. When Lori held out her arms, the child hurtled into them.

26 ● Dr. Preston's nurse beckoned them back into the office. Diana walked beside John's wheelchair, her expression unreadable. Vi was at home, on a morphine drip, but the hospice nurse had assured them that she would not die while they were gone. Lori followed, and Claire saw that she was unable to take her eyes off the girl, this child of hers who had been lost. Havi came behind his wife, his face as expressionless as his daughter's. He had moved back into their house, and they were slowing repairing their marriage. Claire brought up the rear. Both parts of Diana's family had asked her to be here. Charlie was at home, watching both Max and Zach. Two days after Claire found Diana, Zach had been declared again in remission.

Both of Diana's families had agreed that she would live primarily with her adopted family. Later, Diana might begin to spend some weekends with her newfound family.

Dr. Preston waited until they were all gathered around his desk. Claire stood a few feet from Diana, who leaned against the wall in a studied slouch.

"Diana and Zach match on all six HLA antigen tissue markers and are mutually nonstimulative in the mixed lymphocyte culture test." The doctor must have seen how blankly they were looking at him. He cleared his throat. "What I mean is, Diana's a perfect match for Zach."

Claire watched as John signed the news to Diana, too fast for Claire to see more than fingers pointing, splaying, fluttering, wrists turning, hands moving toward the body

239

and then away. Sign language was like dancing, and Claire, who had decided to try to learn at least the alphabet, was barely able to crawl.

Diana tilted her head and raised the black wings of her eyebrows as she signed back to John. Sign language was as much body language as it was hand movements, so Claire could tell that Diana was asking a question. John answered with a nod. As Claire looked from Diana to Havi, it was easy to see that they were related. They had the same dark almond-shaped eyes, the same prominent noses and knifelike cheekbones. Diana's hair was brown, not black, but otherwise she was clearly Havi's daughter. But it was also clear from the way Diana and John acted toward each other, that he was her father, too, in ways equally important.

"What's the next step?" Lori said. She asked the question of Dr. Preston, but she kept her face turned toward Diana, enunciating well enough to allow her to lip-read.

Lori's cues reminded Dr. Preston to lift his head and speak directly to Diana. "For Diana it's not very complicated or painful. About a week from now, we will put her under total anesthesia and use a needle to harvest an adequate amount of marrow from the back of the large flat hipbone." He stood up, and with one long-fingered hand he patted the back of his khaki Dockers. "Diana, all you will have is a week or two of soreness." He smiled. "Probably wouldn't want to go out horseback riding."

He turned to Havi and Lori. "The procedure is a little more complicated when it comes to Zach. In order for Diana's bone marrow cells to survive and grow, the recipient's own marrow and immune system need to be killed. Normally, we are limited in how much chemotherapy or radiation we can give a patient, because enough to kill the diseased bone marrow would result in the death of the patient. When we do a bone-marrow transplant, to put it crudely, the total body irradiation and the intensive chemotherapy kills both the leukemia and the patient. We then rescue the patient—but not the leukemia—through bone-marrow transplantation." Claire saw Lori shiver. Havi put his arm around her.

"So, before we can infuse the marrow, we have to put Zach through a very difficult course of chemo and radiation. It's going to be worse before it gets better. He will experience nausea, vomiting, and fatigue. We'll have to keep him in isolation, with only a few visitors, and those will have be washed, gowned, gloved, and masked.

"After Diana's marrow is filtered, we will infuse it into Zach's Port-A-Cath, the same way we would a unit of blood. The marrow cells will find their own way to the marrow spaces inside the bones. As far as Zach is concerned, the transplant is not surgery—just a blood transfusion. Again, it's not like a kidney that starts to function immediately. Instead, the cells will slowly repopulate the marrow over the course of a few weeks."

"How long will it be until we know if it's working?" Lori asked.

"Until the bone marrow starts to function, which may take a few weeks, Zach will be totally dependent on us for supportive care to defend against anemia, bleeding, and infection. If the procedure is successful, the transplanted marrow produces a new crop of normal cells. That means mouth sores should heal, and nausea and vomiting will decease. Most importantly, Zach's blood counts will gradually start to come up."

There was a long silence, and then Lori asked the question that was on everyone's minds. "And if we don't see these things, these changes?"

Dr. Preston didn't drop his gaze. "If there are no signs of new marrow growth within four or five weeks, then the engraftment has failed."

In her mind, Claire paraphrased what he meant. If the engraftment failed, the leukemia would be dead. But so would Zach.

27 • The day was perfect, the kind of day that Oregonians like to keep secret from the rest of the world. Eighty degrees and not a cloud in the sky. Boats bobbed on the shimmering blue water of the Willamette River, which ran through Portland's heart.

For two cans of food for the Oregon Food Bank and three dollars at the gate, Portlanders were enjoying a Fourth of July tradition, the Waterfront Blues Festival. The grassy bowl between the Hawthorne Bridge and the River Place Hotel held a cross section of the city. Suburban couples dressed head to toe in Eddie Bauer pushed strollers past blues fans wearing Levi's and T-shirts. A man with a diamond-patterned python looped casually around his neck, its tail stuck in the back pocket of his jeans, cut a wide swath through the crowd. Families spread out picnics in the grass next to people napping, and for once no one seemed to mind if the nappers had the look of people who spent every night lying out-of-doors. One man dragged a heavy wooden cross through the crowd, past kids with safety pins and dyed black hair who hadn't heard that no one dressed like a punk anymore. Old friends stood in clusters drinking beer, college students played games of Frisbee that included the obligatory dog, and kids got their faces painted or stood in line for a balloon hat from Cosmo the Balloon Wizard.

A tiny hunched-over man, about the size of an elf, scooted past in an electric wheelchair without footrests. His stunted feet curled a half inch from the ground. With one hand, he held a large gray bunny in his lap. On stage, the dancers for the current act appeared, having changed into different—but just as skintight—dresses for the next song.

Zach, who had already consumed a fruit roll, a can of apple juice, most of a basket of curly fries, and a corn dog, now ran up with Max to where Claire and Lori were standing, and asked for money for strawberry shortcake. With a grin, Lori reached into the pocket of her jeans and handed Zach and Max two dollars apiece. They ran off, briefly separating to run around a man wearing a top hat and tails and carrying a necromancer's staff.

The adults were eating their way through the festival, too. They ate burritos and Thai noodles and Cajun chicken and pulled pork sandwiches. Fried dough was available from four different vendors. They could choose from elephant ears or Indian fry bread or Dough Boys or something called Fri Do, served by sturdy sweating women who were supposed to be Swedish, got up in some outfit that was a cross between the Flying Nun and a milkmaid in a bustier. And from a beat-up trailer, J.B. was doing a roaring business in cinnamon rolls the size of dinner plates. A representative from Portland's Saturday Market had already given him a card and asked him to call about setting up a permanent booth.

Squinting from the refracted light that danced off thousands of wavelets, Claire sat down on an old quilt next to Charlie, who was tapping her fingers on her knee in time to the music. Dante gave Claire a smile. He had been in Oregon since late June, and he and Claire had been making up for lost time and lost conversations. After a week spent walking along Oregon's beach, exploring tide pools during the day, drinking microbrews in the evening, and spending long nights in bed, they had agreed to disagree about whether she should have ever tried to unearth what had happened to Ginny. They still hadn't figured out how to resolve the three thousand miles between them. Friends and family kept Claire in Portland. And the reality was that Dante's job at the Met could not be matched anywhere else.

Next to Dante, Jean shared a fried onion flower with her new boyfriend, Zed, whom she had met at Shoppers Anonymous. She put another batter-covered slice to his lips, and Zed playfully nipped her fingers, making her squeal. He was a tough-looking little guy, scrawny and wrinkled, who probably weighed a good fifty pounds less than Jean. A teamster, he no longer had a TV in the sleeping cab of his truck, so that he could avoid temptation. Whenever they felt tempted to pick up the phone to buy something, he and Jean called each other long-distance instead.

Dante took a bite of the napkin-wrapped item that Claire had handed him, then spit it out into his palm. "What *is* this?"

"It's a butter-pecan bagel," Claire answered, a little defensive. She herself had liked the taste, like butter-brickle ice cream.

He groaned. "Oh, Lord, I am truly far from home."

IMYRMAN

Author's Note

While I was writing this book, my brother Joe told me the story of a friend of his who had lost his adopted son to leukemia the year before. That morning, a year after his son's death, the father had found a scrap of paper tucked deep inside his wallet. In a five-year-old's hand, it read simply, "I love you Daddy." The father broke down in tears. While he and his wife had spent the final year of their son's life trying to track down his blood relatives, they were never able to find a compatible bone marrow donor.

To learn more about how you can become a bone marrow donor, contact your local chapter of the American Red Cross, or call the National Marrow Donor Program at 1-800-573-6667. Bone marrow donors must typically be between the ages of 18 and 60 and in general good health. Minority donors are especially needed.

For patiently answering my questions, I'd like to thank Mike Allison, Lynn George, Linda Moe, Mark Rarick, MD, Carla Robertson, and Alida Rol, MD. Any errors are my own. Thanks to Bruce Bishop for introducing me to heteronyms, and to Mike Calkum for letting me borrow his poetry fragment. Many people have shared license plate puzzles with me, but Mary Hogan, Tom Hilleary, and Candace Perry gave me some good ones just when I needed them most. Special appreciation to Dave Jennings and John Lyster for handling things with care. Folks on DorothyL have provided me with advice on everything from writing to wonderful books to read. And Jan Bellis-Squires's support—as well as that of dozens of other Kaiser Permanente staff—has been invaluable.

On the publishing side of things, Wendy Schmalz, as always, provided hand-holding and sage advice. Thanks to Carolyn Marino for wrestling the manuscript to the finish line, and to Robin Stamm for her able assistance. Debra Evans in telesales was my first fan not related by blood or friendship. Diana Jackson recommended me to booksellers thoughout the Pacific Northwest. In an often thankless job, Patty Garcia has been an invaluable publicist. Prior to Patty, Brian Jones was organized, indefatigable, funny, cheerful, trustworthy, and brave. And Gary McAvoy treated me like a star.

My brother and sister, as well as my parents, Hank and Nora Henry, continue to offer their love, support, and pride. My daughter might be the only three-year-old on record as saying, "Shouldn't you be writing, Mom?" And without my husband's support this book wouldn't have been possible.

Key to License Plate Terms

10SNE1 = Tennis, Anyone?
1DRING = Wondering
1MORTNG = One More Thing
2DRESQ = To the Rescue
6ULDV8 = Sexual Deviate
ALLLII = All Lies
AMAMTOH = Hot Mama (as seen in rearview mirror)
BAD DOG = Bad Dog
BITEME = BITE ME
BYRLVR = Be Your Lover
CHK PLZ = Check, Please
D8NNE1 = Dating Anyone?
GLFNUT = Golf Nut
GONFSHN = Gone Fishing
HOTMAMA = Hot Mama
IMAUMBN = I'm a Human Being
IMAYSGUY = I'm a Wise Guy
IMYRMAN = I'm Your Man
KID KR8 = Kid Crate
NSTIG8R = Instigator
OWTAHR = Out of Here
SHRSHR = Sure, Sure
TAXMAN = Tax Man

TYMZUP = Time's Up
UDY11 = You Die Once
U8MYPY = You Ate My Pie
UJUSTME = Just Between You and Me
URBSTD = You're Busted
URNNML = You're an Animal
WHO RU = Who Are You?
YW84NE1 = Why Wait for Anyone
YY4U = Too Wise For You